THE LAST VANISHING MAN

THE LAST VANISHING MAN

AND OTHER STORIES
by
MATTHEW CHENEY

THIRD MAN BOOKS

Third Man Books, LLC
623 7th Ave S
Nashville, TN 37203

A CIP record is on file with the Library of Congress.

Cover photograph by Julie Hamel.
Cover and book design by Amin Qutteineh.

Printed in U.S.A.

ISBN: 979-8-98661-450-2

CONTENTS

for
Eric & Paulette and Ann & Jeff
who know where the stories
are buried

I.

under the pain the words emerged

—Hervé Guibert

AFTER THE END OF THE END OF THE WORLD

I have tried to tell her story for over a decade now, but she slips between the lines.

I know that she was born to a father who wanted to take his anger out on the world, and that she escaped him, and that the consequences were terrible, and that she ends somewhere cold, somewhere north, on a glacier perhaps, a frozen place in an ever-warming world.

It is not too much to say that her father destroyed her life.

Who is to blame, though, for destruction?

Who is to blame for life?

I return always to the moment where she finds out what happened. Or, more accurately, I return to the moments before, then the moment where she is notified, and then the moment after. This is what compels me in the story: the moment a life changes forever. The end of a world, and then after the end.

(Let's call her Jane.)

There are only a few ways it could happen, this change of life for Jane. The most dramatic has the FBI approach her just as she is answering a phone call from a friend who has seen something on the television. How much would Jane know then? Enough, I expect. She would know it was her father. How could she not? Who else would it be? She would have repressed a lot of knowledge over the years, repressed a lot of fear, and in that moment it would flood forth and she would know.

Or would she know?

It depends who she is.

Often, she is a woman with a radical past, though her radicalism is the opposite sort of radicalism to her father's.

Often, she came of age during the 1980s and went to Nicaragua as a Yankee Sandinista, and her eventual husband was a young journalist who traveled down to write about the Sandinistas, and he introduced her to what would become her vocation, or else he was another radical who traveled down to join them and she introduced him to journalism, or else he was not a journalist, just a traveler, someone who would do something different eventually. Perhaps, whether a journalist or not, he ultimately proved himself more of a true believer than she proved to be. Or perhaps he aged into the dull conservatism of someone aching to escape sympathies, empathies, memories; someone who just wants to get on with his days.

No matter who the husband was or what he became, the story in the end is always the same, because he was young when he met Jane, and the one constant to his character is a youthful tendency to roam.

He was a bit less monogamous in love than Jane was, and he ended up leaving her for another woman, a Nicaraguan, shortly after Jane, in fact, became pregnant. In all of the versions of this story, Jane and her husband had split up by the time their son was born, and her husband required a divorce so that he could marry the Nicaraguan woman, whose Catholic family insisted that she marry this man if she was going to have anything more to do with him, and so Jane said fine, and she let him go, and she had a baby, a boy she named, let's say, Steven. She returned to los Estados Unidos, worked in the leftwing press for a while, never made a lot of money, but had a pretty good life, traveled a lot, established a bit of a name for herself, perhaps, at least within certain circles. She struggled, of course, when the newspapers couldn't compete with the internet, and she lost jobs, lost health insurance, did her best to live as a freelancer, bummed rooms and food and conversation from friends. A hard life, but a committed one.

(Given all her radical connections, all her political writing, can we really say she would have thought immediately of her father, and not herself or one of her friends or colleagues, when she saw the FBI approach? Might it be possible that she wondered if the feds had finally caught up with her? Could she have been surprised, even relieved, when she found out they wanted to know about her father, not her?)

Sometimes in the story, Jane is not this Jane. Sometimes she has been less successful at getting away from her family and her past. Sometimes she is more conspicuously damaged, an alcoholic, even a drug addict, someone living on the fringes somewhere (probably somewhere deeply rural, or at least somewhere less expensive and overwhelming than a big city). She was married once, yes, and had a son, yes, but they're gone now, husband and son, somewhere far off, and she hasn't heard from them in ages. She has kept in touch with her father, even though he hates her. (Or does he? Perhaps he is just disappointed. Certainly, he is disappointed.) She is afraid of him and she loves him. He would not have talked with her about his plans, definitely not. She is too wild, too unstable, too unpredictable. He would be careful.

It would take some time for the FBI to find her, no matter how high the priority. She is not easy to find, this Jane. She would not have a cell phone, she would not have any friend or boss or neighbor to call her. The FBI would drive up a driveway and discover her in a shack or at best an old, rusty mobile home. They would approach with guns drawn, because you never know what you'll find in a place like this, a situation like this. There could be booby traps. There could be escape routes. There could be an ambush. But there wouldn't be. She would be alone, probably sleeping, as this Jane doesn't wake up before noon on even the best days, and today would not be one of the best days, would it? Perhaps, for the sake of contrast, it would. A day when she felt some vigor and some hope, a late spring day when she did, in fact, wake early, and when she sat outside in a folding chair, a cup of steaming coffee in her hands, and thought about how she would change her life, how she would make something of herself, and just at that moment the sunshine-bleached morning would shatter into a SWAT team pointing rifles at her, FBI agents crackling her name through a bullhorn, the worst day of her life.

(No, too much irony in the tale of the perfect day ruined. Too easy, too obvious.)

(It would just be an ordinary bad day, and then it would turn awful.)

Her ex-husband renounced the life they led together long ago, whatever it was, and in many versions of the story he became successful, rich, powerful. She calls him a sell-out, and sometimes he thinks she is right about that. More often, he thinks he came to his senses and gave up the blind enthusiasms of youth. Maria, his second wife, was happier once he stopped being a radical or stopped drinking so much or doing drugs and hanging out with people whose lives had never been good and were always getting worse. He had a son to raise, after all. Jane would always hold his life against him, and she would always think he had stolen their son, even as she knew the life her ex-husband gave to Steven was beyond anything she could have given him, but still: he was her son, too.

Is that what her father felt? The loss of his daughter to whatever she was lost to?

No, it was different. Affection that becomes distance — love
that becomes fear — is not the same as a life led distantly, a
life where one parent is a hypothesis or a dream. Steven always
had Maria, too, and Jane had never had anyone else after her
mother died when Jane was four or six or, at most, fourteen or
fifteen. It was an entirely different situation.

"What's happened?" she said to the FBI agent who
approached her.

(In one version of the story, she added: "Is it my father?")

They would check her name and driver's license before they
told her anything. They would want to make sure they had
the right woman, the right daughter. She might have seen
something on TV, though no names would be used until families were notified, so she would not have heard her father's
name spoken by an announcer, but once the sirens escaped
the television, she would quickly make the connection and
she would quickly think of her father and it would quickly all
make terrible sense.

"Ma'am, you'll need to come with us."

Yes, they would call her *ma'am*. They always do in every version of the story, because talking that way highlights their seriousness and power. At first, the agents would be wary of her:
she might be an accomplice, especially if she lives somewhere
rural, on the fringes, in a shack or a ragged, rusty mobile home.
Even if they found her in New York or Seattle, wherever she
ended up as a freelancer, they would still be wary, because
the FBI is wary of the press, especially the leftwing press. She
could easily be thought of as the enemy. But she always stops
being the enemy soon enough.

(Soon enough for what? Soon enough.)

(And this because she is white and unreligious. Were her skin darker, were she known to be a Muslim, she would likely be locked up forever, or, just as likely, dead.)

And then they, or at least some of them, these agents of the government, start to feel sorry for her. The more imaginative and empathetic of the agents pity her, because they know she did not want to be connected to anything like this, and she did not want to share a name with a man like that, and now even if she changes her name she cannot change the knowledge that what was once her name is now a hated name, a loathsome name, and these few imaginative, empathetic agents think about what it must be like for your father's life to so determine your own life simply because, no matter what you do or what you desire, you are your father's daughter.

But most of the agents would not think about this at all.

Soon, the television reporters and the newspaper reporters and everyone else everywhere knows the name Ray Draper and the name Jane Draper.

(Draper, my paternal grandmother's maiden name, my own father's middle name. Is this homage or revenge?)

Jane Draper is the daughter of a murderer.

Jane Draper is the daughter of a bomber.

Jane Draper is the daughter of a terrorist.

Despite the efforts of the agents, not only does her name become known, but her face, too. What does she think when she first sees a picture of herself on a television screen? The first pictures would be ones designed for other contexts. Official pictures that accompanied her newspaper articles or her driver's license or her passport. But then other pictures would surface. Snapshots from somewhere, provided, perhaps, by friends or family she hadn't spoken to in a long time, people who hoped to be helpful or hankered for some moment of fame for themselves, or who wanted to emphasize their virtue against hers, or who were susceptible to an offer of money. One would be a picture of herself when she was ten or eleven years old, posing with her father and a rifle. "What kind of man gives a child a rifle?" people would say, people who had never held a rifle, people who would see it as a further sign of her father's pathology to know that she had shot rifles and pistols when she was much younger even. When she was growing up, so long ago, kids would bring their rifles to school during hunting season and leave them in the office with the secretary because they had been out hunting before they came to school. Everybody had guns when she was growing up. Her father just had more than most, and he liked guns other than hunting rifles. She shot her first machine gun when she was eight. None of it seemed strange until she went to college in a city where none of her friends knew anything about shooting except what they saw in movies. They would ask her again and again to talk about her life because it was an alien life. She never told them everything. They probably thought she was making most of it up, anyway, and telling them more would not help her.

"Your father is Raymond Draper?"

"Yes. What has happened?"

"There has been an incident."

"What kind of incident? What happened?"

"Did you see the news?"

"There was something, but then you came and — a bombing, I saw, in D.C., a café and a Supreme Court justice, but that couldn't be him, I don't believe that was him, there must be something wrong."

"Yes, there was a bombing. A Supreme Court justice is among the dead. What else do you know?"

"Nothing, nothing."

"Why do you say it could not be your father?"

"He's never hurt anyone."

"What are your father's political views?"

"Please, why do you think he was there — he's never been to Washington in his life, he hates cities—"

"Why do you say he hates cities?"

"Because he's said so a billion times. 'I hate cities,' he says. The crowds, the confusion, the traffic, I guess. Please, can I call my father, please just let me call him and—"

"When did you last speak with him?"

"Months ago. Maybe a year."

"You aren't close, personally."

"No, we don't really get along. But he's my father and I'm sure that—"

"We found his car. He mailed notes to the *Post* and the *Times*. We found his body."

"His body."

"Yes."

(They would not, of course, tell her what they found of his body. To call it a body was not a precise statement. It had been a body, but it was not a body when they found it. What they found were scraps. Enough for an identification and little more.)

She cannot understand this information in any complexity, but she does not reject the knowledge that her father is dead. She has known from the moment the FBI came for her. The bomb, the dead people, the Supreme Court justice, all that will take much more time to think through, but she knows her father is dead and she knows her life now has two parts, a before and after. She cannot imagine the after.

The Jane who is a journalist soon wants more information.

The Jane whose life has been mostly struggle immediately wants a drink and a cigarette.

There could be other Janes.

Who else might result from that childhood?

A Jane who is a teacher, perhaps. She would have stayed in New Hampshire, close to her family, and she would have sought escape from what she grew up with by trying to help kids make their way in the world. A high school teacher, probably, the last chance to influence children before they harden into the adults they will be. She would teach history, because her father had loved history, but his was the history of someone who didn't do well in school, who had felt brushed aside, and he had not gone to college, had not even considered going to college, and so had taught himself history through paperback books he bought from drugstore newsstands and through television documentaries and through popular magazines. The danger of such a history was that it only provided him what he knew he wanted to know, and he assessed its worth based on how well it fit in the puzzle he imagined for himself. Her own schooling would teach her that history is more complex than that, more filled with paradoxes, messes, and mysteries than anyone really wants to admit, and she would be attracted to the contradictions within the histories she learned, as well as the systems for thinking around and through and between those contradictions, because even as she recognized the flaws and partialities in any system seeking to reconcile the infinite facts of reality with the limited capacity of human consciousness, the quest itself would remain thrilling, and the thrill would fuel her passion for teaching. She wanted to find the students who were like her father, the students who hung out in the back of the room, who skipped class whenever they could, who said it was all boring and irrelevant and stupid, who nursed grudges and resentments because grudgeful resentment gave them some way to think of themselves in relation to the world. She would do what she could for these students, try to help them toward some curiosity about something other than what they already knew, or thought they knew, try to nudge them away from the sense of expendability that shaped their days, and to open even a tiny crack for them to look through so that they might see how wide, how vast is the world beyond what we know, and how exciting — how humbling — it can be simply to glimpse the vastness.

Imagine this Jane in an FBI interrogation room. It would be the end of everything for her. "I'm afraid your father is dead, Ms. Draper." (That would be the first blow, but not the one that destroyed her.) "We found his car. He mailed notes to the *Post* and the *Times*. We found his body." What would destroy her would be what was in those notes to the *Washington Post* and the *New York Times*: a rant, a manifesto. Hatred, yes, of all the politicians and corrupt judges who had destroyed everything good in America — but Jane would see something else, too, a different hatred: the self-hatred of the man who had never been able to be the person he thought he should be, and she would see, because she knew, the resentment that pushed his self-hatred outward so that anyone else was to blame. *Blame,* that's what she would see, the great, aching desire to have someone to blame, someone to pin a life of rotted hopes on, and eventually (after all the anger and pain petrified into purpose) someone to kill. She had seen it in her father all her life, fled from it, built a career trying to save others from it, and now this was what her efforts had brought her to: this: here: a small, windowless room with a buzzing fluorescent light and a metal table with nothing on it and a metal chair that screamed against the floor, and, rising above the lingering scent of bleach and cleaning products, suffusing it all: the inevitable, soaked-in stench of previous interrogations, of loss and fear, of lives obliterated.

(No, there is nothing we can learn from that story. Do not imagine that Jane.)

They would not detain her for long. (A white woman, not Muslim.) She could only tell them what they already knew or what confirmed their suspicions: her father was a man who owned many weapons, who certainly had the knowledge to build a bomb of the type that had blown up the café, who had been filled with anger for as long as she could remember, who lived alone and had few friends, who felt that all the failures of his life could be explained by the successes of other people. She told them that though he was a lifelong resident of New Hampshire who rarely left the state, he hung a picture of Robert E. Lee in his living room and flew a Confederate flag in the yard. She had asked him once about this, and he said his allegiance was to anyone who fought against big, oppressive government. "And for owning people?" she said, and he said, "Don't give me any of your liberal bullshit, you don't know what you're talking about."

In the letters he sent to the newspapers (not just the *Post* and the *Times*, but also New Hampshire's daily *Union Leader*), he said he was making his stand. He did not describe his plan in detail, though he did say his target was at least one Supreme Court justice, because the Court needed a new justice, one who would follow the Constitution and not make things up, a justice who would interpret narrowly, not impose broadly. When the FBI raided his home, the two-bedroom log cabin that Jane had grown up in, they found all his preliminary notes. He had been traveling to Washington, D.C. for almost two years, following various potential targets. The most liberal Supreme Court justice frequently went to a particular café for a cup of coffee and a blueberry muffin. Once he discovered this pattern, the plan was easy enough to enact. He had a shelf of Army field manuals, a chemistry textbook, and a book about the Algerian war. His workshop was filled with various bomb parts, and remnants of test bombs rested throughout the two hundred acres of woods behind the house. It took the bomb squad days to declare the property safe. By then, the house had been almost completely dismantled, its floors and walls and ceilings sliced, torn, shattered in the search for what might be hidden there.

The newspapers would print pictures of the house and diagrams pointing to stashes of guns, stockpiles of ammunition, and the workshop where the bomb was constructed. Only then would Jane think about the house. She had not been back inside since she was eighteen.

(Who was Jane's mother? I've never been able to imagine her sharply. She was a woman who loved too young and hurt too long — a woman who, perhaps, found some way to escape, but who, no matter what, died early, before Jane became the Jane we know. She was not the gravity Jane sought to escape, but the voice Jane heard whisper amidst coyote howls in the wind of black, cold, winter nights.)

She flees the press, the publicity. She flees her friends, their compassion.

Books are written about her father, but she does not read them, and after selling well at first, they are dumped in remainder bins and they go out of print.

Jane makes her way north. She wants to go somewhere cold, somewhere barren. She runs out of money and survives by charity, odd jobs, luck. She is too old for prostitution, though she wonders how she might accomplish it if she could find someone willing — it's not the act that scares her, but the words and nods and glances that convey information, the whole code of the commodified body, and she does not know the key to that code.

She is not always lucky. She goes hungry. She breaks into houses that look empty and she steals clothes, cookies, shampoo, a bit of warmth, some moments of rest. Now and then she encounters people who see her as something less than human, something able to be spat upon, laughed at, a toy to boost their own sense of themselves, and she lets them if they will give her a ride or a meal, if they will get her closer to the glaciers and the tundra.

She thinks of her son.

In some of the stories, Steven goes to school at New York University to study film. He wants to make documentaries that show people truths and help to change the world. He joins an environmental group and protests corporations. He almost gets arrested during a demonstration outside a skyscraper. He falls in love with the leader of the group, a young man named Julian who is a year ahead of him at the university and studying literature or philosophy or something else that will annoy his rich and eminently practical family. Julian loves having an acolyte; Steven loves having sex. They lie naked together in the apartment that Julian's father rents for him on 6th Street, and they fantasize about the terrible things they would like to do to the men who are raping the Earth, and they say that if they had a terminal disease they would strap bombs to their bodies and dive off of giant dams and ignite themselves to crack the dam's wall and let the water out — and this fantasy is so luscious that they can't resist imagining both having a terminal disease, truly terminal, with only weeks or even days to live, and imagining how they would stand on the edge of the dam, the security officers screaming behind them, the sound of police and military helicopters scrambling the air above, and they promise each other here and now in this bed in this apartment on 6th Street that they would jump together (hands together, lips together) just before some Marine sniper's bullet could kill them, and together they would plunge together and they would explode together and the rivers would flow free.

Eventually, Julian grows tired of Steven or Steven grows tired of Julian. They yell. They weep. They console themselves with the friends who were always only *their* friend alone. They can't bear even to look at the other person from across a crowded street. Julian will break up with environmental activism around the same time he breaks up with Steven, who will do the same. Julian will go on to do a law degree and please his parents. Steven will stick with film.

In some versions of this story, Steven finds his way to Hollywood, where he gets one break after another, until he directs a successful small-budget movie that both makes a small profit and earns awards nominations, which gets him hired to direct a big-budget movie, and though the big-budget movie does not get nominated for awards, and, indeed, the critics say nothing good about it whatsoever, it stays in the top ten throughout the summer and makes Steven enough money to buy multiple houses and to finance his own production company. His father is proud of him. (I have never liked this version of the story.)

In other versions of the story, Steven starts making a movie about himself, his feelings and frustrations, and this leads him to ask questions about his family, and soon the project is no longer quite so narcissistic, and he begins to imagine a world before himself and beyond himself. His father does not lie to him, Maria does not lie to him, Jane does not lie to him.

In some of the stories, he interviews Ray before Ray goes to

Washington, D.C. He is haunted by Ray's hatreds and paranoia, but also charmed by his humanity. He turns the camera on himself one night and says, "The words he speaks terrify me, but every time I leave his house, I always make sure to give him a hug, an honest hug, and to tell him I love him, because, I guess, I do."

In most versions of the story, Steven goes to Nicaragua to see what his parents saw. It is futile, of course, because what his parents saw disappeared long ago, but the journey is worthwhile, nonetheless, because Steven discovers he likes the tropics and he likes traveling, so he makes his way to Argentina and to Tierra del Fuego, because that's what the characters do in one of his favorite movies, *Happy Together*. He has all sorts of adventures that are outside the scope of this story, but all we need is to see him down there at the bottom of South America, standing on rocks that lead to the ocean, his bare feet washed by waves, a lighthouse towering behind him. He has a little camera with him, and he films a couple of people far off, a silhouette, they could be anybody — two men, two women, a man and a woman, anybody, any age, any race, anything — and he films them as the sun goes down and their own story continues elsewhere, while his is just beginning.

In one version of the story, Steven does not know his mother is Jane. He thinks he was adopted. He never finds out otherwise. In this version of the story, Ray Draper does not complete his plan. He goes to the café and he sees the Supreme Court justice, but Ray is just not a killer at heart. He is disappointed in himself because of this. It is another failure in what he will only truly admit to himself late at night in the dead of winter has been a life of failure. He leaves D.C. and goes off in search of the house he grew up in, somewhere in central New Hampshire, still rural but far less remote than his own current house.

He finds the place. The house is dilapidated, but the young family living there, two men and their daughter, is optimistic. One of the men is a doctor working at a small clinic, the other is Steven, now a filmmaker who has given up working as a TV cameraman to take care of their daughter and, on the side, to make a documentary about the clinic and the neighborhood. He asks to interview Ray, who then tells a story about being happy as a kid, playing with his sister in the neighborhood. It is a nice story, but it doesn't seem to have much of a point, and Ray knows this, and he's tired, so he thanks the men and says goodbye and drives home toward the dark, nobody the wiser.

In all of the versions of this story, Jane finds her way to a glacier. She stands on it and listens as it cracks and rumbles. The air is warmer than it should be. The world is warming up. The glacier is melting. Soon, the seas will rise and the cities will drown. She won't live to see it, but she knows it is the only possible future. Misery, suffering, death. She wonders where Steven is. She wonders what he has made of himself. She wonders how he will live in the ruining world.

She is alone. Her father is dead. She has not seen her husband in many years, nor her son in at least a few. She wonders if this is her fault. Yes, she thinks, it is. She wishes it were not so, but it is. And it is her father's fault, too, yes, and the fault of his father before him, and his father before him, and all the way back to the colonial settlers who brought disease and murder with them, and then all the way farther back, back to caves and mastodons, to the very first fire, the very first man and woman who uttered a child into the world, a suffering being among other suffering beings, like everyone who would come later, alone together from first to last, birth to death, primordial ooze to the end of entropy. A world is born, and then it ends and goes on ending, which is to say: it changes and goes on changing, each ending a beginning of a new end, until all the heat of the universe is gone and nothing, and no-one, can change anymore.

(The people we love destroy us.)

(The people we fail to love destroy us, too.)

Jane stands on the slowly melting glacier and looks out at the world as light slips away and the air turns to ice against her skin. She does not know what day it is, what time, but if she did she would know she had reached the end of one day and the beginning of a new one. She might shed a tear for the world below, a world of suffering and a world of loneliness, and the tear would turn to crystal against her cold cheek as she stares out across the landscape of blue and white. She might, in these moments, see all the way to the other side of the globe, where a young man with a camera captures the image of two people against a bright sky, and she might smile a brief and tiny smile and wonder what stories might now begin.

THE LAST VANISHING MAN

1.

I saw The Great Omega perform three or four times, including that final, strange show. I was ten years old then. It was the summer of the Sacco and Vanzetti trial, a time when vaudeville and touring acts were quickly fading behind the glittering light of motion pictures and the crackling squawk of radios. What I remember of the performance is vivid, but I am wary of its vividness, as I suspect that vividness derives not from the original moment, but from how much effort I have put into remembering it. What is memory, what is reconstruction, what is misdirection?

What I remember (or what I remember that I remember) is a smoky auditorium, rather dimly lit even for those days of dim lighting, and I remember piano music, and I remember my father eating peanuts, cracking their shells, letting the shells fall to the ground. I am sure he offered me peanuts, too (if there were peanuts there), but my memory is not of myself eating them, but of my father, and of the shells falling to the floor.

Then I remember the magicians, The Great Omega and his assistant, The Great Alpha, standing on the stage. The memory is frozen: it could just as well be the memory of the poster displayed at the front of the Opera House. The Great Omega wears a tuxedo and a cape with bright red lining; his thin face sports a goatee and mustache; a top-hat perches on his head. The Great Alpha wears a beautiful gown, the color of a white pearl, and a headdress apparently made of peacock feathers. I do not remember many of the tricks. Things with cards, things with handkerchiefs, things with coins. The sorts of tricks performed by most other magicians, but even the most familiar tricks were new to me. They fooled me, and I suspect they fooled my father, though when I asked him at the intermission how one of the tricks was done, he said, "Smoke and mirrors, Billy, it's all smoke and mirrors and getting you to look where they want you to look." I remember him saying this because it perplexed me. There hadn't really been much smoke, nor could I see any mirrors.

The one trick I clearly remember (other than, of course, the finale) was a silent routine accompanied by the piano. The Great Omega held a silver bowl in either hand, and the Great Alpha placed a handful of rice into one of the bowls. The Great Omega then gently and quite elegantly tossed the rice to the other bowl, then back. It went back and forth like this, but it quickly became clear that the rice was growing in quantity, and then, somewhere along the way, the rice turned to water. Just as the audience was getting over the amazement of that transformation, the water then turned back to rice, and it dwindled, moving back and forth between the bowls, until there was only one single grain left, which the Great Alpha plucked from the bowl and held up for us to see, or to imagine we saw — one pure grain. I remember it so well because I thought about it endlessly later. What had been in the bowls? When was it only rice and when was it only water? Could there have been a moment when it was both?

The performance ended with the Vanishing Man. I had seen it before, because the Great Omega always concluded his show with this signature illusion, and he had been returning to Littleton with some regularity for at least a year, maybe two or three. I have heard that magicians try not to perform the same feat repeatedly for the same audiences, because with each new performance the chance of the audience seeing through the illusion grows, but the Great Omega seemed to have no qualms about performing the Vanishing Man again and again. Perhaps he was arrogant and thought no-one would be able to see through his trick no matter how many times he performed it; perhaps he did not care. I know no-one who ever explained the trick, though it is similar enough to other illusions that I am sure professional magicians guessed its mechanics.

It was one of his few routines that required a participant from the audience. Unlike many other magicians, the Great Omega only occasionally included audience members in his performance. But the key to the success of the Vanishing Man was that a random man from the audience, somebody we knew was not in on the trick, was at the center of the illusion.

What I remember about that night was that the man who volunteered, Tom Ellison, was obnoxious. Tom Ellison was known for being obnoxious — he drank too much, he was incapable of talking quietly, he seemed to think everyone deserved to listen to his opinion wherever he was, including church — but that night he was especially obnoxious. He had been heckling the show from the beginning, and though the managers of the Opera House tried to throw him out, the Great Omega prevented them. "No no," the magician said as ushers tried to drag Tom Ellison from his seat, "the man may be a boor, but he has paid his money, and he is entitled to a show." Ellison had been drinking steadily from a flask all night, and I expect he replenished the flask during intermission, because it seemed bottomless. By the time the Great Omega started the Vanishing Man routine, Tom Ellison was so drunk he was nearly incoherent. If I had not known of him from town, and had not seen other performances by the Great Omega, I would have wondered if Ellison were not a plant, someone hired by the magician for comic fodder, because his behavior that night, as I remember it, was very much that of a buffoon.

The piano played dramatically. The Great Omega stepped to the front of the stage. "If there is one man in this room that we would all, I expect, like to see vanish, it is *you*, sir!" he said, extending his arm and pointing his finger toward Tom Ellison. "Come to the stage!"

Tom Ellison hooted a cheer for himself and then wobbled his way forward. The Great Alpha stood toward the back of the stage, tending to the apparatus: a large brown box, standing on its end, with a lid-like door in its front, and a few small steps leading up to the door. The Great Omega helped Ellison to approach the box, and held him steady while explaining what he was about to do. "The Vanishing Man is a simple illusion," he said, "that simply does what it simply says: It vanishes a man. Oh, don't worry, we will bring him back. Or maybe not. You never know." The audience laughed.

"Mr. Ellison, sir, we will need you to step inside this box here, and then your contribution to the night's entertainment will come to an end. No great effort necessary, I assure you, no skill required, nothing except the ability to get up these steps and into this box, which I see is quite a challenge for you at the moment — have you been imbibing sir? Oh, well, it's the weekend. We can't begrudge a man a bit of gin, now, can we? Or is it scotch? Hmm, by your breath it smells like both! You are a man of eclectic tastes, it seems!" All of this was said while the Great Omega pushed and cajoled the inebriated Ellison toward the box and its little steps, steps which Ellison needed significant time to negotiate, or at least he seemed to (I wonder now how much was the magician milking laughs and heightening the man's humiliation).

And then he was in. Tom Ellison stood in the box for a moment before tipping to the side and leaning against its wall. "Careful in there," the Great Omega said. "You never know what might happen!"

The piano music played faster. The Great Alpha still hung back at the far edge of the stage. At the time, I barely registered that she had pulled away from the performance, but in retrospect it did seem somewhat strange, as at the previous performances I had seen she had been by the Great Omega's side.

The Great Omega said a few words to increase excitement, and then there was the familiar explosion of light and smoke, and when the smoke cleared, the box had broken into its component parts, its four walls splayed across the stage, its top dangling from a chord suspended from the rafters. The stage was otherwise empty. The audience applauded, the piano kept playing, we all expected the Great Omega and the Great Alpha to return, and we expected them to then gesture to the vanished man now standing at the back of the theatre, as that was how the illusion and the show itself always ended — but no. The moment went on and on. The pianist eventually stopped playing. There was some sort of commotion backstage. Finally, a manager came out and told us the show was over.

It all seemed odd, of course, but it was a magic show. Nobody thought much of it until later, when the police investigated and the newspaper reports came out. I can't say I thought about it for long. Life moves on, after all, especially when you're young and the world seems new every day. I finished high school, and then some mysterious, distant family connections on my mother's side got me into Dartmouth, and then of course there was the war, though I did not go to it, as I was too busy with graduate school and rather old by that point. Well, old for the war. I got married when I was twenty-seven and we had two children. I published a book about *fin de siècle* France and England, and I was able to teach at a college in Boston, but teaching was not for me, and I had grown tired of historical research of the sort I was doing. I just was not an academic at heart. I did some work for the government in the 1950s, but it was desultory work for which I was ill suited by temperament, and in a bit of what I will admit was desperation, I ended up partnering with a friend to open an Italian restaurant in the city, and it did well, much to our surprise, as neither of us knew much of anything about Italian food or restaurants.

Sophie and I had been vacationing up here for years, and after she died, I continued to come up every summer, first with the kids, then, once they were at college, just myself. As bed and breakfasts go, this is one of the best I have known, and once they opened up the cabins, it became the perfect get-away — around the summer of 1964, I think, or at least that is when we first stayed in one. Of course, over time, Alice, Mary, and I became very close friends, and I all but moved up here in the fall of 1968, when Alice was sick and then after she passed away. It was a quiet time, off-season, and Mary told me a lot about their past. And that is when I heard about the Great Omega again for the first time in about forty years.

2.

We moved up here in the summer of 1927. Alice knew the owner. It was just a big old farm then, and the owner was becoming elderly, and she didn't have too many people to help her with the place. A son, maybe, some daughters, or perhaps they were people from town. I don't know. I didn't pay a lot of attention. I had other things on my mind. There was even then some sense of this being a place of refuge, a place people in trouble could come to. I assumed it had something to do with bootlegging, and maybe it did, but the people we met once we'd bought the place were always women. Sometimes women in trouble, yes, but as often as not women seeking some escape, even just for a week or two. That's how we came up with the idea of making it a B&B. Naïvely. We'd planned on becoming farmers. (We were young and crazy and didn't know how hard farming is — and up here, where everything is so rocky and salty, it is especially hard.) That first year, everything died. All the crops died, and the chickens all died one night when we left them out too late and a cold set in, and you might not know this, but chickens are terribly stupid creatures, I'm sorry to say, and those chickens all ran to each other to get warm, and they piled on top of each other, and all the chickens at the bottom of the pile suffocated or were crushed to death. It was a mess. We had a couple cows and had to sell them because we could barely do anything with them ourselves and had so little money by then. We'd brought a good amount of cash with us when we moved up here — Alice's life savings, and what I'd been able to hide away and take when we fled — but by the end of that first year we were not in good financial shape, and we knew we had to do something. We'd had visitors, and we enjoyed having them, and decided that renting out rooms would be a better way to use the property. The house was built for families, and not just a family like we think of now, with a couple of kids, but a family where everyone would be born and die here — the grandparents would live here, and the parents, and all the children, and there'd be plenty of children. That's the only way anybody could have survived up here before the highways were built and the population grew. It's remote now, yes, but it was the far edge of nowhere fifty years ago.

It was hard in the beginning. We certainly worried we weren't going to be able to make it through those first years, but soon enough we had lots of help, and because the place was so remote then, people who came here weren't really on vacation, they were after something else, some deeper escape. We were sort of a commune for a while, and it was good. For a while. Eventually, we shifted toward what we are now, and even as it's become easier to travel up here, we've tried to keep some of the communal spirit. And it's still a place people escape to.

Of course, Alice and I were escapees. Escape artists. Literally, actually.

I suppose it's all right to talk about now, though we never did, not once, to anyone, including ourselves. It was a long time ago, another lifetime. I hardly remember the details.

We had met in New Hampshire, where she was performing as a man. She was a magician, an illusionist. That was not something women did. Women were the sidekicks, the assistants, the people they sawed in half. She did that for a while when she was quite young. I think she ran away from home. That's what she always said, anyway, and I never knew quite how serious to take it. Ran away from home to join the circus. Or, well, not the circus but the vaudeville circuit. Something happened during a tour out west, one of those frontier towns that stayed a frontier town even after the frontier was long gone. She got away by disguising herself as a man. She knew how all the tricks worked, and so she started performing them in out-of-the-way places. Just sleight-of-hand at first, cards and coins, that sort of thing, until she could save up enough money to buy some props and equipment. She slowly made her way back east. Doing everything as a man. It's not so hard to pull off if you're a magician. People expect you to have secrets, they expect you to be mysterious. And she was, of course, even then, I'm sure, quite manly. Big shoulders, big feet, little breasts, always walked like she had something swinging between her legs. Some spirit gum and a good mustache and goatee were all she needed. Nobody looks carefully if they don't have reason to. We don't really see each other, do we? And in those days, clothes were important. It's not like now, where women's clothes and men's clothes can be so similar. Back then, if you put a big, husky, hairy guy into a beautiful dress, plenty of people, probably most of them, wouldn't think twice about it, they'd just think it was a homely girl. Hard to believe, I know, but it's the truth. People saw the clothes, not the person. The clothes make the man. Put Alice in a top hat and tails, call her Henry, and there you have it. But with her, it wasn't even a performance. It was just what she was. Even later. She didn't dare do it too often or too publicly up here, because of all that happened, but she was far happier dressing in men's clothes. There was a kind of safety in it, you know? But then there wasn't. And that's one of the things I regret, one of my big regrets — I took that safety away from her. I didn't intend to. But that's what I did.

And what's sad is that I got my own safety even as she lost hers. Tommy, that was my husband's name, he was a terrible man. Every way that a man could be terrible, that was Tommy. When we were kids in school, I was very attracted to that. He was like an outlaw. But he wasn't. We were in northern New Hampshire. There aren't outlaws there, there are just assholes. But I was young and naïve and romantic. I didn't know. He liked me because I was pretty when I was young and I didn't really know there were better people out there, better men even, than Tommy. It was a different time, too, and a different place. Men hit their women, that's what they did, that's what they all did. My father hit my mother, and his father hit his mother, and so on. *Their* women, yes. Their women to hit. That's how you know they're *your* women, isn't it? Same as a man could hit his dog or his horse or whatever, he could hit his woman, because she was his. And I didn't know any better. It was Alice who taught me, showed me, what my life had become. And what it might be.

I fell in love with Alice when she was a man. I hadn't been able to have any children, and once he took a look the doctor said I wouldn't ever, and I suspect now that it was because of what happened during one of Tommy's really bad times, but I don't want to go into all that, so I'll just say I was hoping for something to get me out of the house, and at that point Tommy didn't care if I worked or what, I think he just wanted me to die and leave him alone. He wouldn't let me go, though. That was the terrible thing. I would have happily left. But no. I was his woman, and it would be an insult to him if I left him. He'd get so mad when I brought it up. Just awful. But he didn't mind me looking for some work. So I read the paper. And there was a notice for an assistant to a magician. That's what it said: "Magician's assistant." It sounded like the most wonderful thing in the world to me. It involved some travel, some mystery, everything I wanted. I asked Tommy if I could apply, and he said he didn't care, so I did. Alice was Henry then, The Great Omega. Stupid name, I know, but it didn't sound so bad back then.

She interviewed me at the Opera House. There were ten or fifteen other women there, all single, all younger than me. I think most men didn't want their women to travel, or to be involved with such a disreputable sort of thing, so I was the only married one. I almost left when I saw how beautiful and young everybody else was. But Henry — Alice — liked something in me. "Are you sure you really want me?" I said. "Oh *dear*, yes," he said. I'll never forget that. He sounded so strange.

I asked Alice later, after it all, why she hired me. Why *me*? She never quite explained it. She said I seemed to be the one who needed the job the most. And I suppose that was true. Or maybe it was love at first sight, even though I can't say I really believe in that. But he was very handsome, I thought.

"There will be many secrets," he told me. "I need to know that you can own secrets." I remember those exact words. *I need to know that you can own secrets.* And of course, I could. An owner undesiring, unjudging, profoundly indifferent.

It took time to learn the tricks, to learn what I needed to do. I had always been a good dancer, and I had done some acrobatics, so I learned it all quickly enough at a basic level. And then experience teaches you, one show after another. I was terrible at first. Scared of the audience, scared of the equipment, scared of messing everything up. But I improved.

It was, I suppose, eight or nine months into our tour — it wasn't much of a tour, just northern New England, but farther than I'd ever been — anyway, it was into that tour maybe a year — no, sooner, maybe seven months — that I figured out Henry was Alice. I'm sure there were lots of signs before, and I just missed them. We were all but living together on the tour. Tiny, dingy theatres with rotten dressing rooms. You get to know a person in spaces like that. Certainly, we became very close. I knew I was in love with him. I hated it, hated myself for it, that blind and terrible love. He was so charismatic, so confident. I didn't say anything. I didn't do anything. My fear of Tommy was stronger than any love I could feel. But still. It was love. And so one day I happened to open the dressing room door as he was changing out of one set of clothes, and he wasn't being as careful as usual, and … I saw. Everything. He didn't seem to mind. Alice smiled and I remember that she gestured for me to come closer. I closed the door. She took off the rest of her clothes. And she embraced me, and kissed me. It was lovely.

I was so scared of Tommy. I tried to go back home once a week, and I usually did, once a week for a day or sometimes two. But even so, he was beginning to get angry. He said people were talking. He said they said he couldn't look after his woman. People thought I must be having an affair with Henry. Tommy said that to me. I was terribly scared.

Tommy got drunk a lot. He was better when he wasn't drinking. But he was drinking all the time by then. I returned to Henry one day with bruises and cuts.

She said we would solve this. She said Tommy could be stopped. She said we would never be apart again.

She spoke the truth. Tommy never hurt me again, never hurt another person. And Alice and I, we were never apart for the rest of our lives. She stuck to me and refused to fall away. Until now.

I could go on and on, spinning a tale, using what tricks I know, but it would always be the same. I'm sorry. I'm afraid I can't talk about it any more.

3.

"And to be honest," William said, "that is all I really know about the Great Omega and Mary. Or Alice and Mary. She never said more than that, and she died a fortnight less than a year after Alice had. I developed the place into what it is now. I thought about renaming it The Great Omega or Alice & Mary's or something, but it already had a reputation, and I thought the best way to honor them was to keep the name they had given it."

"Lolly Willowes," I said. "It's fun to say."

"Yes, indeed. For the longest time, I thought it was some exotic plant. But it is a book both Mary and Alice liked, a British novel, I think."

Neither Cath nor I had ever heard of it, and William said he hadn't gotten around to reading it, though he had a copy somewhere. We were sitting out on the porch, watching the sun set. It was an unseasonably warm October night, and we were the only guests, though a week earlier the place had been almost filled to capacity.

"What a fun coincidence," Cath said, "that you were at their last performance. That you saw it all yourself, but you never knew the actual story."

"Yes," William said. "I have had a lot of coincidences in my life, actually. That one was not even the biggest. I was in London once, at least ten years ago now, back when I was teaching — I remember because it was spring break, and I went to London for vacation. Anyway, I had gone shopping with a friend in Soho, and we wandered around some side streets and then decided we were hungry, so we stopped in a pub and got a sandwich and a pint. I am sitting there, and I see a man walk past, going over to the bathroom, a man who looks just like a good friend of mine from the school, another history teacher. A lovely man, someone I was very fond of — if I had to run into someone from the college randomly, I would have certainly wanted it to be him. But of course it could not be him, could it? The likelihood was simply impossible. Or was it? What were his plans for the break? I had no idea. So maybe... I said to my friend, the one I was having lunch with, 'I think I know that man — I think I know him from the States,' and my friend looked at me as if he thought I were developing dementia praecox. 'Say his name when he comes by,' my friend said. So I did. 'Dr. Carmine,' I said as he walked past. He stopped. Froze. Turned slowly. We stared at each other. It was him. James Carmine. Scruffy brown hair, green eyes, sharp cheekbones. It was him. We stared at each other for a whole minute, I think. Worlds seemed to collide. In talking with him, once we recovered our senses, it turned out he was in London visiting some friends he had never told me about. As was I. Secret lives overlapping. Some sort of fate. For one moment. After, we went our ways. I left the college. Life continued. I have no idea what became of him. It was not so many years ago, but a different world." William lowered his head and looked long at a fading strip of sunlight stretched across the floorboards.

"Did you love him?" Cath said quietly.

William didn't look up. "In my own way," he whispered. "Distantly." He turned toward us and smiled shyly, then offered another glass of wine, and we said sure, and I don't remember what else we talked about. Maybe London, since it was where Cath and I had met, her home town and a place I visited with a radical theatre troupe I was managing back in the days when theatre seemed like it might save the world, and it did save me from the husband my parents had so desperately wanted me to find. Or maybe we mentioned that we'd just sold my mother's house in Massachusetts, sold it for more money than we'd ever dreamed possible — a house that had been, when my parents bought it, an undistinguished two-bedroom in a working class suburb and had become quite valuable after the technology companies settled in along Route 128 and prop-erty values exploded. Cath had been working with a women's group in Boston, but there was a lot of in-fighting and she was tired of it. I'd been managing a restaurant that had just gone bankrupt, a job I'd settled into after a life of traipsing around as an ever-more-destitute revolutionary got to feeling like a caricature of whatever I'd dreamed of for myself. We were taking our extended vacation up to Lolly Willowes because we hadn't quite decided what to do next, and we didn't much want to decide.

That night, we lay in bed for a long time, chatting about nothing in particular, nothing memorable, until I mentioned William. "He seems so forlorn," I said, thinking about some of the men like William that I had known over the years, especially Eddie, one of the actors in our theatre troupe, whom I'd dubbed, to myself at least, The Boy Who Pines. Drunk one night, he told me he'd loved one of the guys who had just left the troupe, but Eddie had always been afraid to say anything, and he hadn't even wanted sex, he said, just someone to touch him, some hand to hold. Last I knew, Eddie had married a nondescript woman and settled down in Idaho or Iowa or one of those places, where he found a job as an accountant or clerk of some sort, something with very regular hours and a modest salary with the potential for incremental promotion, and he's probably got children by now and a mortgage and a couple cars, and maybe he's happy, though if I were to be honest I would suppose he's probably more numb than anything, not happy or miserable, just existing, but how could I ever know, really? I haven't heard from him in years.

"Forlorn?" Cath said. "Alone, maybe. Lonely, perhaps. I'm not sure about *forlorn*."

"He talked about his wife a lot, and his kids. Or kid. One? I don't remember."

"Yes. And what about that story of Soho? Why tell us that? I mean, Soho…"

"Right. And the whole magician thing? Do you believe that?"

"No," Cath said. "But he seems to. And you remember Alice and Mary. They loved a good story."

"They told me they were from Calgary," I said.

"Swingin' Calgary!"

"Or maybe Ottawa. Or one was from Calgary and the other was from Ottawa. I can't remember. But maybe that was just a story."

"A cover story."

"Maybe."

"You know, I swear," Cath said, "the last time we were here, William was living with a man. Or at least, fooling around with one."

"Right! You said you saw him go up to William's rooms. Ronald? Ronnie? One of those. He was nice."

"I saw him — Robbie? — I saw him go up one night when I'd come in to the kitchen to get a glass of water, and then another time, a couple days later, I saw him coming down very early in the morning when I was up for the sunrise. I pretended not to see him and he sort of shuffled by behind my back, then down to his cabin."

"Yes, I remember you told me. I thought William's behavior, so carefully ignoring him, I thought that was very strange. I mean, *here* of all places. When was the last time a straight person even set foot here?"

"Eons."

"So why hide?"

"Habit, I suppose. Easiest just to keep going along as you've always been going along."

"Sad."

"True."

Our conversation drifted off, and soon enough I heard Cath's familiar little snore, a sound that always made me imagine a sparrow whose song had somehow attained a BBC accent.

We held each other close that night, all night.

We woke together to a beautiful morning: the sky clear, the air crisp, the light creamy through the thick old glass of the cabin's window. Cath made tea in an electric kettle we'd brought, and we dawdled about through the morning, then headed up to the house just in time, we hoped, for the end of breakfast. A feast sat in silver serving dishes on the dining room table: hardboiled eggs, scrambled eggs, fried eggs, bacon, ham, croissants, doughnuts, Corn Flakes, strawberries, blueberries, apples, peanuts, carafes of orange juice, milk, coffee, water. No one was around. We ate slowly, then wandered through the house, looking for William to thank him for a particularly sumptuous meal. He wasn't there. He wasn't anywhere. We returned to the dining room and found a large envelope addressed to us on a side table in the back corner. Cath gave me a perplexed look, then opened it.

She pulled out a sheaf of papers: a cover letter and various official documents. The letter was simple: "I leave this all to you. Do with it what you will. I think that is best. Thank you. William." The official documents were a deed and all the necessary materials to sign the property and business over to us, if we wished. It would only need our signatures.

I knocked on the door to the upstairs rooms where William lived. I knocked and knocked. Eventually, I turned the doorknob. The small, sparsely furnished rooms of the apartment looked like a museum, with chairs and a couch and a bed that dated back well into the 19th century. A few pictures on the walls must have been there when Alice and Mary moved in: sepia photographs of people long dead, paintings of farm scenes by someone more earnest than skilled. A tall oak book case filled with a few dusty volumes — a family Bible, a dictionary, a collection of Longfellow's poems, a collection of poems called *Offerings* — as well as a collection of moth-eaten cloth dolls, a couple of blue china teacups, three tattered peacock feathers, a large silver bowl filled with rice. The bed had been tightly made and covered with a threadbare quilt. William was nowhere in the apartment.

We waited. Soon enough, guests came and, not knowing what else to do, we helped them settle in. The pantry and refrigerator were stocked full, and so we cooked breakfast and dinner. Eventually, we had to go shopping, and so we did. Eventually, we brought the deed to the town offices, where the clerk had, it turned out, been expecting us, and all the paperwork was quickly filed. Eventually, we moved into the apartment.

Sometime after moving in, while trying to spruce the apartment up a bit and bring it into the current age, we came upon a newspaper clipping that had fallen behind the bed (or perhaps someone had left it there for us to find). It was so old it began to crumble in our fingers. "MAGICIAN VANISHES MAN — AND HIMSELF" the headline read. So there was some truth to the stories, after all. What sort of truth it might be, we'll likely never know.

It is January as I write this. Cath is making tea for me and our six guests. A storm came in last night, and snow blankets everything. Now, though, it is morning and the storm is gone and the vaulting sky burns blue. I hear muffled voices in the rooms below. I hear Cath laugh. I will stop writing now, I will close this book, I will stand and walk across the ancient floorboards of our room, and I will press my nose against the cold window and stare out at the untroubling, untroubled world.

WINNIPESAUKEE DARLING

"What a dump!" Henry exclaimed after he opened the cabin door and stepped inside. One might assume that this was hyperbole, or the high standards of a New York City interior designer applied to a rustic rural retreat, but, alas, no. Even before I stepped inside after Henry, I could smell the mildew. It was a dark place, and the globs of sunlight that seeped in through the cabin's small windows looked curdled. Dank, rust-colored carpet covered the floors. The furniture was all clearly older than me, maybe even older than Henry.

"This," Henry said, "is not as advertised."

We walked through the cabin to a small porch, then down a path that led past other cabins and then, eventually, to the lake, where a wooden dock reached into the water. The dock looked at least as old as the furniture in the cabin, and I was sure it would capsize the minute Henry stepped onto it, but it held him fine, and I followed, and we stood, arm in arm, looking out at sailboats, kayaks, and motorboats making their way across the expanse of Lake Winnipesaukee.

After a while, we wandered back to the cabin, where we opened all the windows to air the place out, moved some furniture around, brought in our suitcases along with bags of groceries we'd bought in town. Henry popped the cork on a French cabernet sauvignon he had been saving for the occasion, and we raised our glasses in a toast to ourselves, the lake, and Candy Darling.

...

This is what started it all: Henry and I watched a documentary about Candy Darling, and all of a sudden he was obsessed with finding a cabin on Lake Winnipesaukee. Before we watched this movie, Henry had never even heard of Lake Winnipesaukee, but at the end of the movie there's a note from Candy about three things she wanted in life and one of those three things was a cabin on Lake Winnipesaukee (the others were big houses in California and Long Island, and to learn languages and how to sew). "Where's Lake Winnipesaukee?" Henry said, and for once in our relationship I was the one with all the knowledge. "New Hampshire," I said. "About an hour north of where I grew up. We went there for a week during summer vacations sometimes, my parents and my brother and me. Lots of sunlight, people, water. I hated it."

Henry didn't say much that night, but over the next few days the living room coffee table sprouted a pile of library books about Andy Warhol and the Factory (the scene of Candy's fame), and then the word *Winnipesaukee* wormed its way into conversations, first with Henry asking me about those summer trips of my childhood, then asking why Candy might have been attracted to the place, how she even knew about it. Soon he was talking about the cost of cabins there, the ridiculous real estate prices. How had my parents afforded it? "We only ever stayed in dingy, moldy motels," I said. "There are plenty around there if you don't want to be right on the water. The nicest spots are for wealthier people, but it's a big lake, and there are all sorts of little places around the water that are comfy and quaint. I think it made my parents feel like they were able to get a taste of a life they couldn't otherwise afford, so that's why we went there." Had I known the perilous depths of Henry's new obsession, I might have spoken more carefully, might have embroidered tales of marauding rednecks or radical weather or freshwater sharks, might have at least not painted such a cozy picture of the place — but I didn't realize the danger at the time.

Candy Darling did something to Henry, set him off balance, weighting the scale of his always-unbridled appetites even more toward immoderation. One day I came home from the coffee shop where I work to find that Henry had opened our nightly bottle of wine early and made his way through most of it. His words were a little slow and his face a little flushed as he explained that though his savings account was not what it used to be, he nonetheless had decided to splurge on renting a cabin on Lake Winnipesaukee next week, and he had also contacted some of his old friends from his days working backstage at various off-Broadway theatres, and with their help he had managed to put together a series of outfits that he thought would be perfect for me.

"Outfits?" I said.

He tossed me a white silk dress.

I must confess — and risk befouling my faggy bona fides in the confession — that I do not see, and have never seen, the attraction of drag. Drag shows bore me, and I have no interest in pretending to be a woman. I'm baffled by the whole thing, honestly. Women's clothing is uncomfortable and fussy and time consuming, women's shoes are torture devices, and I don't even like the *sight* of make-up, so the thought of smearing it on my skin is nauseating. I don't know why women themselves want to dress as women, never mind why men would want to imitate them. But perhaps I am insufficiently experienced, or buttoned up by prejudiced assumptions, woefully lacking in sensitivity. The topic was forbidden between myself and Henry, as he had been (or so I was led to understand) quite the drag queen in his younger days, and the moment he got a whiff of my indifference to drag, he said we must never discuss it again or he would immediately fall out of love with me. At first, I assumed he was joking, but then I saw the seriousness in his face and I avoided the subject forever after.

What was I to do, though, when presented with a dress? And a pile of other clothing apparently intended for women?

"I thought perhaps we could make a movie," Henry said. "You have the right shape of face, you're exactly the right age, it's perfect. I've got the most divine wig for you."

"You want me to dress up like Candy so you can make a movie?"

"Yes," Henry said, beaming.

"You're out of your goddamned mind," I said.

I stormed out of the apartment and walked through the streets blindly, enraged. Such emotional states are hardly conducive to reflection, but if I had taken even one second to consider how I was responding, I might have seen that — o irony of ironies! — I was all but auditioning for the role of a stereotypically tempestuous drag queen.

Eventually, I calmed down enough to stop at a little shop and get a mixed berry smoothie. The gooey sweetness comforted me. I recognized then that my reaction was all out of proportion to the circumstances, and that really what was upsetting me so was not anything to do with dresses or cabins or Lake Winnipesaukee, but rather with Henry's obsession over a long-dead transgender woman. A woman who was not me; a woman he wanted me to be. It seemed obvious once I saw it. I didn't want Henry to love Candy Darling. I didn't want him to obsess over her instead of me — indeed, I had never felt he'd obsessed over me at *all*. And that was the sore spot. He enjoyed my company, and enjoyed me as a sex partner, but now that he had found Candy, everything that was missing between us came into focus. For a moment, mixed berry smoothie in hand, I considered wallowing in self pity. But that's what a diva would do, I reminded myself, and I did not want to be a diva. Instead, I decided to seize this opportunity. If Henry was going to be obsessed with Candy Darling, then, well, why not — why shouldn't I give in and let him shape me into her? Why not let his desires play out as they would, and submerge myself beneath them?

...

Henry had bought a small video camera shortly before we left the city, and at the cabin he unpacked it before anything else. He wanted to get some shots of the lake as the sun went down, its last rays breaking like shards of stained glass over the water. I finished unpacking everything else while he was off with his camera. There was a little closet in the cabin's one bedroom, and I hung the Candy clothes there. I hadn't really looked at them before. They were lovely, there was no denying: lots of lace and sequins, but tasteful, even classical. A couple of print dresses that screamed 1960s to me. A stole that I hoped was not real fur. Some strange feathery accoutrements. A gorgeous blonde wig. A trenchcoat that made me think of Inspector Clouseau. Nothing I would be too embarrassed to wear. In fact, as I hung them in the closet, a tinge of excitement teased me. I was actually curious what these clothes would feel like on my body.

Henry returned and began making a beef carbonara for

dinner. We had soon finished the first bottle of wine and opened another. We sat on the porch, watched the sun set, ate our food, drank our wine, opened a third bottle. (Though we only each drank a glass from it, it is that third bottle that I blame for everything else.)

As the night wore on, I became obsessed with trying on some of the Candy clothes. Henry enjoyed stripping me, and then I him, and we spent some giggly minutes relieving our urges together on the floor of the bedroom. A quick shower afterward got us clean and a little bit sobered up, and then Henry helped me put on one of the print dresses. I had thought I would feel silly in a dress, but I did not. At first, I assumed it was just that I'd shared a lot of wine and a jolly orgasm with Henry, so we were in quite a good mood, but there was something else, too, some sense of comfort that exceeded the circumstances. Henry put the wig on me, then went to work on my makeup, turning a face that had been scarred by acne and Scottish ancestry into something soft, smooth, and elegant. Looking in the bathroom mirror, I said, "You should have been a beautician."

Henry had mentioned that there was a mansion across the street, and in my wine-besotted state I became obsessed with going over to introduce ourselves to the neighbors. Henry thought this was a delightful idea and that he should film it. Laughing and stumbling, we made our way across the street and up a long, steep driveway to what was, indeed, a very large house sitting atop a ledge overlooking the cabins below and the lake beyond. The front of the house was shaped like the prow of a ship, filled with massive windows. Lights were on inside and out, and muffled strains of orchestral music drifted toward us. The front door was tasteful but unobtrusive; for a moment, we didn't see it at all. Then Henry walked right up and pushed the doorbell.

The music got quiet and soon the door opened. A small bald man stood in the doorway.

"Yes?" he said tentatively.

"We're tenants in the cabin down below and happened to be wandering around. We saw your lights on, so thought we'd say hello to a neighbor."

"Ah," said the man. "Well, then, hello. My name is Max."

"I'm Henry, and this is Candy."

The wine doing the thinking for me, I said, "I have a penis."

Max smiled. "They can be handy gadgets," he said.

Henry laughed. "We're from New York. It's terribly quiet around here. Lovely, but quiet. Anyway, we just wanted to say hello."

"Would you like to come in for a moment?" Max said.

"Are you an axe murderer?" Henry asked.

"Not as far as I know. I'm not sure I even own an axe."

"Well then certainly," Henry said, "we would be happy to take advantage of your hospitality."

The interior of Max's house was modern, with distant ceilings, twenty-foot-high windows, and the minimum walls necessary for the structure to stand. We entered into a kitchen apparently designed to serve a battalion, and then we passed through the kitchen to a living and dining room that seemed to me about the size of a whole city block. The windows at the end of the room appeared even taller from inside.

"I'm unprepared for guests, I'm afraid," Max said. "I don't have a lot of food or drink to offer. I need to go grocery shopping tomorrow. I have some orange juice, some milk, and the tap water is actually quite good."

"A glass of water would be wondrous," I said.

"Certainly," Max said, taking a glass from a cabinet and filling it with water at the sink.

"This is a lovely house," Henry said. "Have you lived here long?"

"No, not at all," Max said. He handed me the glass of water. We made our way to the largest couch I had ever seen in my life. "This was my sister's house. She died last year, and there was nobody else to take care of it. I'm going to sell it, I expect. I haven't had much of a chance until now to visit. I live in Mexico, myself. Puerto Vallarta."

"That sounds lovely," Henry said. "What did your sister do to be able to have a house like this?"

"She married well. I always admired her for that. Never had children and married for money. A great achievement. Even when she was young my father told her that a girl of her tastes would need to marry rich. And she did. Three times, in fact. To terribly bland men with lots of money. Divorced two, out-lived the third, then died a few months later herself. She had seemed perfectly healthy, just passed away in her sleep of a massive heart attack. Not a bad way to go, really. I've certainly seen worse."

"Indeed," Henry said. A silence descended. I wondered if the man had any inkling of what I knew to be true: that Henry had, in the years just before my birth, seen more death than most people who haven't been on a battlefield ever do. Before he changed his career entirely, Henry was a nurse and worked on an AIDS ward. It got to be too much. It had seemed, he said during one of the few times he ever talked about those years with me, that everybody he encountered was dying: his friends, his patients, his neighbors, clerks at stores, bus drivers, everyone. It frightened him so much that he stopped having sex for years. Didn't even have an urge, he said. Perhaps that was why he was HIV-negative, or perhaps he had been scru-pulous about safe sex (*we* had been, certainly — only recently had we stopped using condoms with each other), or perhaps he had simply been lucky when so many other people were not. *Lucky* was not the word he would use to describe himself, I'm sure. Once, after I blithely told the tale of my coming out in high school and how I and my queer friends still joked about how uptight I was about it all even though nobody else had ever cared and everybody had always known I was whatever it is that I am, he said he hardly knew any gay men his own age anymore.

Max said, "What brings you to this part of the world?"

"I've always wanted to see this lake," I said.

Henry nodded and said, "It's nice to get out of the city now and then. Nice to visit someplace a little slower, a little less stressful."

"What do you do there, in the city?"

"He's an artist," I said.

Henry said, "An interior designer."

"While I," I said, "am a hanger-on, living off his coattails. I hope perhaps I might stumble into celebrity if I just end up at the right soiree, perhaps get my picture in *Life* magazine if the paparazzi drift by."

"Fifteen minutes of fame?" Max said.

"Certainly," I said.

"We're working on a movie," Henry said. He held up his camera. "A movie about Candy here at Lake Winnipesaukee."

"How interesting," Max said, apparently meaning it.

"It's a low-budget thing," Henry said. "Nothing grand. Kind of verité, kind of avant-garde." He turned the camera on and pointed it at me. "Say hello, Candy."

"Hello, Candy," I said.

Henry glanced at Max while he kept the camera on me. "Do you want to be in the movie?" Henry asked.

"Oh, I don't think you want me in your movie," Max said. He stood up and walked to the kitchen to refill his glass of water. "I don't feel dressed for it."

"We have plenty of dresses and accessories," I said.

Max chuckled nervously. He stood in the kitchen and sipped his water. "All right," he said. "What the hell. I'm too old to be embarrassed."

"Fabulous!" Henry said. He turned the camera off. "I'll be right back." He dashed out the door like a little kid.

"How long have you two … known each other?" Max asked.

"We've been together for a little over a year now," I said. I told him the outline of how we met, how it was only Henry's second time ever using a dating app, whereas, unlike Henry, I never had any success in bars and relied, instead, on the gentle vibrations of my phone to alert me to the various men whose names I've now forgotten, or, as often as not, never knew.

"An exciting life," Max said.

"It's better as a story than a life," I said. "Tonight is more excitement than I've had in ages."

"Oh?"

"Can you keep a secret?"

"Certainly."

"This is my first time in drag. Isn't that *scandalous?*"

"Scandalous!"

"I'm usually rather preppy, to be honest."

"As am I," Max said. "This will be a new experience for us both." He quickly added: "I was married, once. To a woman. A happy marriage. But I was better off alone."

"So you went to Mexico?"

"I was in the Merchant Marines. For a long time. Went to Panama, Costa Rica, Nicaragua, all over Central America, occasionally South America, and then afterward I kept travelling, until I found myself in Puerto Vallarta, and I didn't leave. Taught Spanish and English at schools there for a while, eventually I got tired of it, and I'd saved up some money, had a bit of a pension, so I gave it up and instead, well, I don't know. I just existed for a while. Easy enough to do there. I live frugally. I've never needed lots of money. It's a beautiful place, Puerto Vallarta, especially the older parts of the city. Easy to let time slip away. Then my sister died, and her estate has taken up a lot of my attention, but also relieved me of any real concern for money, except what to do with it all. A better problem to have than the opposite."

"And you're happy alone?"

"Oh yes," Max said. "I have friends. But I'm terribly solitary. My wife said that, in fact. Complained. That I was complete in myself, didn't need her. I don't think that's true, especially after she left and I missed her quite a lot. But I can see why she thought it."

Henry bounded back into the house, his arms loaded with clothes and a grocery bag that he had filled with our opened bottle of wine plus one more, a couple of boxes of crackers, and a variety of cheeses. I took the clothes while he prepared drinks and snacks.

"See anything here you like?"

Max wrapped the stole around his neck. "How do I look?" he said.

In truth, rather ridiculous, his boring and conservative clothing only made more boring and conservative by the boldness of the stole, but I said, "Fabulous! Do you want to try on a dress, or is this enough for you right now?"

"This is enough now," he said, which didn't surprise me in the least.

We drank and ate, and Henry filmed us. "Just talk to each

other," he said. "Pretend I'm not here."

"Let's give Max a new name," I said. "Tonight you will be Alexandra. Like the Empress. There was an Empress Alexandra, wasn't there?"

Max laughed. "Certainly," he said. "And so I shall be Alexandra, though perhaps not an empress."

"Tell me, Alexandra, do you enjoy this cabin on Lake Winnipesaukee?" I said.

"I do, indeed. I am thinking of doing some upgrades, maybe adding a floor or two."

"Yes, I was just thinking it feels a little cramped."

Max laughed. We continued on with empty, delightful banter, and we ate and drank, and soon enough I had my arm around Max and we snuggled up together on the couch while Henry continued filming. "You've been lonely, haven't you, Alexandra?" I whispered.

"Yes," he said quietly. "The world is a lonely place."

I swirled the wine in my glass. "Does it need to be?" I said. "A lonely place?"

Max sighed. "I don't know. I just know it is."

The night seemed somehow to have opened wider around us, the whole world gone quiet while we nestled there together on the giant couch, Henry sitting on the floor pointing the camera up at us. Despite being larger than Max and me put together, Henry seemed to have shrunk down almost to nothing. I didn't notice him, didn't think about him, and I don't think Max did either.

"What was the music you were playing before we came in?" I asked.

"Bartok," he said. "Concerto for Orchestra."

"Ah," I said knowingly, though I didn't actually know anything about it. "You should play it again."

He seemed to hesitate, then sat up. He went to a small CD player that I hadn't noticed over on a table at the far side of the room. The music started soft and slow from speakers set up in the ceiling.

Max picked up a black lace dress. "I think this might fit me," he said.

Henry said, "Try it on."

"Excuse me for a moment," Max said, slipping away to a bathroom next to the kitchen, dress in hand.

Henry stopped his camera. "What a lovely night it is," he said. He refilled our wine glasses. We stood at a window together and stared out at the vast night, the moonlight sprinkled across the water. Reflected in the window, I saw Max float out of the bathroom. He looked both ridiculous and lovely in the dress.

The music suddenly rose in a crescendo of strings and I grabbed Max in my arms and we danced an impromptu, awkward, hilarious dance. He laughed and I laughed. The music slowed. Henry aimed his camera at us. "This is not dance music," I said, chuckling.

"It is certainly not," Max said.

"But it is gorgeous, just like the Empress Alexandra."

We were still holding on to each other, moving in dance-like motions, but not to the rhythm of the music; rather, to a rhythm of our own. Max's hands held me close. He ran fingers through my wig gently while resting his head on my chest. He looked up and I saw tears in his eyes.

"I'm sorry," he said, pulling away.

"Nothing to be sorry about," I said.

He sat on the couch and I sat beside him, uncertain whether he wanted to be close. He did not.

"I had too much wine," he said.

"Sure," I said.

To Henry he said, "Do you mind not filming anymore?" Henry put the camera down. He sat next to me on the couch.

We listened to the music and looked out the windows at the night.

Eventually, Max spoke, almost too quietly to be heard over the orchestra. "I did have some experiences with men. I was a sailor, after all, stuck in the middle of the ocean for weeks and months at a time. We did what we needed with each other. For each other. It was nice. I haven't thought about that in a very long time, though. I'm not sure we ever *thought* about it much at all. It was what it was."

He reached for his wine glass, which was empty. Henry went to the kitchen, brought a bottle back, and filled Max's glass.

Max drank, then said, "I went to Mexico after my wife left. First to Mexico City. I had a little apartment there. It was not a great neighborhood. There were prostitutes, and eventually I got up the courage to hire one. She was nice, we'd seen each other around. But I couldn't do anything. It was humiliating. We tried a few more times. She was gentle and understanding. I paid her, of course. One time, she brought a friend of hers, a young man. Not especially young, maybe twenty-five. I was horrified, honestly, but there was also something about him, something in his eyes, and she left us, and we did what we did. He returned a few more times. I paid him, too, more than I paid her, but I stopped thinking about him as a prostitute, I thought of him as a friend. That sounds ridiculous, or pitiful, or something, but it's true. I taught him some English. He came by more and more, and sometimes it didn't feel like I needed to pay him for what we did together, so I didn't. We were friends. I gave him little gifts, things I found at the market, little carved animals, that sort of thing.

He was very grateful, almost childlike. I began to feel some power over him. I had always had power over him, since I was the rich American — not rich by our standards, not at all, but certainly by his. I hadn't recognized this as power at first. That sounds naïve. It was naïve. And ignorant. But then I eventually realized the power I had over him, and I liked it. I liked that I could make him do more or less anything I wanted. Not sexually, I don't mean that. What we did together was gentle and friendly. But when we were not in bed together, when we were clothed and up and about, he became something of a servant to me. We would go out to the market together, to shops and cafés, and I would treat him terribly, as if he was worthless. He put up with this for a while. And then one day he didn't show up. And the next day, the next. I sought out the woman and asked if she had seen him. She said he hated me. She said I should be careful because he might try to kill me. I laughed. Why would he try to do anything to me? How could he? I was a rich American, after all, and he was just a poor, dirty little Mexican, unimportant. I told her I would give him no thought at all. She spat in my face. I'll never forget that. Then that night he came back. He said I was a maricón and a rapist and I ought to give him all my money. I laughed at him. Rage filled him. I thought he was going to hit me. I think he thought that as well. But he just left. I never saw him again. I never hired another prostitute. I moved to Puerto Vallarta soon after. I wanted to live somewhere with clearer air, somewhere with more sunlight and ocean, as I did not feel like a real person in Mexico City, or a good person. I thought of the young man often, eventually with regret and shame. And then I stopped thinking about him, I hardly ever thought about the whole thing until tonight. It was twenty years ago. Or a few years more than that. But what hurts me now, what I can hardly bear to admit, is that I don't remember his name."

Suddenly he covered his mouth with his hands and for a moment I thought he was going to be sick but then I realized he was sobbing. Henry and I both went to him, we held him, and soon he dropped his hands to his side and wept.

After a while, the music stopped. Max wiped his face with his hands. I kissed his forehead. He smiled. "I'm so sorry," he said. "I am a silly old man." I kissed his forehead again. He stood up and stretched. "It's a beautiful night," he said, then went to the bathroom and changed back into his own clothes.

"I'm afraid I'm terribly tired," he said, handing me the dress, neatly folded. Henry and I gathered our things and said goodnight. As we stepped outside, I turned around and said to Max, "Will you be all right?"

"Certainly," he said. "Better than ever."

"Goodnight, Alexandra," I said, then Henry said the same.

"Goodnight, Henry," Max replied. "And Candy. Goodnight."

We made our way back to the cabin without saying a word, nor did we speak as we cleaned up the kitchen, then made our way to the bedroom, where I slowly undressed Henry, then held his glorious belly while he pulled my dress up. I let go of him as he guided the dress over my head, the wig almost coming off with it, but he held the wig on and repositioned it. "How's my makeup?" I whispered.

"Lovely," he said. "You are a delightful Candy."

"She's now been to Lake Winnipesaukee."

"Yes," he said. "She has."

Henry took my wig off and set it on top of the dress. Then he pulled down my underwear, and we drifted together to the bed.

...

We woke late in the morning, and after some coffee and fried eggs and a shower, we decided to check on Max. We crossed the road, ascended the driveway, and Henry pressed the doorbell. Everything was quiet. Henry pressed the doorbell again. I looked in a window, but saw nothing amiss. Henry found the garage and was able to open the door. There was no car. The house was locked. "I guess he's out," Henry said.

We checked on Max and the house a couple times each day, but we did not see him again. On our last day at the cabin, we talked about calling the police to see if they might do a welfare check, but we decided against it. There was no sign of Max at the house at all, and neither of us believed he was there.

Once we got back to the city, we downloaded Henry's footage to his laptop and watched some of what he had shot. It was nice to see Max again and I was impressed with how much I actually did look like Candy Darling. But there was a lot of footage.

"This is very Warholian," Henry said.

"You mean boring as hell?"

"That's one way of putting it."

"What are you going to do? Shall we have Candy go on other adventures?"

"No," Henry said. "I think she's done what she needed to do."

I nodded. I wanted to say something, but what was there to say?

Henry pressed some keys on the computer. "There," he said. "All gone."

"Erased?"

"Yes, indeed."

"Why?" I said, some hesitation in my voice.

"Ghosts ought to get to stay ghosts," he said.

In that moment, I felt overcome with loss. I didn't speak to

Henry for most of the rest of the day. But he was right; I knew it then and know it now.

We still remind each other about Lake Winnipesaukee, about Max and Candy Darling, but Henry sold the camera, he gave the clothes and wig back to the people he had borrowed them from, he returned the Warhol books to the library, and he even decided to cut down on wine and carbs, a vow that was easier to make than keep, but he is doing his best, we both are, and recently he asked me where we should go for our next vacation, and I told him I would think about it, but I'm sure he knows my answer, and I'm sure that he, too, is thinking that before much more time gets lost, we all ought to visit Puerto Vallarta.

II.

that piece of the oppressor which is planted deep
within each of us, and which knows only
the oppressor's tactics, the oppressor's relationships

—Audre Lorde

KILLING FAIRIES

I met Jack at the end of my first year of college, a year that began in misery and ended in something else, though even now I'm not sure what to call it. Jack was two years ahead of me, and like me was one of the few people in our program who wanted to be a playwright and not a screenwriter. He was six-foot-four, scarecrow thin, with short sandy blond hair and green eyes that won all staring contests. We had our first conversation during the height of a frigid winter. This was back in the mid-'90s, when you could still smoke inside buildings in New York City, and the smoking area for the Dramatic Writing Program at New York University was in a stairwell of the seventh floor of 721 Broadway, headquarters of all my shattered dreams. I regret I wasn't a smoker — it would have been easier to make friends, easier to have the casual conversations that led to connections, especially since the stairwell was an egalitarian place where the distinctions between faculty and students disappeared; the only distinction was between those who were fond of nicotine and those who were not.

I ended up in the stairwell with Jack because we were continuing a conversation we'd begun in class. It was a class called, simply, "Cabaret" — we all wrote and then performed two cabaret shows during the semester. Jack and I had somehow started talking about Arthur Miller, a playwright revered at

DWP (he'd taught a course or two just before I enrolled). In class, I had told Jack I thought *Death of a Salesman* was sentimental drivel, and he said he was thrilled to hear someone say that. Class ended, and we walked through the narrow DWP hallway to the stairwell, where a couple of other students nodded to Jack, though he paid no attention to them. As our evisceration of Miller's entire career wound down, and as I told Jack for the third time that no, I did not need to bum a cigarette, he said, "So, tell me something about you I don't know."

"I'm left-handed," I said.

"I know that," he said.

"I'm from New Hampshire."

"Everybody here knows that."

"I used to read a lot of science fiction."

"How cute."

"What about you?" I said.

"Me?"

"It's only fair."

"Fine," he said, exhaling smoke. "I kill fairies."

I'm sure my face displayed exactly what he wanted: wide-eyed shock.

"People give them to me," Jack said. "Fairies. Plastic or glass. Dolls. Icons. And every one of them, I smash with a hammer, or I cut off their hair and wings, or I throw them in front of the subway, or I bite their fucking heads off and spit them to the ground."

Perhaps I chuckled nervously. More likely, I stood silent.

"You should come over sometime," he said. "It's fun. We can have a fairy-killing party."

...

I had a dorm room to myself at that moment, a welcome relief after my first roommate. His name was T.C., which stood for Thomas Charles, but for some reason T.C. was considered more appropriate, or at least faster to say. He came from a place that still holds a legendary aura in my mind, though I've never been there: Cherry Hill, New Jersey, which I imagine to be a Disneyland of medical specialists and corporate lawyers, a place where taste is not cultivated but bought, like everything else. No other such place could have produced a creature like T.C., a high-wire act of pointless energy and yammering self-involvement unhindered by self-reflection, the human apotheosis of gregarious kitsch.

He was, of course, a Musical Theatre major. Or not exactly a Musical Theatre major per se, because NYU's acting program was broken into various studios — studios for people who wanted to study along the lines of the pioneers of American Method acting such as Stella Adler or Lee Strasberg, or who wanted to study experimental theatre, et cetera. Or who just wanted to sing and dance and be happy. T.C. was one of those creatures.

His favorite movie was one that had been released recently, *The Mask*, starring Jim Carrey's face. "I *am* The Mask," he told me the first day I met him, when we were hauling our stuff into a dorm room that was much smaller than either of us had planned for. He spent at least five minutes showing me all the great contortions his face would bear. Then he plugged in the TV he had brought with him and which was, I soon discovered, an extension of his being.

"I've memorized *Charlie's Angels*," he said. "Every episode."

The show was on one of the New York stations in the afternoon, and when it came on, he demonstrated to me his skills, first by lip-synching, and then, to prove that he wasn't just good at anticipating lip movements, by saying lines before they were uttered on the show.

I didn't know how T.C. found enough time in his life to memorize every episode of *Charlie's Angels*. If he had enjoyed solitude as much as I, then it would have made more sense, but he hated to be alone and he hated anything resembling quiet. People constantly came in and out of our little cinderblock room, and wherever we went, it seemed everyone knew T.C. During the first week, we did a lot together, trying to get to know the city and the school. We went out to cafés and clubs, and, because they were free, to uninspiring NYU events. I fell into the habit of identifying myself as "T.C.'s roommate." At a party somewhere in the dorm one night, a woman who was openly contemptuous of T.C. stopped me and said, "Why do you call yourself that? Why not just be you?"

"Because," I said, "in T.C.'s world, you are defined by your relationship to him. And I am T.C.'s roommate."

"Yeah, in T.C.'s world," she said. "But it's a pretty fucking empty world to be stuck in, don't you think?"

I did, but I didn't dare admit it. He's fun, I'd say to anyone who asked me about him. He makes life more exciting. It's better than being alone with myself. And I tried hard to believe it.

T.C. quickly managed to get a job at The Gap, a few blocks from our dorm. If he couldn't be the Jim Carrey character in a musical version of *The Mask*, being an employee at The Gap seemed to him to be the best possible alternative. "They require us to wear their clothes," he said, "and I told them they didn't need to require *me*, because I already wear them, and all I want to do is wear them, because, my friend, I am a Gap Man."

Much was amazing about T.C., but perhaps the greatest amazement came when he told me, quite early on and quite emphatically, that though some people occasionally and thoughtlessly assumed he was gay, he was in fact one of the most heterosexual people I would ever meet. I don't know what sort of heterosexual people he assumed I would meet in my life. Perhaps in Cherry Hill, New Jersey an encyclopedic knowledge of *Charlie's Angels*, an obsession with musical theatre, and a worship of The Gap are markers of macho, hetero virility. To a naïve boy from New Hampshire, they had been signs of something else.

Moments before T.C. came out as straight, I had been about to tell him I was gay. I decided to wait on that, and continued waiting when, soon after announcing his profound heterosexuality to me, he looked out the window and saw two men holding hands. "Why do they have to rub it in our faces?" he said. "They're disgusting. They're all disgusting. I mean, I know there are lots of gay people in the theatre, and I can live with that, but I really do wish they'd just *die* already."

...

I had come to New York to be a playwright, and I had thought I would take the city by storm. Through the first semester at NYU, though, the city had stormed me more than I had stormed it. Once classes began and T.C. made friends at his studio, I was cut out of his life. I had expected to make lots of friends in the Dramatic Writing Program, but that didn't happen. Most of the people in my classes wanted to write movies, and I thought only sell-outs and hacks wrote movies. They would rhapsodize about the steam coming out of a manhole in *Taxi Driver*, while I wanted to write abstract plays that would give Samuel Beckett scholars a headache. Later, an attentive playwrighting teacher would point out that everything I wrote, no matter how abstract or absurd, was about somebody torturing and interrogating somebody else.

Those first months in New York were the loneliest of my life. I am not a person given to loneliness; I like solitude and privacy. The problem was that I had desperately wanted to escape New Hampshire and I had built up an idea of the city in my mind that made it into the opposite of everything I hated about my home. New York wasn't a city, it was a savior — a mecca of culture and intelligence, a place where I, because of my own inherent sensitivity to culture and my, I thought, better-than-ordinary intelligence, would finally be recognized for the prince I was. I think I'd been reading too many science fiction stories, too many tales of awkward, unheralded people who possessed the secret that saved the universe. What I found was that New York was a mansion of locked rooms, a magical maze that defied all maps, a place one could get to know only by already knowing. Guidebooks didn't help, because no guidebook told me how to find the person who would recognize my genius and give me a fan club and a Pulitzer Prize. I should have explored the city more, but I mostly stayed within the small precincts of NYU, rarely venturing more than a few blocks away from Washington Square. Anything farther became terra incognita, the realm of dragons. I spent most of my time lurking in the Strand Bookstore and the NYU library, opening favorite books to familiar pages — revisiting these, my oldest friends.

I hadn't the slightest idea how to make friends, because I'd never really had to make friends in my life. My friends had been the children of my parents' friends, and we all went to school together. Friends, for me, had never been something to *make*; they were something that was just there, whether I wanted them to be or not.

Thus, after the first week, once T.C. realized I glittered about as well as a chunk of old cement, I had no-one within three hundred miles who knew much of anything about me, or cared that I was alive. Even for someone invigorated by solitude and privacy, that was a lonely realization.

Things got better after a few months, once I had a job working for the AmeriCorps program at a high school on the Lower East Side, once I'd become at least a familiar face going to classes at 721 Broadway. Disappointments and disillusions still swirled around me, but we'd grown familiar and even almost fond of each other.

The best things that happened, though, were that T.C. almost died and I got my own fag hag.

After six weeks of making friends with everyone in Manhattan, T.C. came down with jaundice, hepatitis, and mono. He left school for a few weeks to recover, and shortly after he came back he told me he'd found an open room at another dorm and would be moving into it. NYU's housing office didn't seem to pay any attention, and I had our room to myself for the rest of the school year.

Meanwhile, I had somehow attracted the interest of an ebullient sophomore in Dramatic Writing, a woman who aspired to write sit-coms, and who came from the same town in New Jersey as Kevin Smith. "I know everybody in *Clerks*," she told me. (I had no idea what *Clerks* was — the film had only hit theatres that month.) Her name was Melissa, and she talked faster than anybody I'd ever met in my life. Like T.C. (and, for all I could tell, everybody from New Jersey), she was a social extrovert, but she wasn't as skilled as T.C. at attracting groupies. In fact, many people thought she was insane. Perhaps she was. Nonetheless, she was the only person who paid any attention to me, the only person who seemed to find my company enjoyable, and that counted for a lot.

"I'm your hag," she said to me one day while we were walking up Waverly Place to Broadway.

"What?"

"Your fag hag."

"Oh. Okay."

"You don't have any idea what I'm talking about, do you?" she said.

"Nope."

"I'm like your boyfriend, but we don't have sex. Because I'm straight and you're gay. Which is hard to understand, because I have way more fashion sense than you and I'm much more of a diva, so maybe I'm a gay man in a straight woman's body and you're a straight woman in a gay man's body, I mean that would make sense, don't you think, unless it's just that you're from New Hampshire and they do strange things with moose there so even the gays are not like *gay* gays but more like, I don't know, lesbians or something. Maybe I'm a lesbian. I've often wondered. I should experiment. They say college is for experimenting, so I think I should get a girlfriend. What do you think? Maybe you should get a girlfriend. Maybe I could be your girlfriend and we could experiment. But that wouldn't make a lot of sense, though, because how could I be your hag if I was your girlfriend, and you need a hag much more than you need a girlfriend, so I think we should just stick with things as they are."

"That's probably a good idea," I said.

Melissa was determined to turn my sexuality into an identity, something I had failed to achieve for myself. To signal my gayness, I tried to cultivate more effeminate behaviors, but I've always been more nerdy than effeminate, really. I attended a few meetings of the Tisch School of the Arts gay club, but it seemed to lack any purpose beyond the social, and any situation that lacks a purpose beyond socializing makes my personality hibernate. And the one fundamental element of homosexuality — the having sex with men part — frightened more than inspired me. There were guys I saw that I found attractive, but the attraction was more aesthetic than lustful. They were pleasant to look at, and aroused in me a faint desire to be near them, but if any had offered to spend a night in bed with me, I would have been terrified, and my desires would have immediately shifted to revulsion, because their bodies would produce odors and secretions and words.

"What's your ideal man?" Melissa asked me one night in her dorm room while we played Uno. (She loved Uno.)

"A deaf-mute," I said. "Blind, preferably."

"You want to fuck Helen Keller's twin brother? Ewww."

"Don't be prejudiced."

"You don't need a boyfriend, you need an inflatable doll."

"Probably true."

"We can get you one."

"Thanks. No."

"Suit yourself..."

...

During my second semester at NYU, Jack and I started spending time together after the Cabaret class. Sometimes we'd go to a café with a few other people from the class and share gossip while drinking strong coffee, but usually it was just us, and usually nothing more than a fifteen-minute walk in Washington Square Park to finish a conversation we'd begun earlier. He always had somewhere to go, something to do in another part of the city. "Well, I've got to go this way," he'd say, and then, "See you later." And I'd say, "See you later," and he'd be gone, across the street or down into a subway station, lost in the crowd.

People were fascinated by Jack, but they were wary of him too. His sense of humor was sharp, and he cared too little for most people to protect them from its edges. But he wasn't a performer; he didn't seek out moments to display his wit, and most of the time he seemed indifferent, aloof. He had a disconnected presence, an ethereality. Conversations seemed to happen around him, not with him. I've met people similar to Jack over the years, but never quite the same, because everyone else like him has an arrogant, misanthropic streak — talking with them, you feel judged. It wasn't that way with Jack. Once he chose to pay attention to something or someone, he'd done all the judging he needed to do.

But his attention carried no loyalty in it. I often felt that if I dropped dead in the midst of a conversation with him, he would shrug and move on to something else of interest. Life, he seemed to think, was too short to bother getting all worked up over.

And then one day in the spring he didn't say, "See you later," but, instead, "Show me your dorm room. I want to see what books you own."

In my room, he stared in silence at the stacked milk cartons I used for bookshelves. "Kafka," he said finally. "Glad to see that. One of Kafka's stories, any one, is worth more than any play ever written. Büchner, excellent. Chekhov. More Chekhov. You like Chekhov, it seems."

"I took a class last term on Chekhov. It was great. I'd never understood how to really read him before, it just seemed—"

"Why so much Brecht? I mean, who needs a copy of *Saint Joan of the Stockyards*?"

"They were cheap at The Strand."

"But you're never going to read them all."

"I might."

"No, you're not. It will make you a terrible writer if you read that much Brecht. Read a few plays, his famous ones, read the poems and essays, and then move on and call it a phase and look back on it with nostalgia and shame."

"Okay," I said, mostly to get him to change to another topic.

"The Greeks, Shakespeare, Büchner, Chekhov, and Beckett. They're the only playwrights you need to know. Well, plus some of the Japanese theatre, that's important. A bit of Brecht to know why political theatre even at its best is shit."

"No Americans?"

"Theatre in America is light entertainment for people who want easy emotion. There's not a single American playwright who is as significant a writer as even our most middlebrow novelists. Steinbeck is more substantial than any American playwright, and I fucking hate Steinbeck."

"Tennessee Williams?"

"Oh, please. Overwrought piffle. Self-conscious poeticizing like some angsty seventeen-year-old. Spare me."

"He's a gay icon."

"So're the Village People."

"You're hard to please."

"Yes," he said, moving closer to me. He put his arms around me. He kissed me. "If this were a campy movie," he said, "you know what I'd say now?"

"What?"

"I like your taste." He smiled and kissed me again.

And then he left, saying he had places to be, things to do, people to see, tra-la-la.

I stood without moving. Twilight inched in, shading everything grey. I sat down on the edge of my bed and cried. I pressed my fists into my eyes, then dragged ragged fingernails down my cheeks, then let myself slide to the floor.

If you asked me, I wouldn't have been able to say why I was so devastated by Jack's teasing, and I don't think it had a whole lot to do with Jack directly — he was the catalyst, an icepick that found the fatal fissure in my defenses and, with just a little pressure, sent cracks cascading across my facade. New York had done me in.

...

"I've seen your place, now you need to see mine," Jack said to me a few days later. We hadn't talked in the time between, hadn't even run into each other, though it's not like I'd been wandering all over the city — mostly, I'd stayed in my room, writing a play about a misunderstood artist and his angst. The artist encounters a beautiful, mercurial young man, convinces him to be a model for a painting, captures his heart and soul, then sadistically kicks him out into the street and refuses ever to acknowledge his existence again. I finished a draft of the play and decided to get a sandwich at a deli a few blocks down from my dorm, and as I waited to cross the street, Jack walked up to me.

"Hi," he said.

After writing for two days straight without much sleep, I was not capable of quickly negotiating social interactions in the real world, but I managed to remember the word "Hello," and to say it.

"Feeling okay?" Jack asked.

"Sure," I said. "Fine."

"What are you doing right now?"

"Standing on a sidewalk with you," I said.

"Perfect. Let's go to my dorm."

There are many things I should have said to him then. Some

of them were things I had written a thousand variations of as I worked through my new play, dreadful lines like, "What, you want a quick kiss and then goodbye again? You want to feel powerful over a puppet — over me, your little toy?" I knew such words were overwrought and melodramatic, but I'd needed to write them. I couldn't *say* them, though. Not in real life. Not without stage lights and makeup and hours of rehearsal.

"Sure," I said. "Okay. I mean, I don't have a lot of time. I just. Well. Yeah."

"Do I need to kiss you again?" he said, then smiled. "Come on, it'll be fun, I promise." He grabbed my arm and led me up Broadway.

...

Jack had a single in Third Avenue North, one of the newer dorms at NYU (and the dorm to which T.C. had moved). I could never get a sense of the building's actual size — it was like a couple of giant boxes pressed together, with stores and hair salons on the ground floor, and then dorm floors dominated by the antiseptic decor *de rigueur* in 1990s institutional design, muddling the differences between midscale hotels and university dorm rooms and psychiatric wards.

Jack's room had just enough space for a bed and a desk. A window the size of a license plate offered some sunlight. The room was a mess — clothes and books everywhere, tapes and CDs scattered across it all.

"Pardon the conflagration," Jack said. "Housekeeping is for people who have nothing interesting to do with their lives. Move anything out of the way that you need to."

I was feeling brave, so I pushed a pair of jeans off his bed and sat down.

Jack handed me a pink cardboard gift box big enough to hold a terrier. I remember the box seeming terribly light, as if even its cardboard didn't weigh anything.

"A box of fairies," he said.

I opened the hinged top and peered inside. Dozens and dozens of fairies — plastic, cloth, porcelain, glass; blue, yellow, green, white, pink; piled atop each other — looked up at me.

Jack's hand darted into the box and pulled out a plastic figurine so fulsome with cuteness it would likely even nauseate people who collect Thomas Kincaid paintings. Its hair was bright blonde with streaks of silver, its eyes were giant blue sparkles, its scarlet lips were puckered, giving the face an absurd come-hither undertone that was probably meant to look like sweet innocence. Its thin, breastless body had a lime-green dress painted on it that made the figure look almost like a mermaid clothed in radioactive seaweed.

"Let the fun begin," Jack said. He held a hammer in his other hand.

Jack kneeled beside me on the bed and placed the fairy up against the cinderblock wall. He cackled as he smashed first the fairy's left arm, then its right leg, its right arm, left leg, torso, and, finally, holding the head by the hair, its face. Splinters and shards of fairy fell to the bed and floor. By the end, I was cackling, too.

We killed the entire box of fairies that afternoon and evening. Now and then, we'd pause to talk about something or other, nothing memorable. At the end of it all, leaving the room littered with the sprinkled splinters of our fun, we went out for a celebratory feast at a Thai restaurant half-way between my dorm and Jack's. I thought he'd invite me back to his room afterward, and that there would be another kiss, and more than a kiss. But no. We split the bill for our food, and outside the restaurant,

Jack gave me a quick peck on the cheek and a slap on the ass. "See you around," he said, and dashed off into the night.

...

"He's going to become a serial killer," Melissa said to me after I'd told her about my escapades with Jack. "I've known him longer than you and long before you told me about any of this, I thought he was likely to climb to the top of a tall building and start shooting people with a high-powered rifle, and now I'm absolutely certain of it, though I'm going to revise my opinion of exactly what sort of psychopathic behavior he will display and instead say I expect, as someone who has taken an abnormal psychology class, that what he'll become (if he isn't already) is a stalker and killer of women, probably by capturing them, holding them up against a wall, and beating them with a hammer, that seems obvious, why are you hanging out with him?"

We were sitting in her room, trying to figure out what to do with the evening.

"He's fun. He's smart—"

"Do you hate women?"

"No."

"Because some gay men are awful misogynists. They think to be gay they have to be repulsed by vaginas. You're not repulsed by vaginas, are you? Because if you are, I can't, obviously, spend time with you, because, in case you hadn't considered it, I have a vagina."

"No, I don't mind vaginas."

"You just don't want to put your dick in one."

"Not really. Not right now, at least."

"Do you want to put your dick in Jack? Or have his dick in

you? Or his dick with your dick and your dick with his dick and—"

"No."

"You're lying."

"Possibly," I said. "I don't know. I mean, yes, I hoped, when I sat on his bed, and after we had dinner, I hoped that we would … I hoped something might *happen*. It might be fun, you know?"

"Of course! It's sex! Sex is supposed to be fun! It's supposed to be more than fun — it's supposed to be ecstatic and transcendent and dirty and wonderful and—"

"Right."

"But not with Jack. Jack is a menace to society, and one day the FBI will have an entire section of the Behavioral Analysis Unit devoted to him, and they'll write about him in textbooks and teach him as a case study in classes at Quantico, and if you have sex with him, then they'll be studying you, too, and I don't think that's the kind of fame you want for your future, do you?"

"Probably not."

"Definitely not. So give up on him. I'm going to watch *Friends*, have you seen *Friends*, it's fabulous, it's the story of my life, except it's not, because it's like a fantasy New York where all the people are pretty and white and funny, so it's like perfect in a sort of Aryan Nation kind of way, but pro-Jew. Watch—"

She turned the TV on, and, though I stared at the screen, none of the images or sounds penetrated my brain, since my brain was too busy thinking about Jack.

Years later, though, whenever I happened upon a stray episode of *Friends*, I'd think of Melissa, and wonder what sort of fantasy world she'd ended up in.

...

For our first cabaret performance, I cast Jack in a skit I'd written that made fun of Trent Reznor and, by some extension, myself. I'd been turned on to the music of Nine Inch Nails by a high school friend, and I found its loud, violent, self-pitying bleakness to be the perfect soundtrack for my New York days (it helped that Trent Reznor's voice seemed to me then just about the sexiest thing in the world). My skit had Trent talking with his agent about problems with his new album — he was struggling to come up with appropriately miserable songs, because his life was going quite well, and everything he wrote came out like a Hallmark card. Jack played the agent, and proved himself an excellent straight man.

Outside of the class, I only spent time with Jack once. After a brainstorming session about possible skits for the second show, Jack stopped me in the smoker's stairwell, grabbing my arm and pulling me close to him. "I'm ready to let you see something," he whispered. "Something important. Come over tonight."

I hesitated. I'd begun to enjoy having distance from him. Life seemed comprehensible, even manageable if I kept him away. Without him, my mood swings had settled into mere mood sways, and I had little desire to return to a life of grand hopes and megaton hurts.

"Please," he said, letting go of my arm.

I didn't resist.

...

Jack turned the lights off in his room. He held a grey metal cashbox and sat next to me on the bed. He opened the box.

"Do you see anything?" he said.

I looked inside. As my eyes adjusted to the darkness, I made out some sort of amorphous shadow-shape in the box.

"Watch," Jack said. He moved his hand toward the shadow. The shadow shifted and a weak blue light flared briefly.

"I've almost killed it," Jack said. "It's been centuries, but I think, now, perhaps…"

I reached my hand toward the box, but Jack closed it quickly. "No," he said. "It will … feed."

"What are you talking about?" I said.

"They live off us. It's why they say we can't kill them. They can kill us — they *do* kill us — but because we value our lives, most of us won't do what seems most obviously to kill them. But I think I've finally found another way."

"But what is it, in the box I mean?"

"By day, by light it looks a bit like a worm. A dusty worm. In darkness, though, if they want to feed, they reveal their actual form."

"Can I see it again?" I asked gently.

"Don't try to touch it," Jack said.

"Okay."

He lifted the lid of the box. My eyes were used to the darkness now, and the shadow seemed more defined. It looked like one of Jack's figurines, but more delicate, silken. Like a tiny child crossed with a dragonfly.

Perhaps, though, desire caused me to see what Jack wanted me to see. Perhaps I was just making sense of a meaningless shape, perhaps there was nothing in there at all. An illusion.

"How do you kill them?" I said. "With a hammer?"

"No no. That doesn't hurt them. I've tried. I even shot it once. With a handgun, a .44 magnum. Useless. They love the attention. That's what I discovered. Everybody thinks you have to love fairies to keep them alive, but that's not true. Any attention works. I expect hatred — pure hatred — is their favorite meal. It's so rare. Pity sometimes, yes, and joy and happiness. They get those a lot. But absolute hatred, not much. It must be a wonderful treat. Invigorating."

"So you just ignore it."

"Yes. They never leave you alone. They scream through the night. Laugh, cry, everything. They know every trick to get us to pay attention to them. And then they suck us dry. It took me so, so long, but now I don't care about them, one way or another. Not the real ones, this one. I just leave it in this box. One day, the dust will smother it. A year, a hundred years. I don't care. It'll be dead. And I'll be free, then. Finally."

He closed the box, set it on the floor, and pushed it under the bed with the side of his foot. He leaned over to me and kissed me on the cheek, then the lips. He put a hand on my leg. We lay down on the bed, our hands moving beneath each other's clothes. My tongue touched tears on his lips.

"I'm sorry," he said. "We can't."

He stood up and moved to the other side of the room. "You should go," he said.

I wanted to scream a thousand melodramatic monologues at him, but could only squeak out a word: "Why?"

"I like you a lot," he said. "I do. I wish we could do this, what we're doing. But I'm not free. Not yet. Please. Wait for me. I promise I'll—" But he couldn't keep speaking.

"Please," he said after a long time. "You should go."

I stood up, buttoned my pants, tucked in my shirt, and walked out into the night.

...

During the days after that night, my brain burst with questions for Jack, but I never asked him any. During the nights after that night, I cried myself to sleep more often than not. By daylight, I spent a lot of energy fighting off self-pity; by night, the effort hardly seemed worth it, because who, after all, was there to pity me if I didn't do it myself? I figured Jack got some sort of erotic excitement from teasing me, some kind of sado-masochistic pleasure from letting me get close then pushing me away. Once I'd stopped paying him the sort of attention he desired, once I'd stopped returning after being discarded, he came up with the fairy story to bring me back. It worked.

We saw each other during class, but we never had a con-versation. I hadn't cast him in my skit for the second cabaret show, nor had he cast me in his, so we didn't need to work together during rehearsals.

I didn't tell Melissa the details of what Jack had done, because I felt embarrassed about it all somehow. For a moment or two, I'd believed what Jack had said about what was in the metal box. I'd convinced myself that there was a light there. I'd con-vinced myself that the shadow was something other than a shadow, something that could, in fact, somehow, enslave him. An hour later, I couldn't believe how stupid I'd been, but in the moment, I had believed in Jack, believed in mysterious light and the fairies that hungered within it.

I did tell Melissa, though, that I wasn't really on speaking terms with Jack anymore. "What happened?" she said, eyes wide and ravenous for gossip, as we sat on her bed reading scripts we'd been working on for our different classes.

"Nothing happened," I said. "I just realized he's an asshole."

"Hooray! You came to your senses!"

"Or something."

"We'll find you a boyfriend, don't worry."

"I don't want a boyfriend," I said.

"Of course you do. Everybody wants a boyfriend. Or at least a fuckbuddy. Do you want a fuckbuddy?"

"No," I said. "What I really want, I mean honestly, right now, what I want is to become a monk and live in a monastery."

"You'd have to have some sort of religion. They pray all day. It's central to the job description."

"I know. That's the problem."

"I'm going to write a sitcom about you. I mean, your character will have to be straight, because, you know, even though Billy Crystal's character in *Soap* broke all sorts of new ground, the ground's gotten pretty hard — pardon the pun — and network executives are just *not* going to accept a gay main character, especially if he ever had sex, which is kind of the whole point of our show, or the Macguffin at least, kind of like who killed Laura Palmer, so I think we'll just have to give in to the realities of commercial television and make you heterosexual, though you can still be adorably geeky, of course, because really, that's your selling point."

"Thanks," I said, inching my way toward the door.

"You'll be the lonely neighbor that everybody's kind of wary of, and I'll be the Jewish-mother-in-training who lives upstairs and bakes you latkes and hires a matchmaker and inevitably has the perfect yiddishism for the moment and — I've got to go write this down! It'll be like *The Nanny*, but cuddly!"

...

As the audience was settling in to our second cabaret show, Jack sneaked up behind me backstage and whispered, "I'm working on getting you proof."

I turned around and nearly punched him, mostly from surprise.

"What are you talking about?"

"I'm grateful to you," he said. "I'd wanted things to be

different. But it's not all going according to plan. I need a lot more time than I thought. So I'm going to give you some proof of my affections. And proof of — well, fairies come in all sorts of different guises, you know."

Then the show began.

Afterward, as I was getting out of costume (the last skit I performed in had required me to wear a padded suit under a giant red velvet dress), I glanced through the curtain that separated the backstage area from the audience and saw Jack talking with somebody near the door.

It was T.C. They were laughing. Jack's eyes radiated adoration.

I didn't stop staring until T.C. took Jack's hand and led him out of the little theatre.

I never saw either of them again.

...

Jack didn't return to NYU in the fall, and nobody I asked knew anything about him. What happened to T.C., though, everybody knew. I didn't hear about it until I got back to school, because I didn't have any final exams at the end of my freshman year, so I had gone home earlier than most students.

Melissa, of course, was the one to tell me. "Sorry about your roommate," she said.

I thought she was talking about my current roommate, a club kid who spent more time going to the Limelight than classes.

"Did the police raid the clubs again?"

"What? No, not Danny. You don't know?"

"What?"

"T.C."

"Oh. Yeah, him and Jack. They were made for each other. I always thought he was—"

"No no no." I'd never seen her look so serious and disturbed. "What?"

"Oh god, you don't know. T.C.'s dead. He jumped off the roof of Third Avenue North at the end of last year."

I don't remember how I responded. After that moment, I don't really remember anything from the beginning of my sophomore year.

I didn't see Melissa much after that. I had joined the NYU environmental club, and we spent a lot of time trying to figure out how to be radical environmental activists in New York City. I look back at that time with amusement and fondness; we were ridiculous, going to protests at corporate headquarters, dreaming of trees to chain ourselves to, but it was a good ridiculousness, entirely appropriate for college kids. It gave me a solid group of friends, we had something to believe in, and our adventures helped the rest of my time in New York be less lonely and agonizing.

I knew I was in the wrong place, though. I didn't really want to enter the world of professional New York theatre. I didn't know what I wanted. My disillusionment was complete. I transferred to the University of New Hampshire as a senior, and enjoyed that year more than most of my time at NYU. After college, I got a job teaching English and theatre at a boarding school in central New Hampshire, and teaching satisfied me in ways the quest for fame and fortune never had.

Now and then I thought about Jack and about T.C., but less and less as the years went on. I was too busy with work to think about events I didn't understand; too busy to bother with such complicated love. Sometimes at night, though, real loneliness hit me hard, and I indulged insomnia with wild imaginings about proof and affection.

Three years after I started teaching, I received a postcard of

Aubrey Beardsley's drawing "Withered Spring". On the back, a simple note:

> Why do you always go around wearing black?
>
> Love,
> Saint Joan of the Stockyards

The question, famously, comes from Chekhov's *The Seagull*, where Masha's answer is: "I am in mourning for my life."

...

I am generally contemptuous of celibate people who say they're saving themselves for just the right person, but, like so much else, my contempt is probably an extension of self-hatred.

I'm not sure I believe that, though. I'm not sure what I believe.

No, that's wrong. I believe a lot of things.

I know, for instance, that I believe in fairies.

I know because I'm still waiting for one to die.

HUNGER

It was only a few weeks after my mother's funeral when my father told me never to come home again. If not for the coldness of his voice, I might have assumed he was passive-aggressively trying to shame me for having stayed for so short a time, having returned to my son and my husband. But my father's aggression had never been passive. He was not a talker, never much of a communicator at all, and so, over the years, in order to understand anything from him, I honed the skill of interpreting his every word, gesture, and intonation to a fine art. When he said, "Don't come home," it wasn't a gentle reassurance, it was a warning. "Don't come here," he said. "Never. *Never.*" And then hung up the phone.

I booked a flight to Boston for the next morning and sent my boss an email saying I'd be gone for a few days but would be working remotely as much as I could. I called Sally and Amy, our neighbors across the hall in the building, and asked if they would be able to look after Zack a bit this week, and they were as supportive as always, said he could come have a sleepover with their son Paul if Ron needed any time just to work. Once everything was set up, I told Ron, and he was annoyed at first, then concerned, but he could see that I was in no mood to answer questions, and he didn't ask many. "Are you all right?" he said, and I said yes, but he knew it was a lie.

"We'll be fine," he said. "Don't worry about us. Just take care of your dad."

I barely slept. All night, and all day during the long flight, and then during the two hours' drive north in a rattling tin can of a rental car, I kept trying not to think of my brother Corey, about his death a year before, kept trying to consider everything as separate from that. It wasn't separate, though, and I knew it. If my brother hadn't killed himself, if my mother hadn't withered away, if I didn't blame myself for a heap of it and then hate myself for the blame, I would not have been so quick to fly across the country and drive through the night to a world I loathed.

...

Shortly before he died, Corey told me I was the most selfish person he had ever met. He said I made Ayn Rand look like a philanthropist. He was angry because I wouldn't agree to buy him a plane ticket to Seattle and let him live with us while he bummed around looking for a band to play with or a rich patron who would appreciate his paintings or a vegan anarchist collective that would let him work as their cook. In that moment, he forgot all the money I had given him over the years, all the free meals, all the connections I had tried to make for him that he screwed up in one way or another, all the hours I had listened to him moan about his endless string of doomed relationships.

I keep telling myself all that, keep reminding myself what Corey forgot.

It doesn't do any good. When I think of Corey, I think of him taking me down to Boston for my sixteenth birthday to see the Fourth of July fireworks, staying with college friends of his and hanging out on the roof of their apartment building, which had a great view of Back Bay, and discovering a Corey who, away from home, moved through the world with wonder, who was able to smile, laugh, play. I think of long, barely-punctuated emails telling me of his ever-changing philosophies of life and love and politics in his first year of sobriety: Christian socialism one month, rationalist nihilism another, queer paganism the next. I think of taking him to the airport and not being able to stop hugging him, and him gently disentangling himself from my arms, wiping a tear from my eye, and saying, "Don't be so sentimental, little sis. We've got a million tomorrows." He skipped to the security gate, turned back to blow a kiss my way, and then disappeared. I never got to hug him again.

...

By the time I arrived at the house, it was nearly midnight. I hadn't called my father, and I feared just walking inside — he went to bed by nine o'clock every night, but he had never been a deep sleeper, and more than once during my childhood he grabbed the shotgun from the gun rack in the front hall and went out to see what one sound or another might be. I remembered him twice shooting into the night, once at (apparently) nothing, and once at a pack of coyotes that were making their way across the yard toward the chicken coop. He managed to shoot two of the coyotes as the pack ran off. One, the shot took the top of its head off. The other was wounded, one of its legs destroyed, and even though this was almost thirty years ago, I easily hear in memory the coyote's whimpers, growls, and cries as our father slowly walked toward it, then shot it again. (I was only eight or ten years old, and our mother quickly grabbed me and sent me back to my room before I could reach the front door, but my window looked out over the scene, and I watched it all. Corey was in his early teens, and since he was a boy and older, our father called out, ordering him to help drag the carcasses into the woods. Later, dawn still some hours away, Corey came back to our bedroom, took all his clothes off, left them in a pile near the door, huddled shivering in his bed, and cried himself to sleep.)

Not wanting to end up like a coyote, I parked the rental car at the end of the long driveway, tilted the seat back, and slept until morning.

I woke to my father knocking on the window near my head. The glass had all steamed up overnight. I realized he couldn't see in and didn't know it was me. I opened the door and stepped out groggily.

"Good morning," I said.

"I told you not to come."

"Right. And I hadn't even been considering it. But you hung up the phone before we finished talking. So I figured I ought to come check on you."

"You should go."

"Jesus, Dad, I've flown three thousand miles, driven through the night, and slept in my goddamned car because I didn't want to disturb you. The least you could do is offer me some coffee."

"Eileen," he said, my name heavy on his voice, a sound torn by yearning and fear. He paused then and scrunched his eyes as if a sharp pain hit his forehead. "All right," he said. "I suppose it's fine right now. Come on."

"Hop in, I'll give you a ride," I said.

"No," he said, and so I drove down the quarter mile of gravel driveway to the house while he walked behind. I tried not to go too fast so as not to blast dirt and stones at him. He walked slowly, steadily, his face impassive as always, but somehow in the impassivity I couldn't help but see anger, though now I think it was more likely fear.

In the cool autumn daylight, the house looked as it always had, a farmhouse forever in need of new paint, new shingles, new windows, new boards. Somehow, it kept standing. The barn beside the house was even worse: weatherbeaten, leaning a bit to one side, the hayloft door warped and broken, the roof sagging. Two milk cows and a few sheep called the barn home and didn't seem to mind its sorry state, but I hoped perhaps if I got the promised promotion at work that I might be able to afford to have someone fix up the barn.

When we were kids, there had been more animals — chickens, ten cows we dutifully milked, a dozen sheep, random goats, a couple horses, some dogs, plenty of cats. Once, we even had a llama: certain protection, a neighbor named George Swanson told my father, against coyotes and other predators, because llamas are curious creatures that walk in a straight line toward whatever they are curious about, and this singular focus unnerves more cautious animals. George Swanson knew a guy who was selling llamas and got us what he said was a good deal on one. It was a stupid, spitting creature. A few months after it arrived, the llama got killed by coyotes. "George Swanson is a fool," my father said, and never mentioned the llama, or George Swanson, again.

Inside, the house was just as it had been for the funeral. When Corey and I were growing up, our mother did a good job of keeping the old place as clean as could reasonably be expected, but after Corey's death, she lost interest in most things, including cleaning, and my father had never had any talent for, or interest in, housekeeping. I had been shocked to see how dust-encrusted everything was, how dirty were the kitchen counters, how many unwashed dishes filled the sink, how much laundry had piled up, how thick were the cobwebs clinging to every corner. I had cleaned as best I could, finding comfort in it, even as I was disgusted by how bad things had gotten. It was mindless work, meditative but purposeful, with clearly visible progress. It made me feel generous, like I was able to add some good to a rotten situation. I had felt that if I could get things into better shape, then my father would be able to keep it up and carry on.

He had not. Cobwebs and dustbunnies filled every corner. Thick, rank air hung in the rooms. The kitchen sink was completely filled with dirty dishes, and dishes covered the counters, as well.

I pried the kitchen window open. "Have you done a single bit of cleaning since I left?" I asked. My father stood across the room, silent. "At least the coffee's hot," I said. "Thank god for small graces." I washed a mug out in the sink, poured some coffee, and opened the refrigerator to get milk.

The refrigerator was filled with food: meat, eggs, squash, tomatoes, zucchinis, potatoes — more than I could quite comprehend. I burrowed around and found a bottle of milk, sniffed it to make sure it was fresh, and poured a bit into my coffee.

"Are you stocking up for the apocalypse or just for a big party?" I asked, jostling the bottle of milk back into the refrigerator. I took my mug and sat at the kitchen table. My father continued to stand across the room.

"You should go," my father said.

"I just got here," I said. "I'm pretty exhausted. And I'm concerned." I sipped my coffee. "I'm not leaving."

"It's not what you think."

"Oh? No? Really?" I stared, unblinking, at him. "What I think is that you've given up. You're letting it all go. I understand. I sympathize. We had a life here, a good life sometimes, and now... Well, it's done. Right? What's left? It's done. Maybe it's time to admit that and move on. You could get good money for this land, big money. You could sell and get a nice condo somewhere, live comfortably. Hell, come out to Seattle. A new life."

"No," my father said.

"Why not? What've you got here?"

"You wouldn't understand."

"Try me," I said.

"It's not good here."

"Clearly. And that's what I'm saying. Places around here have been selling for crazy money recently. It's as good a time as ever to get out."

"You don't understand," he said, and walked out of the room.

If I hadn't been so tired, I probably would have chased after him, forced a confrontation, because I was in the mood for it — seeing the state of the kitchen had shocked me, and shock makes me lash out. But I was also exhausted from all the travel. I needed sleep. So instead of chasing after our father, I went upstairs to our bedroom, a room which had stayed mostly the same since Corey and I were kids, and I lay down on my old bed and was soon asleep.

My father's hand on my shoulder woke me. "It's time to go," he said.

I sat up. "What time is it?"

"Afternoon. Three. You need to go."

"Go where?"

"Not here."

"That's helpful."

"*Eileen.*" Once again, as he spoke it, my name sounded thick with meanings I could not parse. "Please. You must. Go."

"The earliest I can fly back is in three days. So you're stuck with me."

He breathed deeply and lowered his head. He said nothing. He stood up and stared at me, his face looking as weathered as the barn, lips tight, eyes conveying not anger or resolution or fear but simple resignation.

"I'm as stubborn as you are," I said. "Always have been. You called me a mule once, do you remember? And mom laughed and said we're both mules, you and I. Corey was the soft one, you said so yourself, and it was a cruel thing to say but it was also true. So no, I'm not leaving, not until I'm sure you're going to be okay."

He nodded slightly, turned around, and walked out of the room.

I sat down on the bed. I felt as exhausted as before I had slept, perhaps more so.

I heard the front door open and close. I looked out the window next to the bed and watched my father walk across the yard and disappear in the barn, then reappear in the hay loft. He stood there, looking out at the horizon beyond the house. I remembered my mother saying that she wanted him to tear down the barn, even burn it down, salt the earth beneath it. But he refused. The animals needed it, he said. The hayloft was off limits, though. Even he didn't go up there.

Staring at my father standing in the loft, looking out at the sky as if seeking some world beyond what his eyes could see, I hated him more than I had ever hated him, more than I had ever hated any person or any thing, hated him more than I hated Corey for the ruin he had caused. Corey, at least, I had understood. Tying a rope to a beam in the hayloft, wrapping the rope around his throat, and jumping off an old chair to snap his neck made a certain terrible sense. I hated him for leaving us, for leaving *me*, for causing pain, but I also knew he had ended his own pain, and partly I hated him for that, too, because I could not follow him; I would not inflict such pain on my husband and son, at least.

Staring at my father, I wanted him to collapse and fall out of the hayloft onto the hard ground, to explode in blood and bone. But I wanted, too, to catch him, wanted him to fall into my arms so that I might comfort him as I would a child, allowing him, for the first time, to let tears fall, let a wail of pain scream forth, let all his harm and hurt go free.

He did not collapse and fall, did not weep or wail. He left the loft and soon I saw him carrying chicken feed out to the coop from the barn. I went downstairs to try to make some sense of the chaos.

. . .

He came in after dark, as I was cooking up ham, eggs, and potatoes for dinner.

"Food's almost ready," I said. "Sit down and we can eat."

"No, it's no good," my father said.

"What's no good? The food? Looks perfectly good to me. Smells great. Tastes—" I scooped up some eggs and ate them. Spat them out.

They were not eggs, they were dirt, sand, a mouthful of sawdust. Dry texture, no taste.

"Cans in the cupboard are fine," my father said. "The milk's okay so far. Water, coffee, dry beans."

"The refrigerator? All that food?"

"Not for us."

I coughed, nearly choked on the remnants of what seemed to be egg but was not.

"It's no good."

I sniffed the ham. With a fork, I cut a small piece, brought it to my mouth, touched it with my tongue. The meat screamed of rot and I recoiled, dropping the fork to the floor.

My father wandered off to some other part of the house as I dumped the food in the trash and then looked through the cans in the cupboard to see what I might make a meal from. Various beans, vegetables, fruit. It was easy enough to put some beans, tomatoes, and corn together in a pot and call it chile. I found an old shaker of pepper and a few jars of spices. The flavor wasn't bad.

"Want any?" I asked my father when he came back into the kitchen.

"Sure," he said. I scooped chile into a bowl for him. We ate together in silence.

...

After dinner, my father told me it would be best if I went to bed, or at least if I stayed upstairs. I asked why, but he wouldn't say anything. Annoyed, I huffed upstairs like the bratty kid I once had been. That was when I remembered to call Ron. He had left a couple voicemail messages and sent texts asking how I was doing. I'd managed to send one quick text saying everything was fine and I would call him when I got a chance. Reception was terrible at the house, but there was a landline phone in the bedroom, a line my parents had put in as a 16th birthday present to me, though it was at least as much a present to them: they would no longer have to listen to me on the kitchen phone talk endlessly with my boyfriends. (Corey had left for college by then. He never talked on the home phone with his boyfriends.)

"Are you okay?" Ron asked.

"I'm fine," I said. "Dad's weird, but he's always weird. Everything's weird here."

"But he's okay."

"I guess so. It's hard to tell. I mean, *something's* wrong. He won't tell me what, though. I'm trying to get him to sell the place. The faster he can do that, the better it will be. There's nothing here for any of us anymore."

"Zack wants to talk to you."

"Put him on."

I expected Zack to complain about school. He hated everything about third grade. His previous teacher had been wonderful, but for third grade his teacher was older and a bit more distant, a very by-the-book sort of woman. But he didn't want to talk about school.

"I took a nap this afternoon and I had a dream," he said.

"What sort of dream?" I asked.

"It was about Uncle Corey," he said.

"Oh?" Zack and Corey had only spent any real time together when Corey visited us that last time, and I hadn't thought Corey had left much of an impression. Certainly, Corey had not seemed interested in Zack.

"He's in the basement and he's sad."

"Basement? What basement?"

"In grandpa's house. He and grandma are down there and they're sad."

"What are you talking about Zack?"

"They're so hungry, mommy."

"Zack—"

"Help them, mommy," he whispered. "Help them."

Ron got on the phone. "He misses you," Ron said.

"What was he saying about Corey, what's that — he was whispering—"

"He's crying because he misses you."

"No, Ron, before that, he was saying about Corey, about grandma, the basement—"

"What are you talking about? He's just crying. He'll be fine. Are you okay, honey, what's—"

The phone went silent. I called Ron's name, but he wasn't there. No dial tone. I hung up the phone, picked up the receiver again, but there was still nothing.

I opened the bedroom door and stepped out into the hall.

A sound like wind through a cave echoed from below. As I approached the stairs, I caught movement out of the corner of my eye. I turned, but saw nothing. I turned back to the stairs and there was something, a shape, hanging like fog in the air, like a nightgown caught in a breeze I could not feel, a face, somehow familiar, like a face in clouds, a mouth open as if wailing, but the whole world was silent, and I thought I saw arms reach out to me, only inches away, but then gone in a gust of wind.

I ran down the stairs to the kitchen. Now the whole house filled with a low, deep sound, mournful and resonant, a sound that ought to have rattled the windows and vibrated through the floors and walls, but the house was utterly still. The lights in the house were on, but they seemed ineffectual, as if the house were dense with smoke, smothered in shadow. The only light piercing the dark slipped out under the door of the basement.

The door was locked. I pulled it, rattled it, but the lock held firm.

From behind the door, down in the basement, my father called out in a desperate tone I had never heard from him before: "Stay up there, Eileen! Go back to bed! Stay away, for god's sake, stay away!"

The basement door and its lock were older than me, possibly older than my father, and they were weak. The kitchen table was small but sturdy, with a metal frame and formica top. I used it as a battering ram. On the third blast against the basement door, the table went right through and I nearly plunged down the stairs, catching myself by reaching a hand out to the doorjamb, then, hardly pausing to think or even quite catch my balance, running down the stairs into the damp, murky basement.

It was, as it had always been, the basement of a farmhouse — not a nice, dry, finished space, but a hole in the ground with walls made of stone and a floor of packed dirt. Light came from a few bare bulbs strung from the beams of the ceiling. I had never much liked the basement (who could?), but Corey had been terrified of it his whole life. When we were children, it was where our father sent us for punishment. As the most persistent rule-breaker in the family, I ended up in the basement more often than Corey, but it was worse for him, and once our father even made him stay down there overnight. Corey was a teenager then; I remember it clearly. At the time, I didn't know what he had done that so enraged our father, and nobody would tell me, but years later, Corey said he had been in the barn loft pretty literally having a roll in the hay with Brad Miller, a guy a few years older whose father was famous in town for murdering a man in a bar fight. (Soon after our father caught him and Corey in the barn, Brad ran away from home and ended up in difficult circumstances in Boston; I never learned the details, but Corey heard from him now and then, heard he was HIV positive, heard he was living on the streets, heard he was dead, maybe of disease, maybe of drug overdose, the stories conflicted. Corey had tried to help him a few times, but he never knew what to do, and I said maybe there was nothing to do, maybe this was just who Brad was, and Corey said no, not at all, that was not who Brad was at all.) When our father caught them together, he dragged Corey out of the barn and hardly paid any attention at all to Brad, as if, Corey told me, trying not to see him, not to see what was happening. All his fury and fear poured into Corey, and our father dragged him into the house and pushed him down the stairs so hard that Corey said it was something of a miracle he avoided broken bones. Our mother frantically asked what was going on, and that was when I came into the room, having been upstairs, working on homework or playing with dolls or taking a nap, I don't remember. Our father wouldn't say anything, wouldn't explain, just said, "He is filth. *Filth.*" I'll never forget the fierce disgust in his eyes, the hatred with which he spat the words: *He. Is. Filth.*

(After Corey's death, I asked our mother why she had never defended him. It was callous to ask the question then, and perhaps a callous question to ask her at any time, but I needed an outlet for my pain, a scapegoat. I don't think she was ever in her life so angry at me, and I gave her plenty of reasons to be angry through the years. "*Always,*" she said. "I *always* defended him." She grabbed my shoulders with strong hands and stared right into my eyes. "Just because I hid the bruises from you doesn't mean they weren't there.")

The air in the basement smelled of earth and mildew, but there was another smell amidst that more familiar one, a smell that brought no memories but which nonetheless I associated with rot, a festering stench of decay.

Our father stood at the opposite side of the basement from me, near a shadowed corner. In the corner, two figures sat on either side of a mound that, as I got closer, I saw to be a mound of food — meats, fruits, and vegetables like the ones that filled the kitchen refrigerator, all indisciminately piled on the floor. The light in this part of the basement seemed to bend away from the figures, which looked to me to be less substance than absence, but once I got closer, I knew they were some form of our mother and Corey. They reached hungrily into the mound of food, but they did not eat it, not with their mouths. Our mother stuffed the food into a gash in her stomach from which steaming, bubbling puss oozed forth. Corey squeezed bits of meat and vegetable matter into a wide laceration in his neck.

I felt words filling my ears, but I cannot say I heard them, certainly not in the way we hear words when spoken.

"This is not nourishing them," I said to our father.

"It is all I have left," he said. "What do they want from me?"

"Nothing," I said.

"They keep telling me they are hungry."

"Yes, but not for this. Not for you."

"I didn't make them come back."

"And yet," I said, "here we are."

. . .

I told the police that I used the table to break through the door, and that my father was certainly dead when I got down there; the shotgun had not left a whole lot of his head intact.

As they asked questions, I barely lied about any of it, but I did not say anything about our mother or Corey, lest they send for a shrink and a straightjacket. A few small bits of food remained in the basement, but otherwise there was no trace of what I had seen. Even the refrigerator was now empty of anything except an old bottle of ketchup.

I also did not tell the police that the shotgun had been upstairs, that I had brought it down to the basement, that I handed it to our father, that I then returned upstairs and waited to hear the shot.

They were incurious, the police men, easily satisfied, repulsed but also compassionate. Soon enough, they let me go home to Seattle.

...

After some weeks of adjustment, medication, and many naps, we pretended to go back to our normal lives, and after a while I realized we weren't pretending any more. I got the promotion I had hoped for. Ron kept busy and said he felt fulfilled. We moved Zack to a small and rather ragtag private school that Ron and I both thought was too much like a hippie commune, but Zack loved it, couldn't wait to go to school each morning, and that was all we wanted or needed. I paid the taxes on the farm and gave the livestock to a neighbor. We talk now and then of selling it, but I am happy to let it rot.

This summer I took a series of cooking classes, trying to find a hobby, some activity that would not be about my job. Ron and I had always split the cooking based on who was busiest or most (or least) motivated, but now I've taken over, and it has helped me feel connected not so much to our mother, who did all our cooking when we were growing up, as to our father, who provided the raw materials. I try to shop mostly at farmer's markets, and the farmers have gotten to know me. I would like to say that I see some of my father in them, but I don't, not usually — Seattle farmers tend to be more friendly and open than any New England farmer I ever knew, which is an unfair generalization, but one I can't shake. It's when I get the food home and start prepping it that I feel my father there, looking over my shoulder with something like pride and even mischievousness as he sneaks a slice of apple or a wedge of tomato for himself, and I do not know if I remember or imagine a similar scene from childhood, our mother at the counter, our father in and out of the kitchen, a rich smell filling the room from roasting ham or baking pie in the oven, our mother instructing us all to bring ingredients or to watch out for steam and heat, telling me to take care of my little brother, our father smiling, teasing us all good-naturedly, and laughter pouring in like sunlight from just beyond my sight.

We sit now each night at our table, a table Zack sets with plates and silverware and napkins, that Ron brings my food to, and we have learned to smile again with each other, learned not to hide the dreams that nightly help us find our words.

"Your mother thought steaming eggs instead of boiling them was ridiculous," Ron says tonight, and I chuckle, because I knew she would think it was a silly West Coast affectation. "But she's impressed," he says. "She might even try it herself."

"Uncle Corey wants you to cook more fish," Zack says.

That's strange, as Corey never liked fish. During his visit he said it was the thing he hated most about Seattle (the ocean, the fish).

"People can change," Zack says. "Maybe he'll cook fish for us one day."

"Maybe," I say quietly, chewing a bit of duck that I think now, from the texture, ought to have cooked a minute less.

People can change. I would like to believe that, Corey. Of myself most of all.

"He wants to know," Zack says, "how grandpa is doing."

"Yes," Ron says to me, reaching for my hand in a familiar way, "your mother is concerned."

Soon, I hope, I will be able to tell them what they want to hear.

I no longer dream of a table strewn with their blood and bones and offal, no longer reach for the sharpest knife whenever my son and wife — my husband — are near. And yet I dread to sleep, dread to be left with myself in the night, a place once wrenched with screams and now silent except for my breath and memory, from which I then fear to wake in the morning and find, despite it all, I still don't trust forgiveness, still cannot taste the nourishment that sits before me.

MASS

The brief obituary for Wendell Hamilton that appeared in the September 30, 2015 issue of the *Coös County Democrat* was not entirely inaccurate, but it was far from complete. I expect he wrote it himself years ago. (Perhaps his lawyer submitted it as a requirement of probate.) Dr. Hamilton's life was significant enough that his obituary should have appeared at the very least in the *Boston Globe*, and it should have been noted by Cornell University, where he taught for nine years, and by Yale, where he earned his PhD, and by Dartmouth College, where he earned his BA. The only notice of his death that I have been able to find, however, is the one in the *Democrat*, the small weekly newspaper covering the northern region of New Hampshire where he was born and grew up, though not quite where he died.

When I tracked him down during the summer of 2007, Dr. Hamilton was living on a dirt road in the very small, eastern town of Pike, New Hampshire, in a 100-year-old house (little more than a cabin) where every spare bit of space was filled with books, journals, magazines, and newspapers. I was twenty-four, had just finished my second year as a PhD student at Boston University, and had been granted a modest research fellowship to study representations of mass murder in contemporary American fiction. Early in that research, I discovered that Randall Curry's best friend had been a literature professor.

Curry is hardly the most famous mass shooter in the U.S. Indeed, he's been mostly forgotten, for though he shot seventeen people (killing nine) outside the Tip O'Neill Federal Building in Boston in 1994, his crimes were not extraordinary enough to last in the public memory, and he was killed by a security guard before he could be taken into custody, leaving little for the media to feast on later. My father worked for the Department of Housing and Urban Development at the time, and he had been in the O'Neill Building when the shooting occurred, so I had a particular interest in it, and my memory of that day remains vivid, though I was only ten years old at the time. (My father came home late, and afterward he never spoke about what happened or what he saw, if anything.)

Soon after meeting with Dr. Hamilton, I dropped out of my PhD program and worked odd jobs out west for a while, mostly in Montana and North Dakota. Eventually, I ended up here in New Mexico, teaching part-time at NMSU in Las Cruces, before recently feeling a need to move on again, somewhere farther away, beyond the borders of the United States, somewhere where the language is unfamiliar and I can't read any of the books I encounter.

I will leave this memoir behind with Ruben Trevino, a research librarian at Boston University's Mugar Memorial Library, who helped with so much of the work that led me to Wendell Hamilton, and who sent me the obituary. He will file it away somewhere where a researcher with similar interests as mine might find it, if such a person ever exists. There is some information here, and possibly even something more than information, but I am currently in no frame of mind to speculate on what that might be. I have learned what I can from this material.

If you, whoever you are, need final words for all this, then let them be these: Do not try to find me.

...

I was working on my master's degree at Dartmouth when I first read one of Wendell Hamilton's essays, "Style as Substance at Century's End: *The Picture of Dorian Gray, The Wings of the Dove,* and *Three Lives*", published in a 1984 issue of *Modern Fiction Studies*. I don't remember how or why I encountered it. It had nothing to do with anything I was working on. I've long been interested in Wilde and Stein, so maybe that was it. (I've also long had an aversion to the writing of Henry James, which perhaps should have led me away from the essay, but didn't.) I doubt that I understood much of what Hamilton wrote, and none of his arguments are what stuck with me. Instead, it was the precision of the mind behind the words, the clarity and elegance of his writing, that fascinated me and compelled me to seek out everything I could find by him.

The list of his writings is not long. As far as I can tell, he never published a book of his own (oh for the days of more lenient tenure committees!), but he did co-edit *Outside the (Meta) Text: Deconstruction and 20th Century American Metafiction* with John W. Rye, published in 1989. After 1989, there was a strange, brief shift in the topics he wrote about, then silence. Simply listing out his bibliography solidified my fascination with his work and my curiosity about his fate:

- "Style as Substance at Century's End: *The Picture of Dorian Gray, The Wings of the Dove,* and *Three Lives*", *Modern Fiction Studies*, 1984
- "*The Making of Americans* and the Making of the 20th

Century Novel: A Study in Discourse", *Modern Fiction Studies,* 1986
- "Obscene Harlem Unseen: Ford & Tyler's *The Young and Evil*", *Studies in the Novel,* 1988
- "'A Squeeze of the Hand': Melville's Radical *Différance*", *Social Text,* 1989
- "Cut-up as Self-Narrating Form in *Naked Lunch, The Ticket That Exploded,* and *The Wild Boys*", *Outside the (Meta)Text* anthology, 1989
- "Fascist Aesthetics and the Adventure of History in Barry Sadler's *Casca* Novels", *Journal of Popular Culture,* 1992
- "John Rambo/John Barth: Lost in the Funhouse of *First Blood*", *Journal of Popular Culture,* 1994

There is much that could be said about that bibliography, but what struck me immediately was the difference between the first five and last two items, the movement from the study of modernist and post-modernist texts (utilizing common theoretical lenses of the time) to the study of popular paramilitary fiction. I read each of the essays and was impressed by the sharp, unaffected writing in them, even when they relied on abstruse philosophical concepts that I've never been especially skilled at parsing. The 1990s essays were as beautifully structured and written as the earlier ones, but there was a difference in them, too, a new sense of, for lack of a more precise word, *urgency.* The sentences were generally less complex than those in the earlier essays, the philosophy was less dense, and the insights led to an unsettling feeling that these items of popular culture matter in a way that everything else Hamilton had written about could not — that, in fact, some sort of life and death struggle was not just represented within books designed for quick and unreflective reading, but embodied by them.

And then Hamilton published nothing else that I or, later, various research librarians could find. Ruben Trevino did uncover his 1983 dissertation at Yale, *Oscar Wilde After Dorian Gray*, and I read it, though with disappointment. Its best passages were early drafts of ideas that would appear in some of the articles, and nothing that had not later found its way into print seemed to me especially insightful.

After my brief original interest in Hamilton, I forgot all about him until I was a student in a seminar at BU on violence in contemporary American fiction. I grew curious to know whether anyone had fictionalized Randall Curry and the shooting at the O'Neill Building, thinking perhaps I could somehow turn the subject into a seminar paper, and in my general search on literary topics related to Curry, I quickly discovered a long profile of him in the *Globe*, published a year and a half after the shooting, which noted: "Curry's closest friend for much of his life until recently seems to have been the Cornell literature professor Wendell Hamilton. Dr. Hamilton declined to be interviewed for this article, and has never spoken publicly about the friendship." Suddenly my interest in Hamilton returned, I dug up all my old photocopies of his essays, and I searched everywhere I could for mention of him in connection with Curry. Their names occasionally appeared together, but no-one had managed to get any more information than the *Globe*, and anyone's nascent interest in Hamilton (if there had been anyone with such interest) vanished as other mass shootings grabbed headlines and, inevitably, fascination with Curry dissipated.

Now, though, knowing the connection between the two men, all of Hamilton's 1990s publications made more sense — or not sense, exactly, since I had no idea what the nature of their friendship was, but rather the change in Hamilton's work no longer seemed entirely, almost comically, random.

The newspaper and magazine articles about Curry said he was someone with paramilitary fantasies. He had been raised in a basically middle-class family in Peekskill, New York (father an accountant, mother an insurance agent), though apparently there was significant tension between the parents; they divorced when Randall was young and he moved with his mother to central New Hampshire. They were, by all accounts, liberal in their politics. Randall was a stellar student, and easily earned a scholarship to a private school nearby, which is where he met Wendell Hamilton, who was one year behind him. Randall's life doesn't get interesting until after high school, however. He attended Harvard for a year and a half, pursuing a double major in computer science and political science. He never fit in at Harvard, kept dropping classes and failing the ones he didn't drop, until finally he just stopped attending, returned to New Hampshire, worked various low-wage jobs (many of which he got fired from; apparently he was especially unsuited for retail jobs), and finally ended up working at a small-engine repair shop in the southeastern part of the state. Acquaintances said Curry was stand-offish and often seemed to think he was superior to the people around him. He became interested in various conspiracy theories, and he developed an obsession with guns and militaria, spending the majority of his income on weapons, tools, accoutrements. He wore a camouflage cap and an olive-drab coat he called his "Rambo jacket". He occasionally had contact with his parents, mostly to ask for money, but never talked about either his mother or father to anyone except to say that they were dead or, if the person knew they were not, that they were mentally unstable, especially his mother, whom he seemed particularly to despise. He subscribed to *Soldier of Fortune* magazine, and told more than one person that he wished he could become a mercenary, it seemed like a good way to see the world. On a Monday in the middle of April, he didn't go into work, but instead drove to Boston, parked his 1989 Ford Bronco illegally outside the O'Neill Building, and started shooting at the building with an AR-15 semi-automatic rifle. He finished with the rifle, got out of his Bronco, walked toward the building with a Sig Sauer P226 pistol in hand, and shot three people at close range before a security guard was able to return fire, shooting him in the head, chest, and stomach, killing him.

Where had Wendell Hamilton fit into this life?

I wrote my seminar paper as a comparison between ideas in some of the *Casca* novels of Barry Sadler (tales of an eternal warrior) and Don DeLillo's *Mao II* and *Libra* — a terrible paper, really, but my goal wasn't so much to write a good paper as it was to think more about Hamilton and his ideas. It also let me put together the core of a research proposal for the summer. Though my ostensible topic was masculine, paramilitary violence in literature and society in the 1990s, my real interest was the connection between Randall Curry and Wendell Hamilton.

Mostly, I wanted to find Hamilton and talk to him. For reasons I couldn't have possibly explained at the time, I sensed that he might somehow offer a key not only to Randall Curry, but to some inchoate feeling lurking in the shadows of my own life. But how to find him? Cornell seemed a good place to start, and so I emailed every member of the English department who had been there when Hamilton had also been on the faculty. Only one responded: Maxwell Corliss, a Milton scholar whose first two years at Cornell overlapped with Hamilton's final two. He replied to my email and told me to give him a call, so I did. (With his permission, I recorded the phone call.)

"Wendell was not as odd as some people will probably make him out to be to you," he said. I told him that nobody so far had responded to any of my inquiries. Either they had no memory of Hamilton or didn't want to talk about him, at least to me. Corliss laughed. "Not surprising," he said. "Wendell was not the touchy-feely type, not at all. People liked him well enough — I don't think he had enemies, per se, at least not any more so than the rest of us — people who disliked something he said in a department meeting or something, certainly, but not more than that, and in any case, Wendell hardly ever spoke in meetings, at least that I saw."

"Did you know he was friends with Randall Curry?"

"Who?" Corliss said.

"The man who killed nine people outside a federal building in Boston. 1994."

"Oh, right, yes," he said in the sort of tone that made me think he didn't remember it at all. "I can't say I paid much attention. Tenure was calling. But no, I had no idea Wendell was involved. How strange."

"He wasn't involved, but he knew the shooter somehow."

"I see." An awkward pause and then I asked if he could tell me anything else about Hamilton. "What do you want to know?" he replied. I said I didn't know anything about his personality, his likes or interests. "Oh," Corliss said, "well that's a bit difficult. A bit personal."

"Personal?"

"He's a very private man. There are so many things I never knew about him, things I don't know about him, and yet we were — well, I'm far less interested in privacy than Wendell, so I'll just tell you: He and I were in a casual, primarily sexual relationship for a lot of my time here. Wendell didn't have any interest in something more than that, at least not with me, but it was very cordial, and I honestly think back on it with fondness. He wanted to know about me, and he enjoyed talking about poetry and books and scholarship, but he rarely opened up much about himself."

"Did you keep in touch with him after he left Cornell?"

"Yes, for a year and a half, maybe two years. He returned to New Hampshire. I assume he's still there. He inherited a house, some money. He really didn't like academia. He liked scholarship, and in many ways I think he actually enjoyed teaching — I think he sees the sharing of knowledge to be a kind of duty, a moral duty — but he has little tolerance for bureaucracy, and even less for the corporatist *weltanschauung* that has so infected higher education, the, well, you know, the endless insistence on *usefulness*, the instrumentalizing and marginalizing of the humanities, all that. So once he was able to, he left. Even when he was here, we'd meet in Manhattan, usually. There were some bars and clubs that he liked, some friends he had down there. This was the '90s, and New York was a different sort of world, a different place from what it's become. Now it's just a playground of the rich. But there was some life still there in the '90s. The last hurrah of the real New York, as it were. We had a nice time, always, but Wendell had become more interested in … well, in rougher trade than I. I'm rather bourgeois in my tastes, I'm afraid. He was not, at least not usually, and less so after he left here. There wasn't a lot remaining for us to talk about, it seemed, nor much passion in the sex, so we drifted apart, and I haven't heard from him in a while. I thought maybe you might have."

Corliss was willing to give me a mailing address he had for Wendell Hamilton, a post office box in Hanover, New Hampshire. "He said he checks his mail two or three times a week, and that it's a good half hour from where he lives. He may still be there, wherever it was. It's been almost a decade since I last heard from him, though."

I wrote a short, stiltedly polite note to Hamilton, explaining my research project, conveying my long interest in his work, and saying that I was planning on a trip to New Hampshire during the summer and wondered if he might be willing to talk to me. I included my address, phone number, and email address. I mailed the note to the post office box and waited.

A week later, I received a response written elegantly in black ink on a small sheet of heavy, cream-colored stationary paper: "Dear Mr. Dalaria: Thank you for your kind letter. I will, indeed, be at home this summer. Please send me your essay, as I would like to have a sense of your work before I commit myself to meeting. Sincerely, Wendell Hamilton."

I read the note over again and again, my feelings a lightning storm of surprise, elation, terror. I had made contact with someone whose ideas had been important to me for many years, and he seemed willing to meet, but he wanted to read my own work — work I had little confidence in. I regretted even mentioning it to him. I spent the next few days revising my essay on *Casca* and DeLillo, trying to make it not quite so insipid, trying to show that I had thoughts of my own and wasn't merely repeating the insights in Hamilton's own essay. I wondered if he would respect me more if I were critical of some element of his work. There was nothing I particularly disagreed with in what he had written, though. I decided not to force it. Better to have him think of me as a naïve sycophant than as an arrogant kid. Finally, I printed the paper out, stuck it in a large envelope, and mailed it to him.

A week and a half later, I received another letter: "Dear Mr. Dalaria: Thank you for sending your very interesting essay. I am generally at home and would be happy to meet you. If

July 16 at 1pm would be convenient, that would work well for me, and you do not need to reply, but simply show up. If it is not convenient, please reply with another date and time and I will make myself available. I have enclosed a map. Sincerely, Wendell Hamilton."

The map was hand-drawn, simple and graceful, with clear indications of where highways turned to small roads, where pavement gave way to dirt, and where moose, deer, cows, chickens, geese, ducks, and dogs were most likely to walk in the road. I found an inexpensive hotel a few miles away from Hanover and booked a room, then spent the long days until our meeting re-reading not only all of Hamilton's own writings, but the various books and writers he wrote about. I was trying to shape my own knowledge to be similar to his.

And then I was driving through the back roads of New Hampshire, through forests and valleys so heavily wooded that I feared claustrophobia would overtake me. I got to the hotel, tried to read, couldn't concentrate, ordered a chicken sandwich from room service, could hardly eat it, tried to sleep, couldn't, took a bath, then spent much of the night lying in bed, staring at the ceiling, and running scenarios through my mind: Hamilton likes me and answers all my questions jovially, Hamilton hates me and doesn't answer any questions, Hamilton is demented and answers my questions in bizarre riddles, Hamilton is not home, Hamilton is a serial killer and slits my throat with a rusty kitchen knife…

In the morning, I drove to Pike. Being nervous and excited, I was early. I think I allowed four hours to drive the forty miles from my hotel to Hamilton's house. I used the spare time to drive around the area until I understood how each road connected with the roads around it. It was a lovely day, sunny and not too hot or humid, so I parked my car and wandered through woods, stopped to look at rivers and ponds, letting myself take in the shape and smell of the landscape that Wendell Hamilton had made his own for more than a decade now. Places, I thought, could tell us about the people who chose them. What was this place — quiet, remote, somehow outside history — telling me about Wendell Hamilton?

I pulled into his driveway a few minutes before 1pm. He lived on a dirt road off of a dirt road, and his driveway was another sort of dirt road, though one with a bit more grass covering it. The driveway led down to a little grey house sitting on a ledge overlooking a brook. Beside the house stood a garage that looked barely large enough to hold one car.

Before I could knock on the front door more than once, it opened and a short, bald man smiled at me. "Mr. Dalaria, I presume."

"Dr. Hamilton."

"Nobody has called me 'Dr. Hamilton' in a long time. It sounds like an accusation. Call me Wendell, please, for the sake of my sanity. Come in."

I followed him into a closet-sized mud room and took off my shoes. "And call me Ted. 'Mr. Dalaria' is not something I'm used to." He chuckled and led me to a living room where two whole walls were nothing but bookcases. Hundreds more books stood in stalagmite piles across the floor. The furniture (couch, two chairs, a coffee table) was old (but not antique); it made my own furniture — relics of yard sales past — seem fresh, modern, affluent. I noticed cobwebs in corners.

"I'm afraid I'm a bit of a Miss Havisham," Wendell said. "I used to be self-conscious about my indifference to housekeeping, but now I am indifferent to my indifference. Entropy always wins."

He offered me a cup of coffee or lemonade, and I gladly

accepted the latter, which it turned out he had squeezed himself that morning. It was sharp and sugary.

I scanned his bookshelves, stepping carefully between the piles.

"There's no real order to it all," he said. "There was once, but I found it oppressive and unhelpful. It is frustrating, I admit, to have to search when you are seeking one specific book, but I find the opportunities for serendipitous thinking far outweigh that occasional inconvenience."

Countless paperback mystery novels, many looking like they'd survived floods and beatings, mingled with pristine old hardcovers of Greek plays and French Enlightenment philosophy. New copies of recent novels sat beside old self-help books from the '60s and earlier. I took Norman Vincent Peale's *Stay Alive All Your Life* from a shelf. "I can't say I expected to find something like this in your collection," I said.

"Oh, Peale is one of my favorites. A blithering idiot and a snake-oil salesman, no doubt, but I can't help suspect he actually believed what he wrote, and I find something compelling in that, something even, perhaps, noble. A feeling that turns the laughter and scorn that fills me when I start reading to shame and then awe by the time I am finished."

I put the book back on the shelf, tucked between what looked to be a lovely illustrated volume of Rabelais and a home repair manual from before I was born. "What do you read these days?" I said.

"Theoretical physics."

I laughed. He smiled. "Really," he said. "Not especially *detailed* theoretical physics, but introductory sorts of texts, popularizations, books for people who don't really ever have a hope of truly understanding physics but nonetheless possess a certain curiosity. And its words are sometimes beautiful — a *tachyonic field of imaginary mass* — who couldn't love such a phrase? I find it all strangely comforting, the more far-out ideas of quantum theory and such. It's like religion, but without all the rigmarole and obeisance to a god. Or perhaps more like poetry, though really not, because it's something somehow outside language, but nonetheless elegant, and of course constricted by language, since how else can we communicate about it? But it gestures, at least, toward whatever lies beyond *logos*, beyond our ability even to reason, though perhaps not to comprehend. At my age, and having spent a life devoted to language, there is comfort and excitement — even perhaps some inchoate feeling of hope — in glimpses beyond the realm of words. There is, I have come to believe, very much outside the text. What is it though? Call it God, call it Nature, call it the Universe, call it what it seems to me now to be — having read and I'm sure misunderstood my theoretical physics — call it: *an asymptote.*"

I had not yet asked Wendell if I could record him, so the above is a reconstruction, but I feel I remember it almost perfectly, because I had never heard anyone speak like him before. At first, I believed he must have prepared what he hoped to say to me in advance, or had said it to many other people over the years, turning it into a performance, a shtick. Maybe this was the case, but I prefer to think not. He ennunciated carefully, his voice a bit high and almost, I thought, English in its accent, and he spoke without haste and without resort to the *umms* and *uhhs* and *like, you know, likes* that the rest of us so often succumb to in conversation. We talked for a while longer about nothing of any real import (certainly nothing I *remember* as having any import), and then I asked if he might be willing for me to record him.

"Why?" he said, suddenly suspicious. I said it was faster

for me than taking notes, and that way I could forget about whether I was getting it all down and instead devote myself to listening, to conversation. He stared at me for a moment, then shrugged and said though he thought it a tad discomforting, he was sure it would be just fine. And so I began the recording. (My transcription here has cleaned up some of what I said, but I've hardly had to edit his responses at all. I have indicated where he took an especially long pause between words, as these silences seem to me as meaningful as what he spoke.)

...

Q: I'm most curious I guess why you switched, or changed — why you made the change from the sorts of essays you were writing in the '80s — right up through the William S. Burroughs piece — that essay — why after that — there's a break — a break in chronology as well as in subject matter — and that's probably the biggest thing that has stuck out to me over the years about your work, the question of why that shift.

A: Yes. There is a shift, certainly, obviously. I've thought about it a lot. [Pause.] At the time, I thought what had happened was that I had simply become bored. I had been doing the same sort of work, the same sort of writing, for a decade or so. I had been ambitious as a young man. I had seen academia as an escape from a fate — from a, though it will sound hyperbolic, a *doom*. It is the right word. I had felt doomed. I also felt that I was a fraud. Given the circumstances of my childhood, it is remarkable that I was ever able to imagine a life for myself different from the lives of the sorts of people with whom I attended public school, the sorts of people, in fact, that I now, once again, live among, and quite happily. But at the time of my childhood it was not happy. I was not happy. I dreamed of escape. School was the only thing I showed any talent for, and so school became my escape. Boarding school, then college, then graduate school. From each of which, of course, I also wanted to escape, because only new things offered the escape I sought, or at least that I thought I sought. It remained so even as I was hired by Cornell. The essays I wrote throughout the 1980s, the essays, we might say, of the Reagan years, those essays are written by a man who wants nothing more than to escape from a fate he cannot even quite articulate (if you'll pardon that unintentional rhyme), a fate which is — though unarticulated, though imprecise and vague and even perhaps mystical — a fate which is, as I said, a doom. The escape that man sought was an escape through literature, or, more accurately, an escape through the *interpretation* of literature. It was an attempt to get the stories right, to find, somehow, the right words, and, thus, salvation.

Q: But? What changed? What was the shift?

A: Not one thing, not one large crisis or such. A series of … it's hard to find the word. A series of insights. A series of catastrophes. Insights taken for catastrophes, catastrophes taken for insights. It was a long time ago. [Pause.] I will tell you this: People were dying. People I knew, acquaintances, and a couple of people I cared about very deeply. They died, slowly, horribly. They wasted away, sometimes neglected, all of them cast out by a society that declared them to be abject. Sinners, lepers. But not deserving of compassion, not even seen as human, at least not fully human. Untouchables. It is easy to forget now, seemingly so far away from it, what it was like for … us … to live then, to die then.

Q: AIDS?

A: Yes.

Q: But you weren't, yourself, you weren't—

A: No. I used to get tested every six months, then every year, then … well, it's been a while. But there's no need. That part of life is over for me, and I will not pretend I'm not happy to be done with it. A friend once called me a Buddhist atheist, and I suppose the label is accurate for me, as I have spent many years now attempting to escape desire, though even as I say it I'm somewhat embarrassed as I know so little about Buddhism that my perception of its precepts, its antipathy to desire — even, as I think of it, war against desire — may be a flight of my imagination. It doesn't matter, though. "Atheist" is close. "Agnostic" more precise, in the ancient sense of agnostic as not-knowing, because it seems to me the height of foolishness to pretend to know anything about whatever there is, or is not, beyond death.

Q: Why, with AIDS, why do you think — okay, this is an impertinent question. I'm sorry. I — why do you think — why — I mean, your health I assume—

A: Why did I not get sick?

Q: Yes.

A: Because most of my practices were not the ones that correlate with the highest transmission of the disease. I would not want to give you the impression that I was *safe*, because I was not. I am, I expect, quite lucky, and perhaps even somehow immune. Or it may just be that since I have never really enjoyed anal sex, and have not sought it out, and have rarely indulged in it, that I was not at as much risk as others. Oral sex, yes, some, certainly, but fundamentally I was interested more in touch than in penetration or the exchange of bodily fluids. I expect the reason, or *a* reason among a constellation of reasons, that I have been able to settle quite comfortably into celibacy is that I have always been somewhat, and sometimes quite strongly, disgusted by bodily fluids. You've seen *Dr.*

Strangelove, I assume — "precious bodily fluids", yes? (Is that the phrase?) Well, I'm quite the opposite. Nothing precious to me about bodily fluids. I all but faint at the sight of blood, for instance. But that's not quite disgust, not quite what I am referring to. (I am, as always, circling my subject.) By disgust, I mean what has been inside the body and is expelled, secreted. Semen, saliva, sweat: they are all equally unappealing to me. To hold a hand, though, to touch a face, to kiss a cheek, to run hands through hair — to wake in the morning and look into someone else's eyes, or to watch them as they sleep peacefully, to listen to them breathe — that, for a while at least, was an exquisite pleasure, a privilege even.

Q: For a while?

A: Yes. Feelings change. Emotions fade. Desires fade, I'm sorry to say. I expect it was because certain people died.

Q: AIDS?

A: Mostly. Not entirely.

Q: Randall Curry?

(I had not planned how I would bring Curry up. In my memory, his name just pops out of my mouth, but I expect I was thinking that the time was right, or that there would, at least, not be a better time, given how honest and personal Wendell had become in our conversation.)

A: [after a long pause] Yes. But. No. Not in the same way. Randall and I were not lovers, I should say that. We were friends, best friends for a time. When we were young. Our ideals were similar, if you can believe it. We wanted to be intellectuals, and we wanted to change the world, to make it a more just, more equitable place. We became embittered and disillusioned, but in different ways, toward different ends.

Q: Were you surprised by what he did?

A: What he did was a shock, and ghastly, and unforgive-able. It was, in addition to being ghastly, and in addition to being unforgiveable — it was, for me, personally — it was a … a disappointment. Randall was a brilliant man. My sense of escape was entwined with my sense of *his* escape. We were, I had thought, similar. I was wrong. Or perhaps not wrong. I have thought about it a lot over the years, of course. How could I not? I never wanted to talk about it at the time because I only wanted to reject him, to cast him out, to make him, as it were, my own abject. To keep him, and his beliefs, and his acts, to keep them outside, untouchable and, most impor-tantly, untouching me. A foolish, if natural and understand-able, emotion. In a narcissistic way, I saw Randall as a failed version of myself. There but for fortune go I. Our given names, after all, are so similar. Wendell. Randall. The same but for a few small letters. Surely, that must mean something? And yet it does not. Chaos torments the pattern-seeking mechanisms in our minds. Catastrophe brings out the fool in the best of us. And I am not the best of us.

Q: Did he have anything to do, for instance, with your interest in the Casca novels?

A: Yes, of course. He was one of the contributors to the shift in my thinking, my desires, my life. His was one of the later deaths, and an entirely different type than that of my friends who got sick. But his decline — I know no other word for it, though the word itself saddens me and, in fact, implicates me — his decline was clear for years, and viewed in retrospect it seems, to me at least, that only a moral monster could have seen it as anything less than a severe crisis. But that is in retro-spect. Still, much was visible, even at the time. How could it not be? My inclination, though, was simply to create distance.

To separate myself from him. To avoid contact. Do not touch. And yet I was fascinated. The fascination of the abomination.

Q: Did you think he would kill people?

A: No. Of that I am certain. (Or I tell myself I am certain.) I had no conscious idea it would take the final form that it did. Does that exonerate me? If anything, I think it shows how unperceptive I was. All the clues were there. I did not see them. I thought I was reading him with great insight, but I was terribly wrong. It's not that I was oblivious. I was afraid for him. But only for *him*, because in the darker moments of night when I thought about his fate, his doom, I thought only that he might kill *himself*. And he did. In the worst possible way, by bringing other people into his own despair.

—But you asked about the books. Indeed, the Casca novels were ones he loved, as was *First Blood*, though in his case the movie and not the novel, which I don't think he ever read. I tried to understand him by writing about them. I tried to write my way out of his doom. It was arrogant and stupid and the only thing I could, at that moment in my life, see to do. [Pause.] What I, in my self-absorption, could not see is that my writing those essays, my engaging with those thoughts, those patterns, would do nothing. And did nothing.

Q: The *First Blood* essay came out right around the time when he died.

A: A month or so after. Yes. Academic publishing is very slow. I had written it two years earlier.

Q: Is there a connection between his death and your not publishing again?

A: Yes. Of course. There is everything outside the text.

Q: The deaths? And?

A: Deaths and asymptotes. Chaos theory and lots of fractals. [Pause.]

Q: I...

A: The story is banal, I'm afraid. I inherited some money, I did not enjoy academia anymore, I had no idea what to write about, I had little interest in sex and none in relationships, and so I came here. [Pause.] How is Max Corliss, by the way? You said he was the one who gave you my address?

Q: He seems to be well. I think he misses you.

A: And I him. I should send him a note. He was the least combative Miltonist I have ever known. They are a fighterly lot. Friendly, but fighterly. The nature of the subject, I suppose. What we study shapes us.

Q: He said you were good friends.

A: Well, yes, we were. We had sex, did he tell you that? Probably not. He was always so shy. I did something unpardonable, I'm afraid. When I didn't understand my own feelings well enough, and didn't understand why I wanted to get away, and mistook my desire for escape as a desire for escape from *him* — I lied to him. I told him a story. He was always so demure, it was easy to make up a story and make up a self. I wanted to believe I was the kind of person who could enjoy pain, who could find pleasure in inflicting and receiving violence. I told a story about that imagined self, and that story was my escape from him. I have always regretted it.

Q: He doesn't seem to hold a grudge against you. I think he'd like to know you're well.

A: Mr. Dalaria — Ted — let me ask you: *Why* are you doing the work you are doing?

Q: Interviewing you? Because I found — I find your work, your writings, fascinating and—

A: No no no. Forget about me. I am flattered by your attention, certainly, and gratified that some things I wrote long ago have whatever ability to communicate still today, but no, that was not what I meant. What I meant was: Why are you doing what you do?

Q: Getting a PhD?

A: In literature. Yes.

Q: It's work that I'm pretty good at. Work I enjoy. And I honestly don't really know what else to do. I mean, I'm not the best in my program, by any means, but I'm not bad, and I, well … it's something to do. I know that sounds pathetic.

A: No, not pathetic. I don't think so. My own reasons were similar. And you are not me and the world is different now, and in any case, numerous people in far more destructive careers have far more pathetic reasons for doing what they do than you have for what you do. But you must know — and yes, I will sound like a meddling scold when I say it — you must know that books and words will not save you, that they are not an escape from whatever you are seeking escape from, but rather an escape *into* something that… [Pause.]

Q: Something that…?

A: [after a pause] Hamlet: "Words, words, words."

He picked up my glass and carried it to the kitchen. "More lemonade?" he asked. I said no, I was fine. He asked me to wait a moment, then went to another part of the house. I heard some drawers open, some items shift around. I stopped recording. Then he came back and handed me a small envelope. "This is the note that Randall sent me before he died. I never showed it to the FBI. Doing so would feel like a violation. And there is nothing they could have used in it. But you should read it."

I didn't want to read it. Just holding it in my hands felt sacrilegious, like touching fire. Wendell did not move and would not look away. I opened the envelope.

"Dear Wendell," the letter began — handwritten in blue

ballpoint pen, almost scrawled — "You will be very angry with me, and I understand that. I'm going to go do something I've wanted to do for a while now. We've become very different. I wanted you to understand me, and I couldn't figure out a way to make you understand. What I am going to do will not make you understand me. But it will do something. Action, not ideas. Reality, not fantasy. No stories, just lives. And deaths. All there ever is. Goodbye, my friend." He wrote his name like an official signature at the bottom of the page. Beneath the signature, with a red pen, he wrote: "Soldier, you are content with what you are. Then that you shall remain until we meet again."

Wendell gave me permission to copy the letter into my notes.

"If you want the answer to me, to my life, it is there," he said. "There is no explanation other than those words. There is no interpretation, no story. I made a life, and then I made what I hope will prove to have been a different life for myself than the life I led before."

"Have you," I asked after I finished copying the letter, "written anything recently?"

He sighed. He started to speak, stopped. Then: "You have not understood a word I have said." He spoke quietly, without anger, without even disappointment. But his words were a wall suddenly between us. I had confirmed his doubts.

I tried to protest, tried to speak, to put words to it all. I don't remember what I said.

"Goodbye, Mr. Dalaria. It was nice to meet you. I wish you the best with your studies."

And so I left.

The sky had become grey, rain was moving in, and darkness shimmered through the hovering trees. I listened to the water in the brook below the house. I listened to birds, though I know nothing about birds and could not identify their calls. I stood in the driveway, fearing to leave. Mosquitoes found me, bit me. Misty dashes of rain touched my hands and nose. I got into my car. Soon, the rain poured down hard, torrential, pelting the metal of the car like pebbles on a steel drum, splashing — smashing — against the windshield in obscuring bursts so that I could barely see even a few feet ahead. The world was dark and the headlights could not penetrate the darkness. Now and then, the lights' glare flashed in the water on the windshield and the rain became a firefly, alive for a moment only. I kept moving forward, as slowly as the car would go, inches at a time, because the bare animal part of me insisted that if I stopped I would die, the car would wash away in a flood, and the flood was here and only here, and if I could get away from here then I could find some dry land, some place to stop and rest without fear. I imagined that the rain was not rain but mosquitoes and flies and junebugs, insect life lured to my headlights and splattered together into a mass and wiped away. I started laughing, nervously, then ghoulishly, and soon in my mind the water on the windshield was no longer bugs but birds and bats and then severed bits of bodies and then eyeballs and then, as somehow the night grew even darker, sprays of maybe ink or maybe blood, I did not know, but surely not water, because how could mere water so menace me? I exhausted what laughter I had left. The night remained dark. The rain continued to fall. All I could do to stay alive was try to keep moving forward no matter how little the car might move, no matter how deafeningly the torrent attacked, no matter the floods beneath the wheels, and to hope that somewhere the rain would stop, day would erase the night, the quiet would return, and I could step outside.

III.

"May we follow along behind?" they asked. "We're lost and not a little fearful. Your robes bring the spirit of the Buddha to our journey."

They had mistaken us for priests.

"Our way includes detours and retreats," I told them. "But follow anyone on this road and the gods will see you through."

I hated to leave them in tears, and thought about them hard for a long time after we left.

—Bashō

AT THE EDGE OF THE FOREST

Throughout the day after the funeral, while puttering around the shop, Bryan caught himself thinking of Julia, her memory like a glint at the edge of his sight. He remembered their constant conversations, her insatiable curiosity, her devotion to both him and Cameron, an odd couple she had herself created through a combination of insight and force of will. She had insisted on bringing Cameron to the shop to meet Bryan, even though Bryan told her not to, that he would renounce his friendship with her immediately, that he was serious, he really, truly, absolutely did not want to meet this man, because he had understood what she was trying to do from the moment she mentioned her friend who was legally blind but not *blind* blind, who lived with his mother even though he was only a few years younger than Bryan, who was a wonderful potter and an artistic soul and a good conversationalist and everybody loved him instantly and she knew they'd both be interested in each other.

"Stop trying to set me up," Bryan had said to her, and she looked stunned. "I don't even know," she said, "if he goes that way." (Cameron laughed at that later. He and Julia had known each other since high school. She was the first person he came out to.)

"Every freak needs a blind lover, is that what you're thinking?"

131

"*No,*" Julia said. She looked away. She walked over to an oak table with a set of mid-20th-century cookbooks on it. She lifted the cover of one of the books without looking at it, her eyes drifting to a wall display of old gas station signs. She came back to the counter. "Okay, I'll be honest. I think he'll be intrigued by your face, your skull. I think he'll want to touch it. And that's good. He's very tactile. It's not like a freakshow thing, not like — like, you know..."

"Not like a fetish?"

"He can't really see anything out farther than his arms. He's okay close up, but to actually *see* something, he needs to be able to use his hands. Is that weird? It shouldn't be weird. He's a potter. It isn't weird with him. It isn't. And, I just, honestly, *honestly,* think you guys will enjoy each other."

On the day that Julia brought him in, Cameron wandered through the store slowly, and Bryan couldn't help but watch Cameron's hands explore the furniture and shelves, his fingers like a piano player's, each working separately over the surfaces. His touch was light, casual, his hands feathery. He paused over an oddly large pink glass vase that someone had brought in a few months ago, and which Bryan had agreed to buy, along with a box of other junk, just to get rid of the seller, an elderly bald man whom he'd never met before, and who started the conversation by saying, "It must be difficult for you, going through the world like that. I admire it. Brave of you." (*What,* Bryan had wanted to say, *would be my alternative? I can't very well chop my head off!* But he did not say it. He was always polite to his customers.)

As Cameron picked up the vase, Bryan said, "Oh, you don't want that."

"It seems a bit out of place here," Cameron said. "An interloper."

"I keep thinking it will go away of its own free will."

Julia looked at the vase in Cameron's hand. "Even I can see it's ghastly," Julia said, "and Bryan will be the first to tell you that I have no taste."

Cameron smiled. "I'll take it," he said. Julia laughed.

"You can have it if you want it," Bryan said. "I won't stop you."

"It says five dollars?"

"I'd be ashamed to take money for it. It's yours. If you promise to smash it to smithereens."

"Gladly!" Cameron said. "I'm Cameron. Julia would have introduced us, I'm sure, but it's more fun to beat her to it."

"Cameron, Bryan," Julia said. "Bryan, Cameron."

"Julia tells me," Bryan said, "that you will want to touch my face."

Julia gasped. "No," she said, "I meant—"

"Perhaps I will want to," Cameron said. "Julia told me that you have an interesting face and that you are an interesting person, if blunt. Or forthright. *Direct*. I forget what word she used. But of course I understand if…"

"Maybe another time," Bryan said.

"After I destroy this vase," Cameron said.

A week later, Cameron returned to the shop. "My mother's gone grocery shopping, so I had her drop me off here," he said. "I have brought you something. Not to sell, but to have. Unless you want to sell it. In which case, I'll accept a commission. But I'd rather you keep it."

From a small backpack he took a ceramic box, dark green with inlaid fragments that Bryan immediately recognized as the remnants of the pink vase, its pinkness now muted against the green of the box.

"I have a friend," Cameron said, "who has a shotgun, and we went out behind his house with said shotgun and we shot,

I tell you, we *shot* the fucking vase." He cackled. "I collected what I could of it, took the shards to my studio, and voilà. Not deathless, perhaps not even inspired, but better than before."

It was a nice box, Bryan thought, a simple bit of slab pottery given depth by the celadon glaze that, on close inspection, revealed a range of hues and smokey shadows. The bits of the old vase added attractive ornament.

"I shall treasure it always," Bryan said. He leaned forward, his elbows on the counter beside the cash register. "And now, I believe…"

"Ah yes," Cameron said, and gently placed his fingers on Bryan's temples, then drifted over the crags of his forehead, his asymmetrical cheekbones, the stub of a nose, the hard skin, the soft skin, the lips covering artificial teeth, the canted wedge of jaw. All the other hands that had ever touched his face had done so from motivations either medical or sexual, but Cameron's hands felt different: no less curious or objective than the doctors' and nurses' hands, no less intrigued than the hands of the men who had taken from him some brief satisfaction, but Cameron's hands explored without awe or hunger, without repressed revulsion. Or so Bryan imagined then. Now, having known Cameron for almost two years, he thought he hadn't been wrong, exactly, about Cameron's perception, but he had learned that such touch was not different in kind so much as in degree from what he had known before.

…

Cameron's studio filled the basement of the rambling old farm-house he lived in with his mother. It had a separate entrance from the house, an entrance that had originally, he told Bryan, been little more than a bulkhead before it was expanded into a room dominated by stairs going down. The front of the studio was a small gallery, with custom-built shelves and tasteful lighting. The rest of the studio spread out behind a wall, a single large cinderblock room with two potter's wheels, numerous tables, floor-to-ceiling shelves that looked to have been built with salvaged wood, and the stout silver octagon that was an electric kiln.

Though Cameron said he had prepared her, his mother could not hide her revulsion at Bryan's face. She brought them a plate of chocolate chip cookies she had made, but she did not stay to see if they enjoyed them.

"She likes you, she really does," Cameron said. Bryan knew it wasn't true. He had seen her eyes looking away from him. Whenever she dropped Cameron off, she never came into the shop. Sometimes, she would park out front, and Bryan would wave to her through the window, but she did not wave back, and she hadn't parked there for a while now.

Though he had enjoyed seeing where Cameron spent so much of his time, and especially enjoyed seeing a collection of Cameron's work, Bryan never felt a need for a return visit.

...

Julia asked about boyfriends once, and he said there hadn't really been any. He told her about the boys who found him in the darker corners of dingy clubs, the boys he spent so much of his late teens and early 20s with, boys whose names he did not remember and rarely knew. In a large city, it is easy enough to discover people whose lusts veer toward what repulses others. They do not yearn for the person, though; they slaver for grotesquerie. For a while, Bryan had been content to let grotesquerie be his selling point. In moments of anger or self-hatred, he had indulged in his ability to repulse. The power to attract was new and thrilling. But newness quickly sheds its skin; thrills dull. By the time he met Tim, even someone's great desperation was barely enough to satisfy Bryan. Tim offered something else, a gleam in his eye that kept Bryan looking, that let him agree to go back to Tim's little basement apartment at the far end of a subway line. Bryan had had dangerous encounters before, men with strong hands or sharp knives, and he thought perhaps this time he had met the man who would kill him — but no, it was just a night together, then some breakfast at a diner the next day, then goodbye. And then their paths kept crossing and they repeated their encounters. They began to know each other's habits and rhythms. They talked about pasts and hopes. Tim never asked, but Bryan told him one night, their lips nearly touching: "It was a car crash. Winter. The highway seemed clear, but suddenly it got cold and wet. My father was driving, my mother in the passenger seat, I was in the back, we were going to see a movie. There was black ice. The car hit a guardrail and flipped over it, flew into the air, toward the edge of some woods. Fell against trees. My parents were killed. The emergency crews at first assumed I was dead. Almost was. Soon wished I was. Parents dead. Arms broken, ribs broken. I barely had a face left. Months in the hospital, years of plastic surgery. This is the best they can do, the best I'll let them do. No more surgeries, that's what I vowed. No more." Tim's lips came closer, touching Bryan's. They kissed softly and gently for what at that moment seemed like days, in memory too few seconds. Bryan had never felt happier or more content. He started applying to graduate programs for archaeology. He stopped going to the bars and clubs where he had found companionship before. Tim was happy to be seen in daylight with him, never seemed self-conscious. "This is my boyfriend," Tim would say to people. Each time, the comfort in those words brought tears to Bryan's eyes, and he would cough or chuckle nervously or look away to hide his pleasure. Bryan never mentioned Tim to Julia. He had never talked about Tim to anybody up here. A year after they met, he and Tim were spending less time together, uncertain where their relationship was going. They didn't end things, and didn't want to end things, but agreed perhaps a pause might help. Bryan returned to the clubs, and kept expecting to see Tim, but he didn't. Eventually, he called Tim's number, but got no answer. He called again a few days later, again no answer, and then finally somebody answered Tim's phone and said Tim wasn't there anymore, sorry, there'd been a terrible accident, Tim was gone. It took Bryan months to piece together scraps of gossip and single sentences in newspaper reports to learn that one night Tim drank too much wine after he had taken anti-depressants and sleeping pills and some mix of pain medication, which he kept in the apartment because he had an old injury to his back that bothered him now and then, or so he said, though Bryan had seen no evidence of that, or any other, injury. Bryan tried not to wonder why nobody had bothered to seek him out to tell him, or at least to let him know about the funeral arrangements.

Bryan said to Julia, "People die around me. People who know me."

"Not *because* they know you," Julia said.

He smiled as best he could, but did not reply.

When she told him she had cancer, he did his best to comfort her, but he couldn't pretend he had not expected it, or something like it. "This isn't your fault," she said. "The world doesn't revolve around you."

"I know," he said.

"Do you?"

There was a coldness between them then, but it lessened as Julia got quickly worse, and in her last week she barely let him leave her bedside. "Tell me about the accident," she said, and he told her about the darkness he felt his parents fall into. "Were you scared?" she asked. No, not at all, not until he woke up in the hospital. Darkness isn't terrifying, emptiness isn't terrifying. It simply is. We had it before birth, we will have it at death. Pain is frightening, suffering is frightening, but emptiness and nothingness are the purest states. He told her he always wished he had been able to go with his parents, he wished that every day, and she got very quiet and bowed her head and told him it was the saddest thing she had ever heard. "Do you still wish you went with them?" she asked at the end, lying in her hospital bed as he held her hand. He leaned close to her ear and whispered, "Yes. Always." An hour later, she was dead.

. . .

Julia first showed up at the shop one day in search of a birthday present for her grandmother, who was turning 90. She spent an hour looking through everything, picking up one item after another (a glass paperweight with a sepia photograph of a stage-coach inside; a woodcut-illustrated copy of *Frankenstein* from 1934; an iron weathervane of a crowing rooster) until finally she brought to the counter a small vessel: pit-fired Guaraní pottery. "I have to admit," Julia said, "I would never buy this for myself. It's got no pizzazz. But it's for my grandmother, and she's a simple woman who likes this sort of thing, and I think it will make her happy, and that's what matters."

"It's from northern Argentina," Bryan said. "I brought it back myself."

"So you like it?"

"Yes, very much."

"You should meet my grandmother, you'd probably get along great."

Julia returned to the shop after her grandmother's birthday party. "She *adored* it. I was the hit of the party. To her, at least. Nobody else much seemed to care, but they were happy she was happy. She was a big traveler when she was young, before she had kids. She speaks Spanish. She knew right away it was from South America."

Julia began to come back every Saturday. She was waiting for divorce papers to go through with her husband; she worked an unexciting job at an insurance company; she said she was tired of the people in town but didn't know where she wanted to go because she had lived here all her life. She asked Bryan to tell her about the places he'd been, and to show her the things he liked most in the shop. "You like the old, weird stuff," she said. He did not disagree. "Do you have any shrunken heads?" she asked.

"No," he said. "But I saw one once, when I was in grad school in New Mexico. A professor from a British school, an anthropologist, came to visit and give a couple lectures. He had been to Ecuador and studied the rituals around head-shrinking there. He got one, I don't know how or where, and he carried it around to lectures to show to people. I suspect it wasn't real, though. I don't think you're supposed to own them. And I'm not sure how you'd get it through Customs. Anyway, he was an asshole. He asked if he could measure my skull."

"No! What did you say?"

"I told him I thought phrenology had gone out of style some years ago."

"I have no idea what that means, but it sounds good."

"It shut him up."

She laughed, and they kept talking, and soon they were going to movies together or out to eat in nearby towns or, in the summer, on long drives through the hills and forests. She needed a distraction from divorce and what she thought of as all her failures in life (lost husband, no children, a solid but boring job), and he relished the companionship after years of solitude. He told himself he would enjoy it as long as it would last, and at the first hint of danger, the first suggestion that the darkness was reaching out, he would disappear to somewhere far away, somewhere even more remote, and start again.

One spring Sunday, they drove across the Kancamagus Highway from Lincoln to Conway, a favorite trip of Julia's childhood, a journey through mountains and forests. She asked Bryan what got him interested in archaeology. Why had he spent years in South America? "Why not?" he said, but she persisted, and he told her the truth: He had been desperate, tired of how expensive everything in New York was, worn down by the fact that even though he had money from his parents' life insurance policies, it would be gone quickly if he stayed in the city. A friend had said there were good archaeology programs at universities in the southwest, so he applied to some, and ended up in New Mexico. It was just a whim, really. He heard about a fellowship for some work in South America, and he had all sorts of idiotic ideas about finding lost civilizations. And not just that. He hoped to find wisdom. He had built up in his mind an idea of indigenous cultures as possessing wisdom that isn't otherwise available, and he wanted to know more about the realm of death. (He expected her to laugh at that, but she didn't.) All of his thesis work was on rituals of death and mourning, and while now he thought that this work was mediocre at best, and that he was lucky they gave him a master's degree at all, it truly had been an obsession, and writing the thesis only made it more so. He heard about a fellowship to travel to South America for archaeological work, and he didn't have anything else lined up, so he applied. Another whim. He traveled to Peru, then Chile and Argentina, working here and there at various sites, all the while looking for traces that would point him toward the wisdom and knowledge he didn't think any living person had access to.

"And what did you find?" Julia asked.

"Nothing," he said. "Good work had been done for decades by far more knowledgeable and talented people than I could ever claim to be. I was just an outsider, an interloper, and — in ways that pain me still — a typically arrogant and oblivious white guy. When I was there, I didn't see myself as that at all, quite the opposite, but I realized it later."

"So you stayed down there for a couple years and nothing came of it?"

"I have a knack," Bryan said, "for always being just a bit too late to everything that matters."

...

He had told Julia most of the truth about his time in South America, but he left out the story of the cave that Sebastián took him to. Sebastián who, like Tim, found fascination not only in Bryan's ruined face, but in something of his personality. Bryan would not let him get close, though. Sex was one thing, easy and fun, but Bryan never lingered, never spent days and nights with Sebastián as he had with Tim, never learned much about Sebastián's family and friends or revealed anything about his own. One night, they got drunk on some local concoction made of various fermented fruits, and Sebastián led Bryan up to a series of caves in one of the hills overlooking the town.

Sebastián had a flashlight, and the light bouncing through the caves made Bryan's head spin, so he sat down, thinking he was about to throw up. Sebastián kept going deeper into the cave, but Bryan stayed behind in the darkness, leaning against the cave's cool wall. He thought he might pass out. Then someone sat next to him and took his hand. Bryan could see nothing in the darkness. Had Sebastián lost his flashlight? Bryan let his head loll onto Sebastián's shoulder, but then he knew it wasn't Sebastián sitting beside him, but someone else, someone with short hair and a beard. "I love you," whispered a familiar voice, Tim's voice, again and again, growing fainter until it was gone. Bryan wanted to speak, wanted to scream out for Tim to stay, or, better, to let Bryan come with him, but his mouth was filled with silence, and then Tim was gone.

Bryan woke later to find Sebastián sleeping beside him in the cave. Every bone in Bryan's body ached, his head throbbed, his skin felt like stone. Sebastián had wrapped himself around Bryan, but Bryan was able to slowly pull himself away without waking him, and he climbed out of the cave and down to the town, where he packed up his backpack and walked a mile to the bus station without ever saying goodbye.

He did not know what became of Sebastián. In all likelihood he was dead.

. . .

Bryan had considered it before, multiple times, imagined countless ways to do it, conjured just as many excuses not to, but Julia's death made him more certain than he had been in many years that the only way out was to die. It might not be too late for him to save Cameron, and it was certainly not too late for him to save someone else, someone who might suffer the bad luck of getting to know him in the future. He had thought going north would be enough, but it was not, because though he was far away from any population center, he was still bound to people. Lacking survival skills, he could not live somewhere truly remote, a cabin in the woods with no electricity, no need for any human contact. He depended on civilization, and so he kept living into the future at the expense of other people's lives.

A gun would be the easiest. He had never had trouble with the law, so would not have trouble buying a gun. But he knew nothing of guns. What kind should he get? A shotgun seemed the best choice, but he had imagined the ways to put a shotgun to his head and hadn't quite been able to figure out the mechanics to avoid it all being awkward (his arms were too short, the likely gun too long) or, worse, a missed shot, the gun slipping and wounding him in the shoulder, for instance. He could put the barrel in his mouth, but the image made him laugh and cringe, the sexual parody obvious and puerile: a final, literally explosive orgasm. Nonetheless, a shotgun still seemed a good option, especially if he wanted to finish the work of destroying his face. But a pistol would be easier. They must make big pistols, something with which to kill a bear, for instance. Put that against his head, pull the trigger, be done with it all. (But *where* against the head? he wondered. He had heard of people wounding themselves gravely, and he did not want that. He did not want to be hooked up to machines in a hospital. No more hospitals.) He wished he could ask someone, wished there were an anonymous service providing answers about the best ways to die.

...

A few days after Julia's funeral, Bryan picked Cameron up in the morning on the way to the shop. They hardly spoke during the drive, but that was normal enough; they both liked quiet mornings. At the shop, they made coffee with an old electric percolator. Bryan poured the coffee into mugs that Cameron had made, which they kept under the counter at the store. Both mugs had a thick, rough glaze that reminded Bryan of lichen. Bryan had first seen one at Cameron's studio and exclaimed over it. "You have a potter's taste," Cameron had told him. "Most people — ordinary people — think these sorts of things are ugly. We love them for the chunky texture, the weirdness. You could only ever give this sort of thing away, or sell it for a few grand at an upscale gallery maybe."

"So why don't you sell it at an upscale gallery?" Bryan had asked.

"Because I need something to drink my coffee from each morning."

This morning, Bryan and Cameron mostly sat silent.

"How are you feeling?" Cameron asked.

"Not great," Bryan said.

"Anything I can do?"

"No," Bryan said. "Sorry. Didn't sleep well."

Cameron reached for Bryan's hand, but Bryan pulled away. He didn't want to. He wanted to take Cameron's hand in his, press it to his lips, hold it to his cheek, let Cameron's fingers drift over his face — he wanted to pull him close, embrace him, kiss him. But that would be a mistake.

"I'll drive you home," Bryan said.

"Why? What's wrong?"

"Nothing, I'm fine. I think I'll close the shop for today. I'm very tired. I think I'll just go home and rest."

"I can come with you, keep you company."

"No, I'll take you home."

"I'm worried about you."

"I know. But I'm fine. Really."

...

After a week of Bryan's carefully-cultivated distance, Cameron demanded that they talk. A friend of his, Sophie, a woman Bryan didn't know well, drove Cameron to Bryan's house one Tuesday night, unannounced. She drove away when Bryan opened the door.

"What's going on?" Bryan said.

"I was going to ask the same of you."

"She just left you here?"

"Yes. I told her to."

"Why?"

"A good place, no? My boyfriend's house."

"Okay."

"Can I come in?"

"Sure. But what's going on?"

"Maybe I'm horny. Or maybe I just want to talk. Or both. I'm out of sorts. And I don't know what's going on with you."

Bryan offered to make coffee, but Cameron went to the cabinet in the kitchen where Bryan kept a couple old bottles of liquor. "I think we need bourbon tonight," Cameron said, and poured generous amounts into two glasses.

"I'm not really in a mood for company," Bryan said.

"Drink your bourbon. It helps."

They sat together on the couch in the living room.

"I know a psychiatrist," Cameron said. "A good one. A woman. Really smart, compassionate. She's in Concord, so a bit of a hike, but worth it, I think. I'll go with you. She helped me a lot."

"I don't need a psychiatrist," Bryan said.

"Of course you do. Everybody does. But you especially right now. I'm *worried*." Cameron took both of Bryan's hands in his own. Bryan tried to pull away, but Cameron held on. "I'm not letting you go," Cameron said.

"You need to."

"Why?"

"It's not good for you. *I'm* not. This will end like it always does, always has—"

"No no no," Cameron said. "You don't get to go with that bullshit *everybody dies around me* thing. You use that, Bryan, it's an excuse, it lets you feel better about disengaging with people."

"I wish that were true. But people are dead. One after another. Julia. Others. I haven't told you about all of them."

"Please stop. Tell me you'll see Renee. The psychiatrist. I'll make the appointment for you and everything. You won't have to do anything except drive there. Hell, I could even ask Sophie if she would—"

"No," Bryan said. He stood up. "I'll take you home now."

"*Will you just listen to me!*" Cameron screamed.

The house creaked. The wind outside blew a branch against a window.

"I'll take you home," Bryan said.

Cameron collapsed into himself on the couch, his arms over his head, and sobbed.

"I don't want to lose you," Cameron whimpered.

Bryan stood up. He listened to the branch against the window.

Eventually, Cameron called Sophie and asked her to drive him home.

...

As he lay in bed in darkness, Bryan saw shadows against shadows, and the shadows swarmed into shapes. Arms and legs writhed across the ceiling. Whispers slipped from the walls and settled into something like words, sibilant sounds swirling across plosive echoes, no language Bryan could understand, though he had heard it many nights through the years.

…

For a while, Cameron called every day, and Bryan said he was fine but no he didn't need company, no he didn't need Cameron's help at the shop, no. Cameron stopped by the shop anyway, whenever his mother needed to go into town, and he made a point of calling to talk to Bryan every night, but then one night he didn't call, but he called the next night, and then not for a few nights after that, and then Bryan realized that Cameron hadn't called or been to the shop in over a month, and despite a pang a sorrow, this gave him comfort.

…

He tried to sell the coffee mugs Cameron had made, but no-one would buy them. For fun, he listed them with a reserve of $2,000 on an auction website, and they sold for more than twice that, the bidders assuming, apparently, that a couple of mugs with such an absurd price must be rare, indeed. He sent Cameron a brief note and a check for the entire amount, and when he got his monthly account statement, he was pleased to see that the check had been cashed.

He kept the box Cameron had made with the inlaid fragments of the pink vase. He set it on his bedside table beside the alarm clock. When morning light came through the bedroom window, the fragments sparkled.

...

By the time winter brought snow, Bryan didn't bother opening the shop. He could sell what he had left for inventory
on various websites, and that was enough to keep him busy,
enough to pay the bills. Usually, he only went in to the shop at
night. He would package the day's orders, bring them home,
then take them to the post office in the morning. The only
people he spoke to with any regularity now were clerks: at the
post office, the grocery store, the gas station.

The snow that covered the trees and the yard muffled the days
and nights. The days and nights were mostly the same. The man
he paid to plow his driveway came in the mornings after a storm,
and Bryan dutifully mailed him a check each time. The truck
from the heating oil company came to fill his tank each month,
and he hid away from the windows while they were doing it; the
payment automatically got deducted from his bank account, no
need to speak to a person, no need to risk encounter.

If the wind wasn't fierce or the temperature too cold, Bryan
spent time each night outside, looking at the contoured darkness. Julia had been a night-owl, much more than he had ever
been. Whenever he looked up at the stars, he thought of her,
because the sky inspired a poetic sense she never otherwise
showed. "Night is when the universe is biggest," she said. "Go
out some night after midnight, the whole world quiet, and
look up. Even when it's cloudy, you can get an idea of just how
small we all are. On a clear night, that's when everything feels
like what it is — just a moment, a blip."

After he made his trip to the post office each morning,
he spent his days reading history books or mystery novels,
or watching old movies on tv, or searching the internet for
new inventory for the shop, or, most often, taking long walks

through the forest. Now, he could sit alone and rest alone. He could walk alone, unwearied, unwatched.

When he looked out his window each morning and each evening, the forest delighted him. In the summer, he found the trees' shadows comforting, cooling; in the autumn, the blaze of foliage thrilled him, the scent of fallen leaves on damp soil invigorating. If he stood still long enough, birdsongs surrounded him. In solitude, he rarely thought of his face, and he had grown more relaxed and comfortable than perhaps he had ever been since his parents' deaths, but nonetheless, he would have liked to share moments with someone — with Julia, with Cameron. That yearning tinged the days with melancholy. He tried to console himself with philosophizing, reminding himself of beliefs he had long held: all matter is interconnected; all time is an illusion; everyone who ever lived is, in some sense, here with him because they had always been and would always be, the atoms of their breaths still lingering in the air he breathed, the electricity of their thoughts and memories mingling with his own. But he had grown weary of philosophizing. Old thoughts could not console him.

...

When the lease on the shop came up for renewal, Bryan decided not to renew. He could store at his house the few bits of good inventory he still had. The website was working well. There was no need for the shop, and he was tired of thinking about it. He spent the fall cleaning it out. He was surprised at how much he ended up bringing to the dump. In his mind, the shop was full of treasures, but in reality, he had put a lot of items he hadn't wanted to deal with in back corners and on forgotten shelves. A whole bookcase full of cheap toys was covered with at least ten years of dust. He had no memory of putting the toys in the bookcase, no memory of acquiring the toys.

Near the bookcase slumped the brown leather rucksack he had carried through South America, a stout and hardy companion he had nicknamed (for reasons long forgotten) Barney. He had thought Barney got lost years ago. He had moved from one place to another enough when he was younger that losses were common. But Barney had been sitting here, sitting for a long time, waiting to be found or to be remembered.

Bryan picked the rucksack up and slapped it a few times to get the dust and dirt off. There was something inside it, likely some relic or memento he'd long assumed gone. He brought Barney back to the front counter, where the light was better, and pulled a strap to open the central pocket. Inside sat a large, dark yellow envelope, and inside the envelope twenty or thirty pages of graph paper covered with handwriting and another envelope, smaller, but thick with photographs.

The photographs looked faded, but it might have been an effect of sunlight or the camera, a misjudged exposure. He recognized the landscape, recognized people from his grad school days, but he had no memory of the pictures. His face had taught him long ago to turn away from cameras when they were pointed at him, and he was, at best, a haphazard photographer himself. Images seemed to him something to discard, not hold onto. These pictures were pleasant, though, not only because he had been the photographer rather than the subject, but also because they evoked no specific memories, only vague and gentle thoughts of a lost era, a different life.

Until he came upon a picture of Sebastián. Then another and another. Sebastián sitting beside a pool; Sebastián on the edge of a dirt road, pretending to thumb a ride; Sebastián standing outside a taqueria in Cuernavaca.

Bryan had stopped in Cuernavaca on his way home at the end of everything. He had spent a couple weeks there, not doing much of anything, wandering. Sebastián had not been there. They had never been in Mexico together at all. Mexico was later, after Sebastián, after the cave. The pictures must have been taken by somebody else, someone who sent them to him.

Or had Sebastián been the one who told him about Cuernavaca, given Bryan these photographs, and that was why he went there?

He could not remember.

He stuffed the photographs back into their envelope and set it on the counter.

The pages of graph paper were letters. A series of letters in a mix of simple English and complex Spanish. The handwriting made Bryan catch his breath — he knew it immediately, and the signature on the first letter confirmed it: Sebastián. (How had he known Sebastián's handwriting? He did not remember Sebastián ever writing anything. He had thought Sebastián was likely illiterate.)

He threw the pages to the floor. A glance at a few sentences was enough, sentences about San Cristóbal and Oaxaca and Cuernavaca, something about leaving Sebastián at the hotel in Mexico City, a "scene" in the lobby. He knew, without reading more, that the letters pleaded with him to write back, even a simple postcard, anything — some words to explain himself, or merely to signal that he was alive. They had done good work together, the letters said, and they had cared for each other, and maybe Bryan hadn't thought of it as love, but Sebastián had, for a little while at least, and hadn't they been happy together, if never else then during that crazy time when they were crossing between countries, riding overcrowded buses driven by suicidal madmen, when they were making their way through little villages and sleeping at the edge of forests — hadn't they been happy then?

Bryan leaned against the counter to hold himself up. He could not breathe. He coughed, retched, and slid to the floor. This was all wrong. The history was wrong, the time, the pictures, the letters, Sebastián, it was all wrong. He had traveled alone through Mexico, he was sure of it, traveled alone after leaving Sebastián at the cave. And yet if that were true, how could he now remember these letters so vividly, and how could he know that one of the pictures he hadn't looked at was one they had asked a British tourist to take of them together outside the Palacio de Cortes? (Even though they were careful and didn't touch each other in public, didn't give anything away, the tourist said, "You two look like you could be in love.")

He got to his feet and walked slowly out of the shop. He did not bother to lock the door. It didn't matter. He would never come back. Or, he might come back one last time — with a can of gasoline and a match.

...

A storm filled the night with snow.

At dawn, Bryan dashed into the drifts and between the trees, frantic for the morning light and the comfort of the waking forest, hardly noticing that he had neglected to put on a coat or even boots, his feet covered only by the wool socks he had worn to bed.

Bits of breeze caused the trees to shake clumps of snow from their branches, the clumps exploding in air, sugary smoke raining down through sunbeams. The world was silent, cold, and timeless.

Shivering, Bryan stood in a clearing between white pines,

snow up to his waist, snow grasping his outstretched arms, snow sticking to his shoulders, his hair, his face.

He would return to the warmth of his house soon, probably, and when he did, he would pick up the phone and call Cameron and apologize for whatever he needed to apologize for, try to explain, though he wasn't sure what sort of explanation was possible. Instead of explanation — which could be at best a shard, a grain of dust, a mote of light — he would offer Cameron escape. They should skip town together, he would say, get away from memories and obligations, spend some time in a warmer place, somewhere south, Mexico or farther even, where maybe Cameron would allow Bryan to show him around some of his favorite sites, the little churches, the marketplaces, the murals, the monuments to struggle, the quiet ruins, the roads through forests and plains and villages in Guatamala, Honduras, Nicaragua. They could spend a few days on the beach at San Juan del Sur, get a cheap motorcycle in La Cruz and ride around Costa Rica, maybe even keep going farther south, depending on their mood, their whims, desires. Maybe they would go in search of pottery, find some far-off village where for a thousand years people had been burying vessels in fiery ground.

When the time was right, he would return to the house and call Cameron, and they would make plans, he was sure of it. When the time was right.

He took a deep breath. (Life is breath. Keep breathing.) Soon he would have enough breaths to be able to pull himself through the snow, to leave the woods, go back to the house, and he would call Cameron when the time was right.

He closed his eyes. He breathed. He stood still, breathing, his breaths caught by a breeze, indistinguishable from it. The breeze shivered through the woods, it tossed little whirlwinds of snow around Bryan's house, it tapped the branch against the window gently, then fled down the hill and into the town, gaining strength; it dashed through the streets, tossed the ends of the scarf wrapped around the postmaster's neck as she locked up the post office for the night, jostled shopping carts against each other in the parking lot of the grocery store, passed by Bryan's shop without a pause, wending its way out toward Cameron's house and farther, until it slowed and scattered and the night settled still and quiet and dark.

In his studio, Cameron slapped a lump of clay onto the wheel and began to shape it, uncertain exactly what he would make tonight, letting his hands guide the clay toward form, tossing some away as the shape asserted itself and he realized he was making, for the first time in many months, a simple cup — or maybe, if he stuck a handle on it, a mug. Wind rattled the windows of his basement studio and he shivered at a slight draft. He continued working, longer than he had ever worked at a vessel of such simple shape. He continued, unhurried, without any sense of time passing, to seek a form that might hold.

WILD LONGING

Early in my time as a college student in New York City during the final years of the 20th century, I saw Oscar Wilde's play *The Importance of Being Earnest* performed by a small theatre troupe in a loft somewhere in Tribeca. Aspiring to be a playwright, I attended at least a hundred shows during those years, and have forgotten most of them; this particular production remains vivid in my memory now, decades later, because it stripped away my commitment to artifice while also revealing the impossibility of escape. I knew *Earnest* well, having performed the role of Algernon in a high school production, and it was during rehearsals that I first admitted to anyone (tentatively, obliquely) that my own desires were of the Oscar Wilde type. Aside from my high school experience, I had never seen a performance of the play, and so I attended the one in Tribeca enthusiastically, but also with assumptions and expectations not only of what I was about to see, but also what I *should* see. I found the show via a listing in *New York Press*, a free weekly newspaper that in those years had the most comprehensive schedules of far-off-Broadway plays. Until I arrived, I did not know the play was being performed as a showcase production in a loft space (one that hadn't yet found a more permanent resident) rather than as a full production in an actual theatre. For a contemporary play, this would not have bothered me, as I was then a devotee of both Samuel Beckett's sparse stages and Jerzy Grotowski's manifesto of minimalism, *Towards a Poor Theatre*. But Wilde, I firmly believed, ought to be *extravagant*. The sets must be meticulous representations of the late Victorian era, the costumes must take the actors at least half an hour to assemble onto their bodies, and I would not have objected to a theatre space decorated with plentiful and aggressively aromatic flowers. Anything else was certain to be boring and likely to be homophobic.

Sitting down on a folding metal chair among no more than fifty other such chairs and perhaps ten audience members, I stared with unconcealed disdain at the playing area in front of us, a wide, narrow space backed by massive windows, the whole decorated only with large cream-colored curtains and a few painted wooden blocks for furniture. When the actors appeared, I probably gasped. They all wore t-shirts and jeans, with the t-shirts each a different color to help us distinguish between the characters. When they spoke, they spoke simply, they did not declaim, they did not recite, they did not demonstrate extraordinary enunciation, and, worst of all, their accents were American. In the first five minutes, I was overwhelmed by righteous fury and something resembling panic, as if what I was watching was not just bad but harmful. But my curiosity was (only semi-consciously) piqued, and I did not leave, and within fifteen minutes I was entranced, suspecting something that, by the end of the play, proved true: in terms of its effect on me, this was one of the greatest productions of any play I had ever seen or, likely, ever would see.

And I knew Jasper Stevens would have hated it.

Dr. Jasper Stevens had spent most of his career as a professor of music at the college where my mother worked as a secretary when I was growing up, and it was he who first told me to read *The Importance of Being Earnest*. He also loaned me his videotape of the 1952 film of the play with Michael Redgrave as Ernest, Michael Denison as Algernon, and Edith Evans as Lady Bracknell, which led, among other things, to my adolescent tendency to fill silent moments in conversation with a fervent impersonation of Dame Edith warbling out the words, "A *handbag*?!" I was eleven years old when Dr. Stevens (as I always knew him) retired, but his interest in me grew after he no longer had dozens of students to teach each day, and, as he was a bachelor, he often spent time at our house, particularly holidays. He gave my mother piano lessons and wrote some small compositions for her; she had played piano when she was young, but had given it up around the time she married my father. With Dr. Stevens' encouragement, she purchased a small upright piano that lived in our front room, much to my father's annoyance. My father, whose car repair business sat on the other side of the road from our house, was not much interested in music other than Johnny Cash and Waylon Jennings, but Dr. Stevens' hobby was vintage British motorcycles, of which he owned four, and he was thrilled that my father not only was able to provide loving service to them, but also was excited to join in long rides through the hills of Vermont and New Hampshire (sometimes on one of Dr. Stevens' spares, but most often on his own 1975 Harley-Davidson Sportster).

After seeing the workshop production of *Earnest*, I wrote Dr. Stevens a letter describing it and trying to explain why it excited me — the sense of lightness when the play's sets and costumes were stripped of any Victorian accoutrements and distilled to shape and form; also, the rhythmic delight from actors who treated the language not as sacred words but as conversational weaponry, sometimes tossed aside like hand grenades, occasionally spat forth like bayonets, now and then sprayed like machine-gun cover toward every horizon. I did not write to Dr. Stevens about the aspect that had thrilled me the most, the subtext the actors so clearly played, which was that Jack Worthing and Algy Moncrieff were more than just friends. It was not hidden. No line of the script was altered, but the actors liberally bestowed knowing glances and surreptitious touches on each other. Jack and Algy's physical affection included a brazen kiss right at the beginning in a pause between when Algy says, "How are you, my dear Ernest? What brings you up to town?" and Jack replies, "Oh, pleasure, pleasure! What else should bring one anywhere?" As he said "pleasure, pleasure," Jack slipped a hand into Algy's pants. The actors were young, beautiful men (neither of them with the lily-white skin of inbred English aristocracy but rather the mixed hues of American history) and there was enough passion between them that I almost expected, and certainly hoped, that they would strip off their jeans and t-shirts right there for a bit of fun. In their scenes with other characters, they were far less openly lustful, but the lingering effect surprised me, because it inflected the scenes with Gwendolen and Cecily in a way I had never imagined before — despite all of their declarations of love to these women, Algy and Jack showed no physical attraction to or affection for them. This felt wonderfully subversive to me at the time, and perhaps accounts for most of my enthusiasm for the production, but I knew I should not mention it to Dr. Stevens.

I did not receive a reply to my letter. In fact, sometime shortly after I went to college, I never saw or heard from Dr. Stevens again. I thought of him now and then, most often when I encountered something to do with Gilbert & Sullivan (a particular passion of his) or the Renaissance composer Orlando Gibbons (subject of his doctoral dissertation). Our

last encounters had been quietly tense, because in my final
years of high school I had grown more and more liberal in
my political beliefs, while Dr. Stevens was deeply reactionary
in his own. After my parents divorced during my first year of
college, he became distant. My mother moved to Arizona and
I never heard her speak of him again; my father, shortly before
his death during my senior year of college, said he had seen
Dr. Stevens a couple of times when he brought a motorcycle
in for repair, but other than that, not at all, and not recently. I
didn't know his exact age, but I knew he was born in the early
20th century, and as the years went on, I assumed he had died.

In fact, Jasper Stevens outlived both my parents and died
peacefully in his sleep at the age of 103. I learned this when his
lawyer called me at the town library where I work and asked if
I would be interested in helping go through some of the items
of the estate, particularly the books and music (vinyl records,
compact discs, sheet music). Having been executor for both
of my parents' estates, I had great sympathy for the lawyer's
task, and great wariness about getting involved, but I agreed
to serve as a consultant.

I met the lawyer, Donald, at the house, a vaguely Gothic
building of Jasper Stevens' own design, set atop a hill in a
forest, ten miles from any town center, nearly a mile from
any other building. I was surprised that I remembered the
way to the house, but it was a place I had been many times
when young. It was one of the first places I drove to with any
frequency after I got a motorcycle license of my own, since
my father had insisted that I ought to ride with him and his
friends. I did not like my father's friends, all of whom inspired
my most snobbish tendencies as a young man who felt himself trapped in the uncultured wasteland of the rural north,
and so I had resisted the idea, but my father fixed up a cheap

little Honda for my sixteenth birthday, and I soon discovered I actually liked riding — indeed, I reveled in the solitary freedom it provided. Best of all, Dr. Stevens would let me park my Honda at his house and take out one of his spare bikes, usually the 1974 Norton Commando, which fit me well and was a lot more powerful than my Honda, much to my mother's consternation, but she trusted Dr. Stevens more than she trusted my father, and as tensions rose between my parents in the year or two before their divorce, I spent as much spare time as possible riding the Norton.

Entering the house, I flashed back to those days. The front door was the same teal-painted wood, the same brass handle (though more worn than I remembered), and once I stepped through the little entrance room into the main living room, the unique smell overtook me, a smell I had never encountered anywhere else, pungent but not unpleasant, a smell of wood and stone and earth, the amalgamated product of the rich, dark soil outside combining with the granite segments of the house's exterior, the timber beams, the floor-to-ceiling bookshelves spanning the right wall of the living room, and the various antiques that Dr. Stevens had inherited from his family, all from the 19th century and earlier: a massive dining table, numerous cabinets and bureaus, a battalion of chairs. And of course his Bösendorfer grand piano, the piece of furniture the house was designed around (a gift, he once told me, from his grandmother when he earned his PhD). While I don't actually know what created the scent of Dr. Stevens' house — whether furniture or materials or environment or some secret perfume he sprayed every evening — it was so distinctive and so specific to that place that upon encountering it again for the first time in twenty-five years, I had to pause for a moment and gain my bearings as I immediately remembered those wonderful days of escaping my parents, getting the keys to the Norton, riding off into the world; and often, before or after my ride, having Earl Grey tea with Dr. Stevens and listening to one of his LPs of *The Gondoliers* or *Ruddigore* or countless other shows, rarely talking but never feeling (myself, at least) awkward or uncomfortable.

Books, records, and CDs were scattered in piles all over the floor of the main room. Most of the bookshelves had been emptied. "A friend of mine's helping sell things online," Donald said. "He's mostly interested in the books. Nothing much he can do with the records. Apparently classical records aren't really worth anything. Jazz and rock, people collect those, but not classical. Take any you want. Probably just going in the trash otherwise. There's already an offer on the house, so we need to get it emptied quickly."

"Where will the proceeds go?"

"A few charities. There's a third cousin, or fourth or something, in Montana, but he doesn't want anything. I don't think they ever met. So it's all going to some organizations, and a bit to the college music department. Take anything you want. It doesn't really matter."

"Are the motorcycles still here?"

"Motorcycles? No," he said, apparently amazed that someone like Dr. Stevens would have even one motorcycle.

What I most hoped to be able to claim for myself was the early printing of *The Ballad of Reading Gaol*, a mustard-colored hardcover that did not have Wilde's name anywhere on it, but rather listed the author as "C.3.3." — Wilde's number in prison. I remembered Dr. Stevens showing it to me and telling me that though this wasn't one of the extremely rare and valuable first printings, the book had sold so well that all the early printings were within months of the first; it wasn't until the seventh printing that Wilde's name appeared, though of course everybody immediately knew he had written it. I had long loved the poem, especially the wonderfully morbid, romantic, decadent line stating "each man kills the thing he loves."

I found a pile of other Wilde items, but not *Reading Gaol*, the only one of real interest to me. The others were mostly books I already owned or was familiar with, and none were more recent than Richard Ellman's 1987 biography, a popular and well-written tome filled with errors, including (notoriously) a photograph supposedly of Wilde in drag that was, in truth, a photograph of a Hungarian woman. The Wilde of Dr. Stevens' collection was one whose life and work were predominantly analyzed by straight people who saw it as a life of tragedy — a life of a cultivated and talented man undone by his desires. Another Wilde was possible, visible in what were lesser-known works when Dr. Stevens seems to have been most actively interested, then in any number of books, both academic and popular, from the 1990s forward.

Nearby, in another pile, I found books that surprised me far more — two Signet paperbacks, both from 1952: *The Promising Young Men* by George Sklar and *Finistère* by Fritz Peters. It was the cover of *Finistère* that caught my eye: a picture of a young man in the foreground looking thoughtful as he stares off a balcony, behind him a man on a couch with a woman in his lap, the man's eyes, though, clearly on the younger man. The top of the cover said, "A Powerful Novel of a Tragic Love." The first page inside offered quotes from reviews, including one from Gore Vidal: "At this moment in our social history it is difficult for most American authors to write a novel about a homosexual affair without making a tract or an apologia. Mr. Peters has done neither … A fine and passionate novel." *The Promising Young Men* was less openly gay, with a cover picture of a blond man in a leather jacket talking to a redheaded woman in the driver's seat of a convertible, but in the background two men seemed to me suggestive in the way things had to be suggestive in 1952: to most people, they would look like a man leaning against a wall while another man (apparently wearing the same clothes) walks by, but to me it screamed of cruising. The plot description on the back of the book spoke of "a young man on the make" who gets involved with three women. "And there were men too, who were attracted by his youth and vigor."

If Dr. Stevens had bought these books when they were new, which was likely, then he had kept them for over fifty years. Though collectors' items now, they had been nothing more than cheap paperbacks for most of that time, disreputable ephemera, not the sort of thing one keeps for decades unless they have meaning for you. I tossed them both into a box I had begun to fill with books about Gilbert & Sullivan that I was myself interested in and also thought would be good additions to the library.

Soon I saw (scattered occasionally among the thousands of middlebrow novels, biographies of composers and musicians, and a surprising number of military histories) a few other books that helped make sense of the paperbacks: *Homosexuality: Its Causes and Cure*, *Homosexuality: Disease or Way of Life*, *Sexual Inversion*, *The Problem of Homosexuality in Modern Society*. There weren't many (six or seven out of a few thousand books) but there were more than any straight person would likely have kept over the years, especially at the time these books were published — all before Stonewall, before Gay Liberation, before AIDS, before *Ellen*, before marriage. I began to search more carefully, thinking perhaps I might find a stray

Edmund White book or maybe *Angels in America* or, most likely, the script of *Gross Indecency*, the well-known play about the trials of Oscar Wilde that I saw when I was in college, and which I had thought about writing to Dr. Stevens about, though at that point I knew it would be futile, so I didn't bother. But the only openly gay material I discovered in the house was all at least a decade older than me. And it wasn't like Dr. Stevens had stopped buying books. There were plenty of more recent books of history, collections of essays, biographies of musicians and writers and military leaders, and quite a few books by people like Pat Buchanan and Rush Limbaugh.

"Find anything good?" Donald asked me.

"A couple things," I said. "Sentimental mostly, though some books I think our library patrons will appreciate. Don't have much use for the vinyl, I'm afraid. I don't even own a record player."

"You could have his. It's nothing special, but I expect it still works."

"No thanks," I said. "I appreciate it. But my house isn't very big, and I barely have room for the books and CDs I've got already."

"Too bad. I think he expected you would want a lot of it."

"Oh? We really hardly knew each other."

"He talked about you. He said you used to listen to records together, and that you have excellent taste in books. He made sure I sought you out."

"I thought it was just coincidence. I didn't realize you knew I knew him."

"Oh yes. I should have said. He left instructions that you could have whatever you wanted."

I continued looking for *The Ballad of Reading Gaol*, but it was nowhere to be found. Perhaps he had given it away himself before he died. (Or, most likely, Donald's friend already got it and sold it on eBay.) I thought about grabbing one or two of the Gilbert and Sullivan records as mementos, but decided against it. They would just gather dust. The two old paperback novels would be enough for me, and the library would benefit from a couple dozen other books, as histories and biographies tend to be popular with our patrons. Empty cardboard boxes had been heaped in piles in the kitchen, and I soon began filling boxes for myself with any books that seemed of value, because I could guess what sorts of organizations the estate's money would go to and I felt obliged to do my part to keep at least some of it from them.

After I loaded the boxes of books into the trunk of my car, I asked Donald what Dr. Stevens' later years had been like.

"He was in good health even up to the end, and he always seemed to have a good mind. A nurse came in every day, but he was pretty mobile and quite self-sufficient. I don't really know what he did with his time. After the trial, I don't think he had many friends around here, if any at all."

"Trial? What trial?"

"His trial."

"I don't know anything about a trial."

"Oh," he said. "Well. That's a surprise. But I suppose it wasn't big news. Or, rather, it *was*, at least around here, but only briefly. He nearly went to prison. It took everything we could do to avoid that, and it was mostly only because of his age. Judge and jury took some pity."

"Trial for what, though?"

"Forgery. Mail fraud, really, that was the serious charge. He forged some letters supposedly by Oscar Wilde and sold them to collectors. Salacious stuff, quite dirty, all about sex with men. The quality of the forgeries was impressive, and I think ultimately he was caught mostly because some of the content just went too far and ended up being unbelievable. But I don't know. I was just starting out in the office then, and my predecessor was his primary lawyer."

"When was this?"

"He did the forgeries in the late 1980s, a few more in the mid-'90s, and then he was arrested in 1997."

"I was in college in New York."

"There were a couple articles about it once in the *Boston Globe*, but not much more than that. Collectors weren't all that excited to have the word get out, so I don't think anybody worked hard to publicize it."

"I can't believe my parents never told me. Maybe my mother didn't know. Probably. She was in Arizona by then. And my father died that year."

"It was a long time ago now," Donald said.

I closed the trunk of my car and drove away from Dr. Stevens' house for the last time.

...

Once a week or so, I would have dinner with the Assistant Director of the library, Rebekah, and her husband, Tom. Rebekah had worked at the library at least a decade longer than I had, and I expect she would have been happy to have my job if it had been offered to her, but she did not have a degree in Library Science, so the Board of Trustees would not consider her application. When I began, she was wary of me, but I did my best to make it clear that I respected her and thought the Board was quite wrong in valuing a credential over experience. Soon, her wariness eased into collegiality, collegiality into friendship and, occasionally, a certain motherly concern. Her son had just gone off to college in Minnesota when we first met, and some of the attention she had bestowed on him now transferred to me, as she worried that I did not eat well or exercise enough or develop a satisfactory social life. I told her it was hard to have a satisfactory social life as a gay man in this rural town, and she said that someone with an advanced degree in Library Science ought to be able to research how to get a boyfriend, or at least a nice guy to spend a night with occasionally.

Tom was a carpenter, and had built their house himself thirty years ago, soon after they got married. He had never lived in another town in his life, nor had he traveled much, which Rebekah often complained about, because even though she had occasionally been able to go on trips with friends, she would have liked to have seen more of the world. Tom was an enthusiastic reader, despite never graduating high school, and it seemed to me that he and Rebekah traveled the world together through the books they shared. They rarely read about rural America, instead preferring books about cities and about any country other than ours. Hearing of their latest literary discoveries was one of the joys of our dinners together, a true education — when Kazuo Ishiguro won the Nobel Prize for Literature, for instance, Rebekah thought it was a good choice and Tom argued quite passionately that while he liked some of Ishiguro's novels, Ngugi wa Thiong'o was obviously the most deserving writer, a man who had influenced the world and literature to a greater extent than Ishiguro or pretty much anybody else, and the Swedes' continued snubbing of him proved without a doubt that they were fundamentally biased against black African writers.

At the first dinner after I brought Dr. Stevens' books to the library, Rebekah mentioned the books to Tom, since he hated Gilbert & Sullivan and she enjoyed teasing him. "I bet they sit on the shelves," Tom said, "and nobody ever takes them out and eventually you sell them for a dollar at the library sale."

"I'm going to create a display of them," Rebekah said.

"Call it 'Books About Shallow Cleverness and Music That All Sounds Alike.'"

"I'm going to call it, 'Tom Heylind Recommends.'"

"That would be grounds for divorce."

Without thinking about it, I said, "He almost went to prison."

"Which one?" Tom said. "Gilbert or Sullivan?"

"Jasper Stevens."

"For what?" Rebekah asked.

I told them what little I knew. I hoped Rebekah might have remembered reading about it, but she did not.

"Oscar Wilde and Gilbert & Sullivan," Tom said. "And a bachelor. It must have been a lonely life. Hard enough to be gay up here these days. Can't imagine what it must've been like for him all those years ago."

"I don't know for sure that he was gay."

Tom raised an eyebrow.

"I never even considered it," I said, "until the other day when I was going through his books."

"Porn?"

"No. Things from the '50s and '60s that suggest he at least was interested in reading about homosexuality. Old stuff, though, nothing from the last forty, fifty years." I told them about the books I had found, as well as the books by Pat Buchanan and Rush Limbaugh, the things published by the John Birch Society, the books about military uniforms.

"Bizarre," Tom said.

"There's always been a certain type of gay man attracted to fascism," I said. "The hypermasculinity. The desire for power when the world has disempowered you. That sort of thing."

"I can understand conservatism," Tom said. "That's common. Misguided, but normal. Even fascism. But the *John Birch Society*? The fluoride-in-the-water-is-a-Communist-plot people? Didn't they fade away in the '60s?"

"Some of the pamphlets and newsletters he had were pretty recent."

"Loneliness," Rebekah said, "makes people fall into themselves. They lose sense of the world."

I sat back in my chair and stared out a window at the meadow behind the house, the town a dim sprinkle of light beyond it. "I don't know that he was lonely," I said. "Alone, yes, for a long time. But I'm not sure that means lonely."

"Did he have pets or anything?" Tom asked.

"Four motorcycles."

"You can't love a motorcycle," Rebekah said. "He should have at least had a cat."

Tom said, "Plenty of men love their motorcycles."

"It isn't real love," Rebekah said.

"Don't be a bigot," Tom said. "Love is love is love."

I helped them clean up the dishes and then we sat and drank a bit of port together, something that had become a ritual, though the first time I was at their house for dinner and they suggested a nip of port afterward, I thought they meant it ironically, as I had never before heard of anyone who drank port except old women in British movies. But no, there was no irony, no parody, no deeper meaning. They just liked port; soon, I did too.

"The forgeries, they're what I still don't understand," I said. "All the time he was teaching me about Wilde, he was creating fake letters by Wilde. I don't know what to do with that. I can't wrap my brain around it."

"What's there to wrap your brain around?" Tom said. "He

forged letters, sold them or tried to sell them, got caught."

Rebekah said, "But *why* did he do it? It sounds like he was trying to give Wilde a more public sex life."

"I thought that, too," I said, "but it doesn't really make any sense. Because of Lord Alfred Douglas's father and the trial and all the publicity it got, Wilde had one of the most public sex lives of the whole 19th century."

"Maybe," Rebekah said, "it wasn't so much about Wilde as about himself. Maybe it was like writing imaginary love letters of his own."

"Would you then go and sell your imaginary love letters? He didn't need the money. He could have written all the fake letters he wanted and never showed them to anybody. But he sold them."

"That makes them real," Tom said. He finished his port and set the glass down on the table next to his chair a little harder than he probably intended. The sound made me think of a judge's gavel. I finished my glass, too, and soon got up to leave. Driving home, I couldn't help but wonder what sorts of imaginary letters I might write.

...

The library has a book club, where patrons sign up each month to read a book and then discuss it together. It began after we renovated the library and built a meeting room in the base-ment. Some of our part-time staff members choose the books and lead these discussions, though now and then we bring in a professor from the local college if the month's book is on a topic for which there is a specialist. Rebekah bakes cook-ies for each meeting, and always leads the December reading of a Dickens novel. For a few years now, every June, I have led an extra discussion of a book for Pride month. (It's extra so that the regular members don't feel obligated to embrace perversity.) I resisted the idea of a Pride reading for a while, assuming nobody would come, but Rebekah pushed for it, and I gave in. Though the first year wasn't popular (*Giovanni's Room*; seven people signed up, five attended the discussion), I got better at promoting it later, and better at choosing books more people in the area would like to read. This year's choice, for instance, was *The Talented Mr. Ripley*, and that discussion was better attended than the regular book club that month (*The Wright Brothers* by David McCullough).

We were cataloguing Dr. Stevens' items when it was time to choose that year's Pride book, and I declared, without consulting anyone, that it would be our first paired reading: *The Picture of Dorian Gray* alongside *The Importance of Being Earnest*. Rebekah scowled and said she had read *Dorian Gray* in college and had thought it was outdated and boring. I said I hoped to show her that it might be otherwise, though I didn't, at the time, have any idea how, because in truth my own memory of it was of a book rather fussy and dull. Still, how could it not be fun, especially alongside *Earnest*? But it wasn't just about me, the books, or the library. I was excited at the idea of exploring *Dorian Gray* because it would give me an excuse to study Wilde, something I had not done for many years.

Unfortunately, as much as I looked forward to burying myself in Wilde before the book club meeting, I nonetheless dithered with work, watched too much tv, aimlessly wandered the internet, and generally procrastinated. Such is my behavior with any obligation, even when I am excited about it. The evening of the discussion getting close, I rushed to read the play, dragged myself through the novel (which was, indeed, a bore), and found the most pleasure in watching the 1945 film

of *The Picture of Dorian Gray*, where George Sanders was perfectly cast as Lord Henry, Hurd Hatfield sublime as Dorian
Gray, and a very young Angela Lansberry marvelous as Sibyl
Vane — all making up for the occasional liberties the film
took with the text, most of which sought to add a veneer of
(inevitably unconvincing) heterosexuality.

Attendance at the book discussion was the worst we ever
had, then or now. There was me, plus Rebekah, and one other
person: a young man who had also come the year before.
Though I did not remember seeing him around the library
otherwise, I remembered him, because he was serious about
the reading, utterly beautiful, and Hispanic, three qualities
rare in this town, where seriousness is reserved for discussions
of how to lower taxes and most of us are physically unremark-
able people who probably share a Scottish ancestor from the
thirteenth century. He said his name was Pedro, which surprised me, because I thought I remembered a different name
from the year before, and I began to wonder if I was conflat-
ing him with someone else, though it seemed unlikely. How
many well-muscled Hispanic men with fierce cheekbones and
haunted eyes could possibly find their way to our little library?

Though I wanted to discuss *Earnest* far more than *Dorian
Gray*, Rebekah and Pedro felt differently. *Earnest*, Rebekah
said, was fun and of course a perfect comedic machine, but
it's all surface, no depth, whereas *Dorian Gray* allows both,
which is what she didn't recognize when she was younger and
unable to appreciate all it had to offer. Pedro nodded. "Out
of the unreal shadows of the night," he said, "comes back
the real life that we had known." My face must have radiated perplexity, because he held his book out to me to show
me the page the sentence appeared on. "That sentence is so
beautiful," he said, "that I had to stop reading when I first

saw it. I kept reading it again and again. And then the rest of the paragraph, I savored it — 'a wild longing, it may be, that our eyelids might open some morning upon a world that had been refashioned anew in the darkness for our pleasure, a world in which things would have fresh shapes and colours, and be changed, or have other secrets, a world in which the past would have little or no place, or survive, at any rate, in no conscious form of obligation or regret, the remembrance even of joy having its bitterness, and the memories of plea-sure their pain.'"

He paused and looked directly at me. "Does that not move you?"

"Yes," I said, struggling for breath. "When *you* read it."

I chuckled nervously, ridiculously.

We continued talking for a few minutes, then Rebekah made some excuse that she had to run home to Tom.

We were alone, Pedro and I.

We smiled at each other, him beautifully, me awkwardly.

"Last year," I said, "you came to the book club discussion then, didn't you? For *Oranges Are Not the Only Fruit*?"

"Yes," he said.

"But you gave a different name. Not Pedro."

"You have a good memory."

"You made an impression." He cocked his head slightly. "You're very insightful," I said, "about the reading."

"Thank you."

"Is Pedro your name? Actually?"

"It's the name I use now. Before recently, I was Michael, sometimes Miguel. That is my parents' name for me, the name I had when I was in school, but I have stopped school now, I did not have the patience for it. I like the name Pedro. There's something simple about it. Do you know the Chilean writer

Pedro Lemebel? His novel *My Tender Matador* would be a good book club book."

"I haven't heard of it. I'll look for it."

"It was an enjoyable discussion tonight."

"Thank you."

"I am glad it was just us."

"Me, too."

He stood up. He looked around the room absent-mindedly.

He smiled and then walked toward the stairs leading out of the basement.

"Goodnight," he said. He walked up the stairs.

I wanted to stop him, wanted to ask him if he would like to go to dinner at the restaurant just down the street, or if not that, if he might come to the next book club meeting, even if it wasn't about books like Wilde's books, or if he might just stop by the library sometime, if we might talk some more, perhaps get to know each other, because it would be nice to have someone here who understood that side of things, a man who read Wilde, because I didn't have anyone like that at all, and I suspected he might not either, and perhaps we might be that for each other.

I heard the front door of the library close and suddenly I was filled with nausea at myself, not for failing to talk to Pedro more, but for entertaining the idea for even a moment that there could be anything between us, anything at all that he could see in me, a paunchy, balding white guy who must be at least twenty years his senior. I nearly ran to the bathroom to vomit, but the nausea passed, and soon enough I walked out into the familiar, empty night.

...

I avoided Rebekah as best I could the next morning, but soon enough she cornered me at the circulation desk.

"Well?" she said.

I pretended confusion.

"Pedro," she said. "Did you and he have a good talk? How did the rest of the evening go?"

"It was fine. He left soon after you did."

She sighed. "I really thought there was a spark between you two."

"I could be his father," I said.

"All the more fun."

"*No*," I said, my tone more forceful than I had intended, but it made it clear I did not want to continue the conversation.

That afternoon, Rebekah told me she had been reminded by our book club discussion of Wilde that Dr. Stevens had nearly gone to jail for forgery, and since it had been a quiet morning, she had begun to search the *Union Leader* and the *Boston Globe* for any record of his arrest or trial. "There wasn't much," she said, "but I did find some brief mentions." She handed me articles she had printed out. "They really only prosecuted him for one sale of a couple of letters. But he admitted to a few more, and they seemed to suspect quite a bit more, but it doesn't sound like they really had much evidence."

I had seen the articles before, found them myself in the days after I first learned of the trial, but I did not mention this to Rebekah. The articles said little about the content of the forgeries, just that they were supposedly letters by Oscar Wilde and contained evidence of homosexuality. An article in the *Globe* reported that the letters would be destroyed after the trial to prevent them ever returning to the market. Inspired by Rebekah's interest, hungry to know if even just the text of one of the forgeries has been recorded, together we searched for more information. Rebekah convinced Tom to call around to police stations to see if anybody knew anything, something I was far too cowardly to do. They told Tom to contact the courts, which Rebekah did. I visited an elderly librarian at the college, an old friend of my mother, and she remembered Dr. Stevens, but though she vaguely recalled hearing something about him and forgery, her sharpest memory was of a prickly man, distant, demanding. Not someone she had ever spent any time thinking about after his retirement. "To be honest," she said, "I thought he was dead long ago."

Though Rebekah and I contacted rare book dealers, and I continue even now occasionally to glance through catalogues of auctions if there happen to be Wilde items, we have not yet found any evidence of one of Dr. Stevens' letters surviving.

...

Pedro has never returned to the library, at least not as far as I know. I sought out Lemebel's *My Tender Matador* soon after he mentioned it. It is, indeed, a beautiful novel, and that summer I overruled the part-time staff and instituted it as the September book club pick, which caused much controversy, not so much for the content of the novel as for my imperiousness. I talked the book up a lot, and was thorough with publicity, so we ended up with a larger discussion group than we had had all year — twenty-three people. Even Tom, who derided all previous book club discussions as vapid, came to this one, and Rebekah tried hard, and mostly succeeded, at keeping him from usurping the whole conversation with a lecture on Salvadore Allende, Augusto Pinochet, and the CIA. I was grateful for Tom's tendency to dominate the conversation, though, because I continually distracted myself by looking toward the door, hoping Pedro might walk down the stairs.

"I'm sorry," Rebekah said to me as we were closing up. "I know you wanted to see Pedro."

"Lemebel?" Tom asked. "Isn't he dead?"

"Another Pedro," Rebekah said.

"Oh? Which?"

"Nobody," I said.

Rebekah said, "We're going for dinner at the Common Man. Want to join us?"

"No," I said. "I'm tired. Long day. Thank you, though."

She took my hand. "Are you all right?" she said quietly.

"Totally fine."

...

That night, for the first time in many years, I cried myself to sleep.

I got home, poured a healthy glass of 15-year-old Glenlivet, put my DVD of the 1945 *Picture of Dorian Gray* into the player, and sat down for some evening's entertainment. I could hardly pay attention to it, though, and soon enough I really was tired, so I turned the movie off and went to bed. Lying in bed, I began to think about Pedro, of course, and then about Dr. Stevens, and I imagined them both together in the library's basement meeting room with me, talking about Wilde. I imagined that Dr. Stevens could find exactly the right way to explain to Pedro that *The Importance of Being Earnest* is more than its surface, and I imagined that Pedro would impress Dr. Stevens with his passion for *Dorian Gray*, and perhaps also his passion for Pedro Lemebel, and then we might listen to a recording of Orlando Gibbons' "This Is the Record of John" together — or, even better, "If You're Anxious for to

Shine" from Gilbert & Sullivan's *Patience*, with its parody of
Wilde — and after Pedro had been entranced and charmed by
the music, Dr. Stevens would say how grateful he was to read
someone like Lemebel, because *My Tender Matador* is such a
different book from, say, *The Promising Young Men* or *Finistère*.
We could talk about what it was like for Dr. Stevens to live in
those years so long ago now, and why he made the choices he
made, and Pedro could tell us about his own life, about choosing a name that was not given to him by his parents, about
leaving school. I was sure that between us, Dr. Stevens and I
could have convinced him to return and finish his degree, and
I would have been there to help him, to support him.

And then I remembered Dr. Stevens saying that English
ought to be the official language of the United States. I was
maybe twelve or thirteen years old and didn't think anything
about it then. And I remembered him saying something about
a family of "pickininies" down the street. At the time, I didn't
know what the word meant and thought it sounded funny,
some silly old slang. I remembered when I was in my last years
of high school and, having discovered *The Nation* magazine and
A People's History of the United States, how horrified I was at
Thanksgiving when Dr. Stevens was praising, for reasons I no
longer remember, Henry Kissinger. I remembered saying that
Kissinger was a war criminal who ought to be in prison, and Dr.
Stevens hissed that I didn't know the first thing about Kissinger.

I remembered waking up one morning in Brooklyn with
Samir and running my finger gently along his chest, thinking
how horrified Dr. Stevens would be at such a scene, at this
skin my fingers touched. (Samir remains the longest relationship of my life: a month and a half or so. I ruined our happiness because I was afraid I was in love with him, and I knew
he was falling in love with me. I told him I didn't think I could

ever love someone like him, by which I meant someone who loved me, though I failed to explain myself, and in any case it was a lie, one for which I continue to feel shame. His lower lip trembled and I knew he was fighting back tears. He turned away from me. "I only liked you because my father would hate you," he said, and though I am sure he was right about his father, the rest I expect was, like my words, a lie. One I chose to believe for a long time.) I had encounters with other men later — sexual encounters — but mostly just a night here, a night there, nothing lasting, nothing satisfying, because I found it impossible to overcome some inchoate shame that made me fall passive in all these experiences, a body to be used but impossible to pleasure. After leaving New York, I got crushes on straight men and sometimes on women, and even tried to have a relationship with one of the women, Connie, who was adventurous and open-minded and rather curious to see if she could mend my gay old ways. We had fun for a little while, but soon an atavistic misogyny consumed me, and I terrified myself and, one awful midnight, her.

I have slept alone ever since.

As I lay in my bed that June night after the discussion of *My Tender Matador*, after watching *The Picture of Dorian Gray* and then letting myself imagine a beautiful scene with Dr. Stevens and Pedro, I couldn't help but then think about Samir, about Connie, about the men whose names I quickly forgot or never knew, about how far I was from New York, how old I had gotten, how forgettable and forgotten. Quiet tears soon gave way to anguished screams, which made me feel ridiculous and melodramatic, and eventually I rolled over and let what tears were left soak into my pillow.

In the morning, I called Rebekah and told her I seemed to have the flu, so wouldn't be in for a few days. She offered to bring over chicken soup, but I said I had plenty of food, and she told me to be sure to hydrate and to take pain relievers and to get lots of sleep, and I said I would.

I drove to Concord and took a bus to Boston, where I found a hotel room in Back Bay and emailed a man who had worked briefly at the library when he was a college student. He had spent the night at my house once, and we got drunk and had sex, and though I was too self-conscious about his age and the fact that I was his boss to be able to perform very well, we chalked it all up to inebriation and somehow managed to stay friends. After he got a job in marketing for a tech company and moved to Boston, we weren't good about keeping in touch, though I knew he'd had a steady boyfriend and they had recently been married, because he sent me an invitation to their wedding. (I did not go. I doubt he expected I would, but he knew I would appreciate being invited.) I wasn't sure the email address I had for him was still active, but he got back to me half an hour later, and we spent a nice afternoon together, then he and his husband and I had dinner at an expensive restaurant, then drinks at a gay bar, one of the few left in the city. "A survivor of the old world," I said, and we toasted it, us, surviving.

The next day, I roamed around the city, and in the evening returned to the bar by myself.

I had ignored numerous calls and messages from Rebekah to my cell phone, but I called her when I got home and assured her I was fine. She said she had almost called the police, but had gone to my house to check on me first, and when she saw the car was gone, she assumed I had either taken myself to the hospital or else was off on a secret mission.

"Yes," I said. "A secret mission."

"I look forward to hearing all the details," she said.

I said nothing. I knew she would ask questions, knew she would invite me to dinner soon so Tom could also ask me what had happened, where I had been, how I was doing, and I knew I would not tell them anything, and I have not.

A SUICIDE GUN

1.

Celeste couldn't understand why Malcolm had to go to Arizona to see Billy, a childhood friend he barely knew anymore, and Malcolm couldn't explain it to her, because he wasn't entirely sure himself. "He is in distress," Malcolm said. Celeste stared at him and he knew she wanted to say something like, "Lots of people are in distress. Why him?" but she said nothing and stood silent, watching while Malcolm packed a suitcase. She gave him a hug and a quick kiss before he got in the taxi to the airport.

Billy's father's house was a small adobe, one storey, with similar houses nearby and a square of something that might once have been a lawn in front of it. As Malcolm pulled into the driveway in the grey Mercedes he had rented, he saw Billy standing in front of the door, smoking a cigarette and drinking a can of cheap beer. Billy looked more emaciated than he did at their high school reunion two years ago. His eyes seemed to be sinking into his skull.

"Nice ride!" Billy said. "Didn't know they paid professors so well!"

"Celeste has a discount through work."

Billy hugged him, covering him with the stench of tobacco, alcohol, and something else, something briny, perhaps urine.

"So," Malcolm said, "you really are giving up on recovery."

"I'm so so so *so* sorry about last night. I honestly, scout's honor, haven't been that shitfaced in years. *Years.*"

Malcolm nodded at the beer can in Billy's hand. "What's this then?"

"Maintenance. I could barely move when I woke up. Didn't want to be a complete zombie when you got here."

"Okay. Well. I'm here."

...

The stench in the house nauseated Malcolm: urine, vomit, alcohol, stale air, old man, sickness, sadness, death.

"When was the last time you opened a window, Billy? Last century?"

Billy chuckled, then pushed a window open, let in a bit of light, a bit of air.

"Got any plans?" Malcolm said. "You going to sell the house?"

"Definitely. I'd like to burn it to the ground, but it's actually worth something, so I'll sell it."

"And then?"

"Dunno. Trip off to the light fantastic."

"You like Arizona?"

"Hell no. Hot as shit. I'm still a New England boy at heart. Not made for this weather."

"Why'd you come down here, then?"

"I was broke and Dad seemed like he could use some help. He offered, actually. Said it would be good to have me around."

"Was it?"

"Sure. Sometimes."

In the little living room, a pile of guns, thirty or forty of them, pistols and rifles both, sat in front of an orange couch. On the phone, Billy had said something about pissing on his father's guns. It seemed he had.

"What's up with the guns?"

"As I said. I was shitfaced."

"Why?"

"Seemed like a good idea at the time."

"Really?"

"I found a bottle of Cuervo and a bottle of some cheap-ass vodka. They were in a cabinet under the sink. Literally had dust on them. They were nasty, but I was bored. Lonely. Low. I dunno. Fuck it. Whatever. I hadn't had the real stuff for a long time, just been drinking beer these days, whatever watery shit I can find, trying to get off it all, you know. *Wean*. Did it before. I was sober for three years. Three years! I'll get back to it. This is my chance, right? A new life, starting over."

"Sure."

"Did it before, I can do it again."

"Okay." Malcolm wanted to say something more, but he didn't know what. He put his hands in his pockets, then took them out again and held them at his side.

Billy said, "Why'd you come out here, Mal?"

"You seemed distressed."

"I've been distressed for twenty years."

"You called me in the middle of the night."

"Yeah. Sorry. I'm pretty damn used to being ashamed of shit, but I really am truly and honestly ashamed, I mean, you came all the way out here, it's kind of nuts."

Malcolm opened a window at the back of the house. The window looked out on flat, brown land.

"I want," Malcolm said, "to see the guns."

"Well, there they are."

"Not the ones you pissed on. The suicide guns."

Billy scowled and looked away.

Malcolm said, "He would never show us. When we were kids. You told me about them and I wanted to see them but we never could."

"It's sick, Mal. *He* was sick. It was some compulsion, some, I dunno, *thing*."

"But it's real? The collection?"

Billy sighed. He sat down on the orange couch. "He kept the trunk in his bedroom."

"Have you opened it?"

"You came out here for that? The suicide guns?"

"I want to see them."

"Why?"

"I don't know."

"Jesus. Fuck. Can we just — here, let me take you out to brunch, there's this good place just a couple miles away, we can go, we can catch up, then maybe you can go do, I dunno, some tourist thing and I'll clean up here and then maybe…"

"I don't mean to be pushy. I just have always wanted to see the collection."

"Yeah, well."

Billy lit a cigarette.

...

It made sense that Billy liked the diner he took Malcolm to: they served scrambled eggs in a big bowl, and clearly understood that a side-order of bacon ought to be as greasy as possible. Malcolm ordered a breakfast burrito.

"Do you remember," Billy said, "how when we were kids everybody always wanted to come over and play at my house because they wanted to go down the road to the shop and see the guns? At first, I didn't know what was going on, but once I stopped taking people down to the shop, that's when nobody wanted to hang out with me anymore. Like, to everybody else, even kids whose parents had plenty of guns, to everybody, seeing the shop was something special, exotic. But to me it never was. To me it was just where my father spent most of his time. I never liked the smell of the gun oil that filled the place, I never liked how cramped it was, I tried to never pay attention to any of it. The guns were just objects that were around and in the way, they were these things my father loved. Sometimes I thought they were the only things he loved, the only things anybody loved. So I was just the weird kid from the gun shop. That's all."

"I don't think that's true," Malcolm said.

"You didn't live through it day after day after day."

"You think you didn't have any real friends when we were kids?"

"I didn't say that."

A waitress refilled Billy's cup of coffee for the third time. Malcolm's remained full.

Billy said, "We would get off the schoolbus, we'd go to my house, and whoever it was, they always asked: *Can we go to the shop?*"

"That seems natural."

"I know, I understand, they were kids and it was fun and exotic and what kids, what *boys,* don't like guns. But it's fucking shitty when you're a kid and everybody's more interested in the stuff your father sells and spends all his time with than they are interested in you."

"I get that. It's self-pitying, but I get it."

"Sure you don't want some bacon?" Billy asked.

"All yours. What you're saying is that my interest in the

collection is a repetition of what you experienced as a kid."

"I'm not saying that. Not at all. It's just, suddenly I remembered all those days in childhood when it felt like nobody on the fucking planet was interested in me as much as they were interested in the guns."

"Okay. I'm sorry. I do care about you. I wouldn't have come all this way if I didn't care about you."

"I know."

"I'm here for you."

"Right. But you still want to see the guns."

"Yes."

...

Billy said he would show Malcolm the collection, he would, he just needed a bit of time, needed to clean up the house, get some things in order, because in a few days somebody from a local gun shop was going to come by and take all of the guns away on consignment, and he didn't want the house to be quite so much of a shithole when they arrived.

Billy cleaned the kitchen while Malcolm did what he could to straighten up and air out the living room. He didn't touch the guns piled on the floor, though he caught himself glancing at them again and again. He imagined holding one, a pistol, imagined standing in the entryway of his townhouse, Celeste upstairs screaming, a man pushing his way through the door, and then the gun fires and the man falls to the floor and Celeste comes running down the stairs to embrace Malcolm, her husband, the man who kept her protected, safe. He told himself it was a ridiculous vision, melodramatic. His hands quivered. He turned away from the guns. Finally, he went to the kitchen to help Billy, who washed dishes in the sink while Malcolm used a bristled sponge to scrub down counters encased in grime.

"How's your wife?" Billy asked.

"She's doing well."

"Corporate lawyer, right?"

"Yes. Celeste."

"*Celeste*, right. And you the professor of music."

"Music theory. I'm less a musician than a theorist."

"*Theorist*," he said, as if trying the word out to see how it worked. "Music theory." He set plates into the rack beside the sink. "You having kids anytime soon?"

"Everybody asks that," Malcolm said.

"Don't you want to do your duty and procreate the species?"

"Not especially," Malcolm said. "And Celeste says she has no mothering instinct. What about you?"

"No, I don't have a mothering instinct either."

"I meant your life. Your love life. Anybody?"

"Random guys from the internet now and then. I don't seem to be any good at longevity. Men, jobs, everything."

"What's the longest relationship you've had?'

"Four months," Billy said.

"Okay. You aren't any good at longevity."

"My problem is I'm a romantic. Nobody ever lives up to the beautiful boy I fell in love with when I was twenty."

"Oh? I've forgotten. Did I know him?"

"You were in college," Billy said, scrubbing an iron skillet. "I was working for Alex Michaud painting houses. It was spring break for you and you came home for some reason rather than go to Florida or wherever college boys go, and we hung out, reminisced about the good old days of high school, and there was a night after we went to a movie — a Jim Carrey movie, I think *Liar Liar* — after the movie we went back to your parents' house on the lake and we shared a bottle of vodka and listened to Nirvana and then Patti Smith and then, once we were really wasted, ABBA. And then while 'Fernando' was playing you let me unbutton your jeans ... unzip your fly..."

Malcolm squirted a spray-bottle of bleach at the counter. "That was a long time ago," he said.

"Yes," Billy said. "When I saw you at reunion, I asked you if you remembered that night, one of the last times we'd been together, and you said no, you just remembered we were really drunk, and you didn't remember anything else. That's what you said. And I saw in your eyes this terrible, what — fear, horror, maybe revulsion, but mostly fear, a fear that I would say something, or do something, touch you too fondly. Kiss you. I saw you were terrified of that, terrified of *me*, because of course despite what you said, I knew you remembered, and you were scared of what I might do, what I might say, because somehow you were ashamed of your feelings, ashamed of me and the memory, *our* memory. I still think how beautiful it is that of all the people in the world, we, us, together, alone share that memory. That was our night. And yet I saw in that moment that for years and years you carried shame and fear with you, while for me our memory was completely different. It was the memory that kept me alive even when everything was awful. So when I heard you were going to be at our reunion, I was so excited, because I was sure you couldn't forget, and I was sure you would remember that night as I did, with tenderness, fondness, regardless of whatever feelings you may have now, regardless of your wife and your commitment to dull straight sex, regardless, I thought: He will remember how tender we were to each other, how special we were together, how perfectly we fit into each other's arms. But no."

Malcolm continued to scrub the counter even though it

was clean. "I wasn't ashamed," he said quietly. Bleach fumes scorched his nostrils.

Billy dried the last of the dishes with a washcloth.

Later, they stood together and looked at the living room. Billy said, "Maybe we could take down the curtains."

"And burn them."

"Good idea."

"What do we do with the guns?" Malcolm said.

"We clean them."

"How?"

"I've got a box of my father's gun cleaners and oils, and probably like five thousand cloths. It's easy enough."

"Aside from the fact that they're covered in urine."

"*Sprinkled* in urine," Billy said, smiling mischievously.

Malcolm took the curtains down while Billy carried the guns out to the kitchen table. They moved the furniture to the center of the room and swept dust and dirt from the corners, then moved the furniture to the walls and swept the center. They argued about where to put the couch, which was too big for the room. Malcolm wanted to get rid of the old recliner that didn't recline anymore, but Billy said it was his favorite chair. Malcolm said it wouldn't be too hard to sand down the top of the coffee table and revarnish it, and it might be better just to throw it out and buy a new one, given how stained and worn it was.

"I'm not you, Mal," Billy said. "I can't just toss everything out and get new stuff whenever I feel like it."

"You can get a new coffee table. You can get a new recliner. Hell, I'll pay for them."

"I don't need your money."

"Well, okay. I offered."

"I'm not going to be living here long. It doesn't matter."

"Okay."

In the kitchen, Malcolm looked through the refrigerator and cupboards, trying to find something with which to make a meal. Rice, eggs, butter, peanut butter, grape jelly, bread. Not much else. Milk, lemonade, rows and rows of beer. "You should buy food," Malcolm said.

"There's a good Thai place down the street, also a pizza place, some Tex-Mex. No need to cook."

"It's cheaper in the long run, cooking."

"I'm not here for the long run. Want a beer?"

They drank beers together while Malcolm cooked rice and fried eggs and Billy made peanut butter and jelly sandwiches. "We're gourmet kings," Billy said as they sat down in the living room to eat.

"So what's next for you?" Malcolm asked. "After you sell the house?"

"See the world. I guess."

"Where do you want to go? Europe?"

"Nah. I'm not a traveler. I mean, I get around, but I don't want to be all touristy and everything. Probably go up to Oregon. I've got friends not far from Portland. It's nice there. Not too sunny, not too hot, not too dry. Here the sun is just fucking evil. I don't know how my father stood it. He said he liked it after all those New Hampshire winters. He had a girlfriend down here, too. That's why he moved here. He followed her. I met her a few times, had dinner with them. She was into crystals, New Age bullshit. He was like the opposite of an atheist: he wanted to believe every religion, so New Agers really attracted him. His girlfriend held out this crystal on a string and then she had me hold it by the string and watch for movement or spinning or something she said was caused by the energy we radiated, and I was like, 'It's not doing anything,' and she said it only works if you believe in it and I was like, 'Well, that's convenient.' After he died she came by the house, wanted to do a funeral and shit. I said no. I didn't want a funeral for him. Nothing. She cried. I told her to fuck off."

"Such compassion."

"Her relationship with my father was her own, mine was my own. And both over now." He lit a cigarette. "I don't want to be part of her relationship with him, and I have no desire for anybody to be part of my relationship with him. She can remember him however she wants. I don't have to share that. She wanted me to keep his memory alive for her. I don't want his memory to be alive. I want him to be fucking forgotten."

In the kitchen, Malcolm stared at the guns piled on the table and on the floor beneath it. Billy brought a cardboard box from the bedroom and set it down on one of the kitchen counters. "Tools, oils, cleaners," he said.

"So how many guns did your father own?"

"Once upon a time, hundreds. At least a hundred just in his personal collection. A hundred fifty, two hundred at the shop. He only brought the best ones out here with him when he retired. Just a few. Relatively speaking. All twentieth century, up through World War Two, that's what he loved. So there's a broomhandle Mauser, a couple Lugers, lots of Walther pistols, various 1911s, an M1 Garand, then just ordinary stuff, the .38 snubnose revolver that he carried, a 9mm Sig Sauer he said was his favorite pistol, back before Sig's quality went down, then a couple Glocks, which is funny because he used to hate Glock, but I guess the more recent designs he liked."

"You sound like an expert."

"Hardly. But I lived with this stuff. He talked about it all the time. A few years after my mother died and things had sort of fallen apart in his personal life, he'd lost a lot of friends, lost a lot of money, he got really obsessive. He literally couldn't talk about anything else. There was nothing else in his life, just him and his guns."

Billy showed Malcolm how to wipe the guns down, how to oil them, how to scrub their barrels. "It doesn't need to be perfect. The guys who pick them up will do their own cleaning."

"Good to get rid of the piss, though."

"Yeah," Billy said. "Better to have them smelling like guns and not like a public bathroom."

Billy drank beer while cleaning and before Malcolm quite realized it, he had himself drunk four cans. The beer combined with the sharp scent of the cleaner and the thick, sweet aroma of the oil made him lightheaded. He enjoyed the work. The guns sat solid in his hands, and once he had cleaned the urine off of them, they began to shine. The black metal especially drew his fascination; he could look into its depths and begin to lose all sense of time and lose all sense of himself. The shimmering, oily darkness reflected his eye, or the inverse of his eye, the sight of all he could not see. What was reflected there, he thought, was a universe, like the animalcule universe in a drop of water under a microscope, yet this was a universe of timeless night, everlasting, a universe of shale and obsidian, of smoke and slag.

After finishing all the rifles and a few of the pistols, they ordered pizza to be delivered. Billy pulled a bottle of Jack Daniels from under the sink. "Forgot I had this," he said, snickering. "Or maybe I didn't." He placed two glasses on the table and dashed the liquor into them. "Here, have a shot."

The pizza arrived and Malcolm paid the delivery guy. He and Billy ate the pizza and cleaned the guns and drank Jack Daniels. As they finished working and eating, Malcolm noticed that Billy was sitting closer to him, and more and more Billy's arm brushed against Malcolm's arm or, now and then, slid across Malcolm's knee; and more and more Billy's shoulder touched Malcolm's shoulder; and then Billy rested his head briefly against Malcolm's head and Malcolm could smell Billy's breath, a breath of whiskey, cigarettes, pizza, Arizona air.

"And now," Malcolm said, "the other guns?"

Billy smiled lopsidedly. His hand drifted to Malcolm's crotch.

"The collection," Malcolm said, removing Billy's hand. "The suicide guns."

Billy splashed the remainder of the Jack Daniels, about a quarter of the bottle, into their glasses. He swallowed his in one gulp.

The guns lay in an old Army trunk in the closet of Billy's father's bedroom. Billy took Malcolm's hand and led him to the room, where they pulled the trunk out together and Billy opened it. "The collection," Billy announced.

Handguns, each wrapped in oiled cloth. Malcolm took one from the trunk and unwrapped it, a silver revolver. A tag dangled from a string tied to the trigger. Written with black ballpoint pen in neat, squarely-printed handwriting: *Arthur Foote 12/23/89.*

"Who was Arthur Foote?" Malcolm said.

"A guy who shot himself," Billy said. "A dead man. A doornail."

"You didn't know him? Do you think your father did?"

"Maybe, maybe not. Probably not. He got the guns from all over. Only a couple were his customers. The people, not the guns." Billy chuckled.

A black semi-automatic pistol with brown grips. *Diana Karaniuk 5/2/95.* "A big gun for a woman," Malcolm said. Billy shrugged. Malcolm said, "I would've expected something petite."

Billy said, "Expectations are shit."

Billy left the room and Malcolm continued to take guns from the trunk, unwrapping them one at a time, looking at the tag, then setting the gun next to the little bed. *Robert Connell 9/12/84. Philip Allen Tewksbury 5/20/87. Brian Hull 2/19/91. Albert Baker 10/5/88. Cynthia Farrell 8/29/93. Stephen McGee 5/9/89. Joseph Tasker 1/1/97.*

Billy brought Malcolm a beer. He put the rest of a six pack on the bed and opened a can for himself. Malcolm left his own can unopened on the floor beside the trunk. *Mary Fuller 6/10/96. Everett Robie 12/19/94. Samuel Conway 3/15/90. Kim Place 5/2/93. Dennis Randolph Stickney 10/24/89. Kelly Ellis 4/14/86. Bruce Zylak 7/4/92.*

"My mother's in there," Billy said softly.

Three more guns and there she was, a black revolver. The only tag without a name. The handwriting seemed slightly less steady, more tentative: *9/2/83.*

"I didn't realize…" Malcolm said. "You only ever said she died when you were young. I assumed cancer."

"I know."

Billy sat down next to Malcolm on the floor and rested his head in Malcolm's lap. After a moment, Malcolm ran a hand through Billy's hair. Billy smiled. He kissed Malcolm's hand. Malcolm let one of his fingers slide across Billy's lips, allowed one finger to slip into Billy's mouth.

"You taste like gun oil," Billy said.

Billy sat up a bit unsteadily. He kissed Malcolm and Malcolm let him. Carefully, with unsteady fingers, Billy unbuttoned Malcolm's pants, unzipped his fly, unbuttoned his boxers. Malcolm ran his hand through Billy's hair.

Later, they undressed each other and moved to Billy's father's bed.

...

Malcolm woke with dawn. (He hadn't slept deeply. Billy passed out half an hour after they got into bed together.) He dressed and then looked around for a piece of paper and something to write with. In the kitchen, he found a pencil and an empty envelope from the electric company. *Billy— I'm sorry for leaving. I fear I led you on. Please get the hell out of here and go someplace where you can have fun. Be free. You deserve it. Mal.* He left the note on the kitchen table.

...

He had intended to drive straight to the airport and take the first flight home, but as he drove through Phoenix his resolve wavered and he found himself sitting in the parking lot of a small hotel. The hotel had vacancies, and he booked a room. "How many nights?" the clerk asked, and without any thought Malcolm said, "Four." He gave the clerk his credit card. The room would be ready in a few hours.

He walked around the city, but the heat soon made him feel tired and hungover, his head throbbing. He stepped into a restaurant and ordered eggs, bacon, and coffee. He nearly fell asleep at the table.

When he returned to the hotel, his room was ready. He didn't bother to bring his suitcase in from the car, nor did he pulls the bed's covers down before lying on it. Soon, he was asleep.

2.

"It'll be a few more days," he said to Celeste when he called that night. "Things are going well. All is well. Billy's much better. I'll be home when I can."

He spent his days wandering the city, trying not to think about anything, trying not to remember or daydream, trying only to live, to let time pass over him, through him. He ate meals in restaurants, he visited museums, he walked across a university campus, he stood in stores and played the role of a customer, and if people smiled at him then he smiled back and if people asked him questions he gave the vaguest, least committed answer that he could, said he was just looking, just browsing, just killing some time, and all the while he tried not to look into their faces, their eyes savage with innocence.

At night, after dinner in the small hotel's small restaurant, he returned to his room and listened to the sounds outside and the sounds from other rooms while drinking from a bottle of Jack Daniels until he fell asleep. He dreamed each night of faces swollen in death, shimmering detached over limbless bodies, floating down dried up rivers all around him.

On the fourth day, he called the gun shop that Billy said he was selling his father's stuff to. He asked if they had bought a collection of guns, a collection in an Army trunk. Yes, they said, they'd just taken possession of them yesterday. The guns weren't inventoried yet, but he was welcome to come over and have a look. He said he was from out of state and expected to buy at least one of the guns but he didn't know how to get it across the country legally. They said they could take care of all that, he just needed a dealer willing to accept them back home. He asked if most dealers will do that and they said yes, all the dealers they've known, and he thanked them and said he would be over in the afternoon.

With his phone, he searched for gun dealers near his and

Celeste's farmhouse in Vermont. There were four. The first he called said yes, certainly, he'd be happy to do the transfer, though he did charge a $25 fee. That was fine, Malcolm said, that was just fine.

He drove to the gun shop immediately. It was only a few miles from the hotel; a large, colorful sign proclaimed its location. Inside, it felt like any other store: brightly lit, spacious, airy, the floor peppered with displays of accessories (holsters, grips, cleaning kits, books and magazines, bumper stickers, camouflage jackets and camouflage hats and camouflage gloves). Toward the back, a glass-covered counter in a square U shape held hundreds of handguns, while rifles of every variety stood in racks along the walls behind the counter. Men wearing identical green t-shirts walked between the counter and the walls. Each, Malcolm saw, wore a pistol in a holster on his hip.

"I called earlier today," he said to one of the men, "about some guns you bought, a collection in an old Army trunk."

"Sure," the man said. "We've got it out back. What are you looking for?"

"A black revolver," he said. "Maybe a .22, a .38, I'm not sure. With black grips. It's all black, the whole thing. And the tag just has a date on it, no name."

"I think the tags got tossed," the man said, "but I'll check."

The man walked through a door in the center of the back wall, then returned a few minutes later, three revolvers in his hands. He laid them on a cushioned mat on the counter. "One of these?" the man asked.

Malcolm pointed to the one he wanted. All black. "No tag?" he said.

"No, we threw them out yesterday when we unpacked."

"That'a shame."

"Why?"

"The previous owner, the collector, he made the tags. There was a ... a lovingness to them. A love."

"Ah. Well. Okay. Sorry. To be honest, these aren't really collectible guns. The others we got from him, they're a lot better. There's a Luger, a Mauser, good stuff. Sure you wouldn't rather something like that? These revolvers here, the guns from the trunk, they're just ordinary, everyday weapons. Not expensive, but they're never going to really accumulate value."

"That's fine. I know what they are. I'll take this one."

He was tempted to ask for them all, to buy the entire trunk. But that would have been pointless. He only needed one, and it might as well be this one, the most meaningful of the guns. He gave the man the information about the dealer in Vermont, he filled out a form about his criminal history, he waited for the background check to confirm that he was not a criminal, and he gave the man his credit card. The gun would arrive in Vermont a day or two after he got home.

...

He did not tell Celeste about the gun. He did not tell her when, soon after getting back from Phoenix, he drove to Vermont to pick up the gun and stash it in the attic of the farmhouse they had bought a few years ago and which she hated. ("We should live more humbly," she said, and he said, "We can afford the house, it's not a problem," and she said, "That's not what I mean," and they almost had a fight, but he had not wanted to keep talking, nor had she.) He had paid more money than he intended for someone to come up from Boston and install a full audio system for the house, putting speakers in every room, so that if he wanted to, he could put a Pablo Casals 78 of one of Bach's cello suites on his Technics turntable and pipe the sound throughout the house. When he first did this, testing the new system, he called Celeste at work and left an excited voicemail. She called back an hour later. "Are you having a midlife crisis?" she asked. "Should I be concerned?"

He could not tell her about the gun. It would make everything worse. They had been doing well, not getting snippy with each other, and they had even discussed selling the farmhouse and getting a timeshare in Hawaii, or maybe Costa Rica. Her parents in Rhode Island were elderly, though, and she didn't want to be more than an hour or two away from them, and Malcolm didn't particularly want to abandon his mother, even though he visited her only a couple times a year and she seemed happy and plenty busy at the retirement community in Portsmouth where he had bought her a condominium. Still, though he rarely saw her, it would feel strange to be far away.

He must not tell Celeste about the gun. She hated guns. It wasn't until he saw the suicide guns that he knew for sure himself that he didn't share her feelings. Before, he had only had suspicion, a yearning, a hunger, and the hunger was deepest for the suicide guns, which he had spent decades imagining — even dreaming about them, wondering what they felt like in the hand, wondering if they bore witness to their history, if their barrels still held bits of blood, flesh, and bone. His imagination failed him when he thought about what they might look like or feel like, the vision was not vivid, the lines were blurred. He yearned like a worshipper dreaming of religious relics, sure that they would emit an aura, that they would impart wisdom or grace, but when he finally reached into the trunk and took one of the guns in his hand, there had been no aura, no wisdom, no grace. The guns felt simply like what they were: hunks of metal. And yet the more he touched them, the more he felt that the metal had a power different from the power of the other guns, the ones he and Billy had cleaned in the kitchen. As he looked at name after name, he began to imagine people, people who were distraught and desperate, he imagined their hands holding the guns, their fingers on the triggers, the barrel pressed to their chest or temple or held in their mouth, he imagined the metal warming in their mouth, he imagined the taste of the metal, he imagined the great strain and effort needed to force yourself to squeeze the trigger, to ease it back such a tiny distance, and then — what? Nothing. The sound of the explosion would travel slower than the bullet. The bullet would do its work before the ears heard anything at all. A silent death amidst great noise.

He did not tell Celeste about the gun, nor did he tell her about the other guns he bought. He had wanted to learn to shoot, but he did not want to shoot the gun from Arizona, so he needed to buy another. He told the dealer that he needed something small but powerful, something for home protection. "A .45 is best," the dealer said, "because you'll be able to stop just about anything smaller than a moose. But you might prefer something a bit lighter, maybe a .38," and the dealer showed him a small revolver much like one that he had cleaned with Billy. He bought it, three boxes of ammunition, protective ear muffs, and some cleaning supplies. The nearest neighbors to the farmhouse were half a mile down the road, and over the last two years he had heard plenty of distant gunshots from people target shooting or hunting, so he felt no embarrassment or fear when he took the revolver out behind the farmhouse and started shooting at trees. The force and recoil surprised him. Even through the ear protectors that gripped his skull, the sound was exhilarating. He paused after the first shot, then emptied the rest of the cylinder quickly. He went through two boxes of ammunition that first day.

As the new school year approached, Malcolm bought more guns: a used Colt AR-15 from the 1980s ("The last time they really knew how to make them good," the dealer said), a Glock .45, a Colt 1911 from World War II, a Desert Eagle .357 Magnum, a pistol-grip shotgun. He only bought one at a time, and he rarely shot them, instead spending hours researching their history and technology. He mused on writing music that was nothing but the sound of the weapons' mechanics, of cocking and sliding, of hammers falling, of powder exploding in cartridges and bullets shooting through barrels, of bullets hitting paper and wood, ricocheting off of metal. He wished then that he had bought the whole trunk from the dealer in Arizona. He could have written a chamber piece for suicide guns.

...

"Are you renovating the farmhouse or something?" Celeste said as they had dinner together at home.

"No," Malcolm said. "Why?"

"You're up there an awful lot these days."

"I'm relaxing. It gets rid of stress, being there."

"Billy keeps calling, trying to get hold of you. He said you don't answer your cell phone."

"Reception sucks at the farmhouse."

"You should call him. He sounds ... unsettled."

"I will," Malcolm said.

"Are you having an affair?" Celeste said.

"What? No no, I'm, what, I — *no*—"

"Jesus, I was joking. I figured maybe you've got a hot young babe in Vermont."

"Very funny."

"We haven't really had sex this summer. Not much. I feel like I'm imposing on you when we do."

"No, I'm just, I'm distracted. Stressed."

"Men aren't supposed to lose their libido too much as they get older, are they? Or are they?"

"I haven't lost my libido."

"Okay. Well. Neither have I."

...

He cherished his nights at the farmhouse, swaddled in dense darkness. The world grew quiet except for the occasional call of an owl or the bark of coyotes. The city repulsed him now, its cacophony, and it was harder and harder, too, to listen to his students and his colleagues. Their voices clawed at him. He suspected that they talked about him when he was not there. He was sure of it. He could see it in their eyes and faces. They did not know how much they gave away, how transparent were their feelings and ideas, or perhaps they did and simply didn't care, didn't see any need for disguise. He used to think they envied him, and he was sure many of them did, envied him his beautiful wife and her lucrative job, their townhouse and ability to travel. Yes, some of his students and colleagues envied him, they had made that clear many times, but there was something else now, something more menacing, an envy that had hardened into malice. If he were to be run over by a truck, they would not hide their celebration, no. If someone broke the windows of his townhouse or smashed in the door and made their way through the halls and grabbed his wife, held her down, tore her clothes, violated her while forcing him to watch (him, the weak and impotent man tied to a chair or left whimpering on the floor with broken legs), he knew this would not bother his colleagues and students, they would smile and mutter about justice and argue over who would get that nice corner office now and what would become of that rather excellent collection of old records, and though they might feel some sympathy for his wife, they would feel none for him, nor would he want them to. Their malice might, he thought, become active, they could take steps, they could do more than jeer and insinuate, they could reach out their hands surreptitiously, they could push him in front of the truck, they could break his windows and smash his door, they could wander hallways he wandered, they could seek him, seek to destroy him. Few of his colleagues were likely to act, but his students were more energetic, more fanatical, less predictable, likely disturbed. Capable of anything. Which was why he now slipped away more and more often to the farmhouse during the week, despite the long drive. He told Celeste he was going to conferences, or giving guest lectures at universities just far enough away that he needed to stay the night. She was busy with work and never questioned him. He had a talent for convincing her. She could probably see he was lying, though. He feared what she might ask. How could he tell her about his colleagues and students, how could he describe their faces and eyes, their voices, and how could he tell her that it was the way voices coupled with the sounds of the city (the car horns and alarms, the shouting and laughter and voices, everywhere voices) that made it impossible for him to sleep or relax. She had already commented on his gritting his teeth at night, which woke her up, and his thrashing around while dreaming, which scared her. She knew he got up from bed again and again to roam the house, and she knew about the new locks he had put on the front and back doors, because he had given her keys, but she said less and less, which puzzled him but also left him relieved.

3.

He was meeting with a student in his office when Celeste called him on her way back from a corporate event in Montreal. He let the call go to voicemail, then got busy working on the agenda for the upcoming curriculum committee meeting, for which he was chair. His students were particularly bothersome this year, each of them, he was certain, convinced that Malcolm was an old idiot who knew nothing about whatever a person was supposed to know things about, and the curriculum committee wasn't much better, with even Malcolm's longtime colleagues seeming to think every opinion he offered to be barely worth a response. He returned to his office afterward, closed the door, and began listening to a CD of Louis Couperin's suite in C major played on harpsichord.

Celeste called again. He remembered that she had called earlier and he had not listened to the voicemail.

"What's up?" he said.

"Explain it to me," she said.

"Explain what?"

"I'm standing here right now in the farmhouse."

Everything in him collapsed, his esophagus and lungs and heart and stomach all dissolved, his legs began to shiver, and there was no air anywhere in the room.

"Why," he whispered, "are you *there*?"

"I called you. Didn't you listen to your goddamn phone? I decided to come home this way. I wanted to see the farmhouse, see why you've been so besotted with it, maybe get some goddamned clue as to why you've been behaving the way you have, and so I did, I came here, I am here, standing here, and what I see in front of me, Malcolm, what I see is a goddamn fucking arsenal."

He knew he shouldn't have left everything out. But there was no good place to store it all. The attic was too hot and humid in the summer, too cold in the winter. He had installed a gun safe in the closet of the master bedroom, hidden it in a crawlspace behind the wall, but it wasn't nearly big enough to hold all he had. And he had been in a hurry last time, late to something or other, needing to get back, so he had left the AR-15 and the shotgun on the couch in the living room and some of the pistols on the coffee table beside a few military instruction manuals he had been reading. Everything else was hidden away. It was hardly, he said to himself, an arsenal.

"It's just, it's a project, that's all, something I've been working on. No big deal."

"I'm going to stop for dinner and then I'm heading home. I don't care how late it is when I get there. We need to talk."

"Right. Sure. Yes. Of course. I love you." She hung up.

By the time she got home, he had worked out a good story for her, a story of avant-garde music and social critique, a story in which he was writing a musical piece for five firearms and working to find exactly the right sounds, a story of himself, not just a professor but an artist, one who stood a real chance this time of getting some good grant money and the attention of the world. A story of a man who would make her proud. He told the story well, and though she knew it was a story, she believed it. They held each other gently that night, and she said, "You'd tell me if there was anything wrong, wouldn't you?" and he said, "Yes, of course, always." He was happy to reassure her.

In the morning, he made breakfast for her before she left for work, scrambled eggs and french toast. He said he would be home late, not to wait up for him, he had a student recital he had to attend, then drinks with colleagues afterward, nobody special, people he could barely stand being around, but he needed their support, so he couldn't exactly ignore the event. She nodded vaguely, then kissed him. "We're okay, right?" she said.

"We're great," he said, smiling.

She did not believe his story, he was sure of that. Something was going on. She had made some decision in Montreal, some decision about him. He needed to know. For months, he had thought about getting cameras, wiretaps, bugs, but he had only looked into it briefly. He should have followed through, should have trusted his instincts. He needed to see what she did when she was alone, who she talked to at work, what she said. Now it was too late. There should be safety in their home together, but there was not. He could not protect anything here.

He called his department secretary and told her he had the flu, he would not be in today, he needed to cancel his classes and meetings. She told him not to worry about it, she would take care of everything, though he was certain he heard something else in her voice, some suspicion. But she was the least of his concerns.

There must be some way to get into Celeste's building and see who she talked to, yet every idea he came up with was impractical, a fantasy, like something out of a bad action movie: stealing a mailman's uniform, setting off firecrackers in the lobby to distract the guards while he dashed to the elevator, pickpocketing someone's ID and slithering through the halls and hiding in Celeste's office, maybe in her closet, maybe under her giant desk... No, no. He needed to be something other than who, or what, he was. He needed to be an insect in a rocky desert, carapaced and thorny, a creature of endurance, armed with pincers and poison, ready for what was coming, because something was going to happen, it had been building up for a long time, imperceptible structures were in place, and now, as his thoughts solidified, he realized the threat was not Celeste, nor was the threat *to* Celeste, she was a small part of a large system, and though he could not identify the threat, he knew she was neither it nor its target. She was vulnerable too. But not nearly as vulnerable as he. The system was a storm front bearing down on the little web of life they had built together, but she would be fine, she was resilient, unlike him, and that's what she must have realized, how exposed he was, pregnable, how likely he was to melt away at the first rain.

On the street outside the townhouse, he was certain that everyone saw how weak he was, and he began to suspect that among the pedestrians making their way along the sidewalks mingled agents of the storm, perhaps even agents of Celeste, for she had always been ahead of him, always known more of the world, and it would be just like her to have prepared already, to have her own cameras and microphones and spyglasses, her own confederates reporting back that Malcolm was outside now in the sun, exposed, and they would speculate about his thoughts, his actions and purpose, they would read him and then write their readings in reports that they would give to Celeste to analyze for portents. Her concern gratified him, but he could not let her be his guardian. He had his own resources. As he walked, he told himself that he must not behave any differently than he would have behaved before. He must not let his face give him away. He looked no-one in the eyes. He walked down into the garage underneath their building just as he had walked countless times before, he walked to the car slowly and carefully, then drove slowly and carefully through streets he drove every day, though he hoped not too slowly and carefully, not giving anything away of himself, and when he looked in the rearview mirror to see if any of the cars behind him seemed to follow, he tried not to let his glance linger any longer than he would have on any other day.

By the time he made his way out of the city, he was sure he was not being followed. He laughed lightly at his concern, but it did not lessen the concern. The person he was a year ago would not have been able to imagine the person he was today. It seemed wondrous to him that he had survived as long as he had. He had not known how precarious everything was in his life. Too much was too clear now. Blissful ignorance had kept him lucky, unknowingly skipping over cracks and chasms that now seethed lava all around. It was a good thing he had gone to Arizona. Without either of them knowing it, Billy had saved him from certain doom.

When he got to the farmhouse, he checked each door and window, spent hours in the attic searching crevices, checked the little pieces of thread he had set in each room to reveal disturbance. Nothing screamed out warnings. The only room with any trace of upset was the living room where Celeste had seen his carelessness, his exposure. She seemed, though, to have gone away without leaving any surveillance of her own. If she had set traps, their cunning was beyond his ability to see. No other forces of the systems had invaded, not visibly. He locked the front door. He cursed himself for not getting an alarm put in. All his attention had been on the townhouse. He could have had security here, but he had not known how quickly necessary it would be.

He investigated the bedroom closet carefully. Everything was as he had left it. She had not snooped here, there were no signs of entry or subterfuge. He pulled back the false panel in the back wall to reveal the gun safe, typed the code into the lock's keypad, and removed his latest purchase: ceramic-plated body armor. He put it on over his clothes, then squeezed his head into the military helmet with night goggles attached. He would not need the goggles for a little while yet, though the days were getting shorter now. The Desert Eagle was loaded and sat in a holster on a belt, which he wrapped around his waist and buckled. This was better. He could begin to breathe again. He took the black revolver out of the safe. It was not loaded; he had never loaded it and never would. He squeezed it inside his armor, against his chest. It pressed against him, against his bones.

He grabbed two of the thirty-round magazines for the AR-15 and brought them downstairs, replacing the empty magazine in the rifle and putting the spares, loaded and empty, into pockets in his armored vest. He would load the rest of the guns before dark, but for now this was enough.

His phone rang. He looked at it: Billy. No, he would not answer. Not now. Soon, though. He would talk with Billy, catch up on all that had happened, hear what Billy was doing with his life, and he would tell Billy that he had saved Billy's mother's gun, that it was safe now, here, with him, and he himself was safe, too, and if he was brave he would tell Billy that he knew Billy needed him, and he was ready to protect Billy, he knew he could do that, he was ready, he was prepared, he had learned — and he would say that he hoped Billy would trust him and forgive him and make his way to him now, because he had saved what most needed to be saved, he had protected himself, he had found refuge, and he could make them safe.

But not yet. He needs to stand here a few minutes longer. He needs to watch the sun sink down below the mountains beyond the forest, he needs the night to come, and he will see through it, he will see all movement and every threat. He is sure that Billy will call back, and he will tell Billy the plan and warn Billy of dangers so that Billy will make his way past every threat and his way will lead here.

It is dark now.

He flips the safeties off on the AR-15 and the Desert Eagle.

Billy will call at any moment.

He lowers his goggles and turns them on.

The night glows alive, he holds the rifle in both hands, and he looks out at the invisible world surging toward him.

IV.

Carl tries to pick up his hands — he can't, he has no hands.
Rod goes to Carl.
He picks up the severed left hand and takes off the ring he
put there.
He reads the message written in the mud.

—Sarah Kane

THE BALLAD OF JIMMY AND MYRA

Jimmy started smoking when he was eight. His father taught him. His father was a drunk and after a couple bottles of rotgut vodka he always thought it was funny to see Jimmy puffing away. Once he learned not to spit, choke, gag, and cough, Jimmy thought smoking was funny, too. Jimmy's mother wasn't around much to tell him it was a disgusting habit. She only came home every few days and spent most of her time out whoring. When she got home, Jimmy would say, "Were you out whoring?" and his mother would say, "Don't listen to that good-for-nothing father of yours. I'm making a life for us," and then she would go away again, which was for the best.

By the time Jimmy was ten, he was up to two packs a day. He couldn't get them from his father anymore, because his father had ended up in prison shortly after Jimmy learned to smoke. Somehow, Jimmy's father had found the keys to the car that he wasn't supposed to drive because he was such a drunk, and he had tried to drive into town on his own and had ended up driving right into Mr. Parkham's living room, killing the whole Parkham family (Mr. Parkham, Mrs. Parkham, little Amy) as they sat on their long white puffy couch watching *Jeopardy*. The police said the car must have been going at least fifty miles an hour, and there was no indication that Jimmy's father had made any attempt to stop, and he had somehow launched up over the hedge on the front lawn and flown straight through the picture window, probably decapitating and certainly crushing all the Parkhams at once. Jimmy's father had been wearing his seatbelt, though, so he was fine. He got sentenced to twenty years for vehicular manslaughter, a plea bargain for agreeing not to fight the charges and clog up the courts with his case.

Three days after his father was arrested, Jimmy's mother came back and said she was pregnant and didn't love his father anymore and didn't love Jimmy anymore either because he just reminded her of his father, so she was going to give him up for adoption because he was too old for her to abort now. She said she had a new husband who was rich and their new house had a heated swimming pool and a crystal chandelier and a garbage disposal unit in the sink. Just before she gave him over to a social worker, Jimmy's mother told him not to use his penis for evil the way his father had. Jimmy lit the last Camel he had saved from his father's last carton. She told him smoking was a filthy habit and would give him cancer. He said he hoped so.

Jimmy was too old to be adopted easily, so he lived at a group home, and it was a cinch to get smokes at the group home if he would give the older boys oral sex. It seemed like a good trade, so he did it with some frequency. Sometimes they just tossed him smokes for free because they thought it was so funny to see a kid his age smoking. ("Look mean, Jimmy," they'd say, and he would scrunch his eyes and chomp his cigarette. "Look like a bruiser," they'd say, and he would grunt and puff and scowl. "Smoke my big cigar," they'd say and pull down their pants.) Sometimes they'd be able to get a bottle of whiskey, too, and they loved feeding him whiskey and cigarettes because he got pretty funny when he was too inebriated to speak coherently. They could also get free oral sex if he was inebriated, and sometimes they would just all end up penetrating him anally because he was too inebriated to fight. He tried not to get inebriated, and he would never touch beer ("I will not be my father's son," he vowed), but he liked whiskey an awful lot. "It's my weakness," he told a new boy, and the new boy quickly learned how to use that weakness to gain pleasure and dominance for himself.

By the time he was fourteen, Jimmy was up to four packs a day and he had a constant cough. He weighed nearly 300 pounds now, too, because even though he had a scrawny frame, the older boys gave him so much whiskey that he became bloated. He was inebriated during most of his waking hours, which made things easier, for him and for them. His whole body ached, and there were sores all over his skin. Sometimes the social workers looked concerned. Nobody could do anything, though. Who, after all, would adopt a boy like Jimmy, a drunk and a smoker and a fat slob with sores on his legs and pustules on his arms and acne volcanoed across his face, a boy whose eyes were always bloodshot and yellow, a boy whose teeth looked like rotten tree stumps? He went to school and did well in math class, but not much else. His math teacher said Jimmy was some sort of prodigy, and if he could overcome his personal problems he might be able to get into Harvard for free and then get a great job at some entity that employed genius mathematicians, and the idea excited Jimmy a lot, but he was too often too inebriated to think about it much, which, in the end, was for the best.

When Jimmy was fifteen, a social worker managed to steal him out of the group home for a night with the goal and hope that they might visit a doctor, get Jimmy a real check-up, and put an end to a few of his major ailments. A couple of the older boys were anally penetrating Jimmy when the social worker arrived, so he was incoherent and bleeding, but she managed to get him out of there and to a hospital emergency room. He spent a few days in the hospital having tests done. Anemia. Alcohol dependency. Perforated intestine. Liver trouble. Lung cancer. Throat cancer. Tongue cancer. Bone cancer.

The doctor, a tall man with short eyes, said, "I'm afraid the outlook isn't good. Your body's a wreck. We can do chemotherapy, but the best case scenerio is you'll be dead in two years at the latest."

"And what's the worst case scenario?" Jimmy said.

"You'll die at any moment."

"Isn't that true for anybody?"

"Sure," the doctor said, "but for you it's more likely."

The social worker gave Jimmy's story to newspapers and magazines, eventually turning it into a book that sold millions of copies, and a gaggle of philanthropic local people agreed to fund all of his treatment, so he ended up going to New York City to detox and then live in a special hospital for cancer kids. He lost a lot of weight and of course had to give up smoking and drinking, which at first made him angry, as they were the only pleasures he had in the world, but by then he'd met Myra, and she changed his life.

Myra was twenty-one and had brain cancer. They met at a support group at the hospital. "My name is Myra," she said, "and I never did anything to deserve this. I was practically a nun. I graduated from MIT at the age of fifteen with a degree in quantum electro-biophysics and was working for one of the most successful digital start-ups in the history of humanity until I parlayed that job into my own consulting firm, drawing paychecks from the richest and most brilliant people on the planet, and now I can't see vowels."

"Vowels?" Jimmy said.

"I'm losing my vision. The vowels have gone first. As the tumor grows, I'll probably lose consonants, but I'm hoping it will be something else. I can read without vowels. I love reading. Do you read?"

"No," Jimmy said. "Not willingly."

"How do you spend your time?" Myra asked.

"Whoring. Or, I used to. I was a booze hound and a smoke addict, too. I did terrible things."

"So you deserve your disease."

"Yes," Jimmy said. "I worked for it. It was all I ever wanted in the world. I love it and it loves me."

"I'm no longer a nun," Myra said. "Are you still able to sexually perform or have you lost that?"

"I don't know," Jimmy said.

"Let's try," Myra said, and so they went back to her room, which was in a private wing of the hospital, and they took off their clothes and sexually performed quite easily and happily. Afterward, Myra showed Jimmy a large gold box of hand-rolled Turkish cigarettes she kept beside the bed, cigarettes filled with tobacco harvested by enslaved children in exotic locales, cigarettes so illegal they had to be smuggled into the country in body cavities. ("*Body ... cavities,*" Myra said to Jimmy, drawing out all the vowels she couldn't see. For the rest of his life, those remained the two most beautiful words in the universe to him.) The allure was overpowering, and they both smoked many of the Turkish cigarettes, and then they sexually performed again.

Exhausted afterward, Myra dragged herself to the opposite side of the room and opened an oak chest of liquors. She poured Jimmy a hefty glass of whiskey and made a martini for herself. They drank all night and smoked all night and sexually performed and passed out, naked and inebriated, together on Myra's bed. Sometime in the night they woke up together and vomited on each other. In the morning, Jimmy suggested that their mutual vomitting was a sign that they were meant to be together forever, and Myra agreed, and they smoked many more Turkish cigarettes and drank whiskey and martinis together and then at exactly the same moment expressed the notion that in honor of their special bond they should sexually perform before they cleaned up the vomit, and so they did.

In the morning, Jimmy could hardly breathe, and the nurses hooked him up to oxygen tanks and scolded Myra, but their scolding was entirely pro forma, as none of the nurses wanted to lose the monthly bonus she paid them to indulge her whims.

Jimmy's social worker came by to collect material for her book, but since he was hooked up to tanks, he couldn't speak, which made him useless to her, and so she sauntered over to Myra's wing to ask, for the umpteenth time, for an interview. This time, Myra said sure.

Q: Do you love Jimmy?

A: No. He is remarkably pliant with his penis, though.

Q: Do you mean *flexible*? "Pliant" is an odd choice of word, especially if he achieved an erection.

A: Yes, "flexible" in meaning, but I prefer *pliant* for the word itself, as the alliteration — or is it consonance? or both? — anyway, it's lovely.

Q: I'll write "flexible" or the copyeditors will have my hide.

A: Well, I don't care, write what you want. And there really wasn't much to his penis, anyway, as it's all shriveled and cracked and thorny. I told him otherwise, as penile pride is very important to him — something about his mother, I don't know what, maybe incest, wouldn't that be delightfully scandalous? Anyway, if I'd told you the true state of it I wouldn't have been able to say "He is remarkably pliant with his penis," and thus I would have deprived myself of a lovely sentence, and I prefer not to deprive myself of anything, given how ghastly is the state of the world and how few our earthly pleasures.

Q: Do you hate humanity?

A: No, I try to give it as little thought as possible.

Q: How's your own health?

A: Dreadful. I could die at any moment.

Q: Couldn't we all?

A: Sure. But for me it's more likely.

After a few days of rest and lots of oxygen infusions, lung pumping, and opioids, Jimmy was able to walk and talk again, though his doctors and nurses repeatedly told him not to get himself too excited, not to exert himself too much, not to bump and grind. Nonetheless, at the first moment the coast was clear, he beelined to Myra's wing, where she waited with open arms and bromides. "Let's quit this place kid," she said, "and trip it as we go on the light fantastick."

"Okay," Jimmy said, then added: "I just read an article about funerals."

Myra kissed his cheek and licked his lips and purred. "We're a couple of wild animals," she said. "You're meat to me. I'm a-gonna devour your body piece by piece and cavity by cavity, Jimmyboy. *Rrrroar.*"

"Sounds good. Let's dash to a liquor outlet along the way."

"Sure thing. We go together, Jimmy. I don't know why. Like guns and ammunition go together. We can blast our way through a boozemart, but then let's rob a bank, like real lovers do."

They zipped and zagged through corridors and down back stairways to slip out of the clutches of the hospital staff. At a far corner of the parking lot outside, a Ford V8 waited for the duo.

Myra jumped into the driver's seat and Jimmy, a bit winded now, a bit under the weather, hobbled over to the passenger's side. He thought for a moment that Myra might want him to hang out on the runningboard, which would surely be the death of him, but she waited calmly for him to find his way inside the car. She was a good girl, Myra. A keeper, Jimmy thought.

They rained terror down on the American midwest for a good year or so, keeping death at bay by offering sudden sac-rifices to vaguely-perceived pagan gods, or at least that's what they told themselves they were doing when they brandished their pistols and fired their tommyguns. At first, they just popped off weasily clerks who lunged for bank alarms, but soon enough they discovered that killing was easy and briefly amusing, so they pumped lead into the hearts of executives and loan managers and tellers, of ladies with little dogs and men with big briefcases, of kids who'd been promised lolli-pops and guards hoping to make it to retirement, of drifters and passersby and good samaritans and cops. It was a joyous way to live, and it made them hungry for meat, so in addition to banks they robbed abattoirs, and in meadows and forests they built campfires and cooked slabs of ungulates and fed each other the gristle and flesh. They grew stronger, braver, happier. Jimmy's penis filled out, and, engorged, it became Myra's favorite thing in the world, the only object she lusted for, the only item in the universe that spilled hope into her dreams. Jimmy was less enlivened by Myra except for the moments where they joined together and took someone's life, and the more they robbed and the more they slaughtered, the more he needed someone else's death before he could get into the state that Myra adored.

As Jimmy and Myra spilled blood through the streets of the heartland, the social worker finished her chronicle of Jimmy's early, awful life, and it was published by a New York magnate who sank half a publishing empire into its promotion. For more than a few months, it was the best-known book in the world. Readers grew weepy as they thought about all the hardships of Jimmy's life, and now when he and Myra rolled into town, they were met not by a phalanx of federales, but by crowds of autograph hounds with easily-opened tear ducts. "Cry cry cry!" Jimmy screamed at them, before shooting them down in the streets. Nobody ever got in their way, and soon enough Jimmy could blow some poor schlub's brains out, then, without pause or interference, in a single movement of inspiring grace, pull down his pants, tear Myra's dress to shreds, whisper "*Body cavities…*", and pump her full of himself.

As the fans clamored for more, Jimmy and Myra made their way toward Los Angeles, the city of angels, the city of dreams. It was the edge of the continent and, they knew, the edge of themselves as well. For all the bloodshed and all the good meat they consumed, they could not escape their fates, and Jimmy's lungs had grown weaker, his bones more fragile, while Myra's tumor had taken half the alphabet away from her and rendered most of her memories as ash.

At night, under the stars, eating animal, Jimmy would tell Myra stories of her lost life: of all the tests she aced, all the boys she made go wild with excitement, all the deals she negotiated with abandon. He told her she was the most loved woman in the world, because she was loved by him, and always had been, and always would be. And she believed him, because half her brain was mush.

Los Angeles frightened them both. The lights were too bright, the cars too fast, the people too underwhelmed by the magic and terror of two kids in love and on the run. Myra shuddered and cowered in the passenger seat, terrified to look out the window. Jimmy told her to imagine the city was gone, all gone. Decades of drought, he said, had scorched the place dry, turning it into a city of husks. The streets were scattered with skeletons. Skyscrapers still rose toward the burning sky, but that sky had long ago scraped all the people away. Myra smiled. Jimmy drove them through the ghosttown streets, making up stories about what he said stood outside the windows Myra hid from. Look there, he said, it's the building where the President once lived, and there's the building where they made that movie about the wizard, and there's the building where all the world's money was stored in golden safes that Jimmy alone knew the combination to. Myra smiled and nodded and drooled a bit as he droned on and on, the pleasure slipping out of his voice with each word, the hope and happiness gone, gone, gone.

He got them out of the city by flashing a pistol and firing a shot whenever the world got in his way. He screeched through alleyways and raced across boulevards, seeking the fastest path he could find to the ocean.

As the car sputtered on its last gasps of gas one late afternoon, Jimmy and Myra rolled down a quiet beach toward the glistening green Pacific. The sun was setting on what Jimmy knew must be their last night together. "We're fugitives from the laughing house, baby," Jimmy whispered, and Myra cooed at him.

They left the car behind and Jimmy carried Myra down the beach to where the water touched the land. He could hardly breathe now. He pulled a few alphabet blocks from his pocket, a little souvenir from a toy shop heist they'd done for fun some months ago. He set the blocks in the sand beside Myra and jostled their letters into a word: L-O-V-E.

"Leave?" she said.

"No, try again."

"Live?" She ran a finger over the top of the O.

"Good try. Close."

"I don't know," she said, "I can't read it."

"Sure you can. One more try."

"It's all gone away. The ocean washed it all away."

"No, it's right here, under your fingers, can't you feel it?" He touched her hand and pressed it on the blocks.

"Just sand," she said, "and ocean and mud."

"That's okay," he said, and pushed the blocks away. He rested his head on her shoulder and she ran her sandy fingers through his hair.

He coughed and spat blood. He wheezed. Pain rippled through him. He squeezed his eyes closed. Myra kissed his forehead.

He imagined what the social worker might say, if she were here. "I can't be all bad, can I?" he would ask her. "Nobody's all bad." He knew what she'd reply: "Well, you come the closest." It was true and he would not deny it. But it didn't matter. Nothing mattered. Everyone was gone. Burned up in the conflagrations, starved and wasted away, diseased. All gone.

"The word was 'love'," he said.

"What word?"

"In the blocks."

"Oh," Myra said. Then, after staring at the waves: "Did you mean me?"

"I think so," Jimmy said. He feared she would laugh at him, but she didn't. She pressed herself closer.

"I love you, too," she said. The waves, now frosted with moonlight, inched in. "Or no. Not you. Not exactly. I love your truck. No, your trampoline. No, I mean: your trauma."

"I don't understand," Jimmy said. From somewhere he produced a cigarette and a butane lighter. He lit the cigarette, then let the lighter fall among the blocks.

"It's why everybody loves you, all the people who read that book, who want your signature. No matter what you do, your trumpet — no, no, your other thing — your wounds — will always be beautiful. We want some part of your treacle — no, your trumpet — *trauma* — also to be ours. It is the one good thing you have that you can give to the world: your pain, your heartbreak, your suffering." She looked up toward his eyes as he stared out at the sea. She took the cigarette from his lips. "We want to witness," she said, then put the cigarette to her own lips and inhaled deeply. He looked at her and she kissed him and blew smoke deep into his lungs. The smoke tore at the last ruins of tissue and clogged the few open pores that had not been filled with tar and tumor. Jimmy coughed lightly, sending a single puff of air, his final breath, back to Myra, who breathed it in and pulled back until she was standing above Jimmy, his body lifeless in the sand, his breath still in her lungs.

That same night, the social worker located Jimmy's mother living in a brothel in Bakersfield, her veins rich with heroin. The social worker helped Jimmy's mother stand, and brought her to a bathroom to splash her face with water, and she led Jimmy's mother out to a waiting helicopter, which whisked them both up to the sky and then down to the beach where Myra stood. The propellers beat sand and water into the air, and the social worker and Jimmy's mother bent down and ran through it all as the helicopter lifted away, leaving the three in peace.

"I breathed his last breath for him," Myra said. "I feel so alive. I can even see some vowels. I'm going to write my own book now. I'm going to call it *Body Cavities*."

"Listen," the social worker said, "I knew you since you were the littlest kid. You were always a regular kind of crook. I never figured you for a louse."

"You never had enough imagination," Myra said, and from somewhere she pulled a shiny silver revolver, a .38 special. She emptied the .38's cylinder into the social worker, who fell to the ground and bled her life away into the sand.

"Now," Myra said, turning to Jimmy's mother, "what about you?"

Up above them, where the beach turned to hills and streets and houses, people had begun to gather.

"Give me the gun," Jimmy's mother said.

"Why?" Myra said.

"You got what you wanted. You'll be free now. And I need something else."

Myra shrugged, then tossed the revolver to Jimmy's mother.

"Go," Jimmy's mother said, "before the cameras arrive."

"But where—"

"Anywhere."

"I might die."

"We all might. Jimmy did. Go while you still can."

Myra said, "I really did breathe his last breath."

Jimmy's mother had turned away from her to look at the people up above them.

"I was a good witness," Myra said, and then, receiving no reply, she ran off into the shadows, never to be seen again.

As the cameras and microphones began to appear, as news trucks and satellite uplinks and klieg lights sprouted up and down the beach, a few pages from a book fluttered across the sand, pages on which anyone who read them would see some names and words they likely recognized, for once upon a time it had been the most popular story in the world, the story of a boy who triumphed over terrible adversity, who yearned for love and found it, a boy who spread hope and wonder. It was a beautiful story, one that made crowds weep, one that warmed all hearts, and everyone who ever heard that story loved it, except for Jimmy's mother, whose tears as she turned its pages were tears of anger, red tears of rage, because every word of that story was a lie.

And so here she stands now, the eyes of the world upon her, the ears of the world waiting for her to break the silence, and after a man in a suit counts down from three to one, Jimmy's mother tosses the pages to the sand and shoots them full of holes, then, once the smoke has cleared and the sound of the gunshots has drifted out to sea, she says, with as much confidence as she can muster and as much clarity as the first rays of dawn light will allow, "Jimmy started smoking when he was eight."

PATRIMONY

1.

For most of my life, I worked in the gravel pit as an overseer. There had been gravel there for a long time, but there wasn't much left. Mostly, we spent our days trying to decide where to set off dynamite. We did not have a lot of dynamite, so we wanted to be precise. We would go for weeks and even months without lighting a single stick. I spent my days — ten-, eleven-hour days — telling the workers to try over here, to look over there, to dig here, to prod there. We sought the best rock, the least sand.

Eventually, the workers went away. I don't know if the supply ran out or if we sent word that we had no more dynamite, and therefore no more gravel, no more need for workers. I don't know. They never told me those sorts of things.

"We're done," my manager said to me one evening. I had noticed how few workers we had left, and I knew there was no dynamite. I did not need to ask questions. I bowed my head for a moment, thought about the good times when we had plenty of workers and more dynamite than we knew what to do with, and then I let the memory go, and I never returned to the gravel pit.

One privilege of being an overseer is that you are expected to take some of the workers home, to provide for them, and

to have them work for you. I had been able to build a comfortable house on Tower Hill because of this privilege. There
is an unspoken privilege, too, one rarely discussed but certainly acknowledged, the privilege of taking any worker as a
lover. Some overseers I knew long ago sought out workers with
whom they could have a procreative relationship, but even in
the early days, I never desired that. We live inside an apocalypse; giving birth is immoral. I tried to love a few of the female
workers, but it was impossible. Despite our precautions, I
could not escape the fear that somehow I would impregnate
her and she would want the baby to live. All very unlikely, but
nonetheless, it made it impossible for me to touch a woman,
never mind function in a sexual way with one. The men were
easier, less threatening, more casual, more anonymous. I did
not form an attachment with any of them but one, and he had
died many years ago, and I worked very hard to forget him.
(Truly, now, I don't even remember his name.)

When the stranger came to town, I had no formal job, since
I was not qualified for any of the salaried work that was available, and no overseer was in the mood to retire from the jobs
that would suit me — the telegraph office, the butchery, the
place where they weigh the water, the treadmill. I spent much
of my day at the town library, and Mrs. Vax, the librarian, told
me she would have happily hired me if there were any money
in the budget, but I knew even she barely made enough to
meet her basic needs. I was one of the only people in town
who went to the library anymore. It had many books, because
though hardly anyone read books, they all revered them and
did not want to throw them out, and so when a house was
taken over after the inhabitants moved away or died, the books
were sent to the library, and Mrs. Vax organized and cata-
logued them all neatly. (The library building had previously

been an immense department store, and there was more than enough room for everyone's books.) Once upon a time, I had tried to read books about science and mathematics, but now I spent my days reading novels about people in love.

The stranger rode into town in a horse-drawn Toyota, some husk he had found in a junkyard, but instead of horses to draw it, he had a pack of dogs, dozens of them. We heard them coming from miles off, at first a sound like distant, dying birds, a shriek across the sky, but as they got nearer, the sound seemed more orchestral, and then when it was within a few hundred yards, we knew exactly what it was, the sound of a thousand dogs howling and barking.

There weren't a thousand dogs, though it sounded like it. A few dozen, perhaps. Mutts, all, but mostly large and seemingly healthy. I was in the library when I heard them outside. Mrs. Vax stood paralyzed behind her desk. "I hate dogs," she said. "I thought they'd all died."

"They'll last longer than us," I said. "We're their servants, really. They've got us trained."

I went to the big doors at the front of the library and looked out at the scene. The stranger ascended from the Toyota, as tall as an old oak tree. He wore a black coat that reached down to his ankles. His head was covered with multicolored scarves. His hands were claws.

And then he stood in front of me.

"Is there water here?" he said.

"They sell it by the pound down at the waterworks," I said.

"I want it by the stream, not the pound," he said. "I have dogs that need water."

"You'll have to talk to them down at the waterworks," I said.

"What's this place, then?" he said.

"The library," I said.

"Ahhh," he said, starting to unwrap the scarves around his face, "so I have, indeed, reached civilization."

He brushed past me and bolted toward the books. He ran fingers along the spines as if they were piano keys in an arpeggio. "Magnificent organization!" he called out across the breadth of the library, his voice oddly powerful in the cavernous space.

"Mrs. Vax is still working at it—" I yelled across the expanse, my voice thin, brittle. "The Dewey system wasn't precise enough, copious enough, and so she's converting it all to Library of Congress, but..." There was no point in continuing. My voice had become dust motes. Meanwhile, Mrs. Vax cowered behind her desk.

Moments, or perhaps hours, later, the stranger strode to the desk and slapped a single thick volume down.

"I am taking this book. *Psychopathia Sexualis.* It was not what I was looking for originally, for I dared not dream to encounter it again. You have exceeded my expectations. I will sign it out for one week. You have my word. Create an account for me, a library card, whatever you want. Use whatever name you will. None of that matters. You know who I am. I shall be in this town. And exactly one week from now, I will return this book to you. Until then, please be well. I look forward to seeing you again."

As the man moved toward the door, I said, "What do you intend to do here for the week?"

He approached me slowly, deliberately, his eyes fixed on mine. "My good man," he said, pressing himself against me, his voice now a whisper, his breath brushing against my lips. "I intend to do what none of you will." The scent of him, thick and earthy, filled my nostrils. "I am the savior of the human race."

And then he was off — out — away.

After a moment, I followed. I kept a good distance, and it was not difficult to listen for his dogs and gauge where he had gone. He surveyed the old residential area, darting into one house after another, until he found one that would suit his needs. It had, I later learned, running water and a sunny master bedroom with a huge four-poster bed and a mattress that had, somehow, not rotted or mildewed into nothingness.

I will not write here of his deeds, for there is nothing in their awful details that could enlighten you. The terror he wreaked was particular for each woman, but for those of us who were not its immediate victims, it was a singular event, a week that could be characterized as a relentless, piercing scream or a razor blade drawn slowly across our ears and eyes.

To my shame, as soon as I knew what the stranger intended, I hid away in my house. We all did. We had become experts at averting our eyes, bowing our heads in darkness, huddling in corners, accepting fate, hoping against hope that we would not be next.

I heard that in the first days, at least, when he saw a woman he told her of his intentions, he offered himself to her, he proposed that he would do anything within his power to make her happy and comfortable if she would not resist him. His desire, he said, was simply to procreate, and he had no care for how it happened. Few women were anything but disgusted, and it was their disgust that infuriated him. His fury fed him, pushed him toward greater and greater violence, until in the last few days he walked naked through the streets, smashing his way into homes and hideouts, tearing and slashing into lives, never satiated — indeed, the more he ravaged, the more he sought to ravage.

On the seventh day, he ceased. Once again wrapped in his

clothes, he assembled everyone he could find on the dead grass of the town common. He brought a girl forward, the youngest and healthiest among us, a mere fifteen years old.

"I have saved this one," he said, "for you. Who will it be?" His gaze searched the crowd. "You—" A boy, only a few years older than the girl. "Take her to that house. It has a fine bed, comfortable, a good place for love. You know what to do, yes? No more of your herbs, no more of the barriers, the socks, the sponges — all that accoutrement of sterility — no more. Just you and her and you inside her until you release, until you implant yourself."

"I cannot, sir." The boy's voice was breathy, timid.

"Cannot? Or will not?"

"I do not understand."

The stranger grabbed the boy, tore at the boy's belt and his pants, and then with his other arm clawed for the girl, pushed her close against the boy, slashed at her dress with his sharp fingers, tore her naked, then embraced the two bodies, manipulated them, aroused their instincts even as their eyes shed tears and their lacerations shed blood, until the deed was done and the stranger stood back and the boy and the girl slumped to the ground. The stranger betrayed no joy or horror. He was, he seemed to think, simply an intermediary, a necessary force, an overseer.

Mrs. Vax stood at the back of the crowd, weeping. The stranger approached her and held out the library's book. "I am returning this, as I said I would. I am a man of my word. You should put this book on a pedestal at the front of the library. You should build churches in its honor." Mrs. Vax held out her hands, but the moment the book touched them, she pulled her hands away and the book fell to the ground.

"I had thought," the stranger said, "that I had found

civilization, finally. A place where men might still be men. Alas. I must travel on."

And then he was back in his car and his dogs were pulling him away from us and we stood until dusk in the town common, listening until the last animal howl had faded to silence.

2.

At first, there was no way to forget the stranger. We went back to our everyday lives, but soon the evidence of his work was apparent. Some of the women died in suicides and hemorrhages, two in childbirth. In the end, eleven babies lived.

I hid away in my house. I could not go back to the library, and I rarely went into town except for provisions, because as long as I stayed home, I could forget. I spent my days working in the yard or reading some of the books I had at the house, old paperbacks mostly, which I had gotten long ago from people I no longer remembered. I became sharply concerned with dust, and I cleaned every room in the house at least once each day. At night, I lit candles and stared out at the stars, or strummed some songs on a ukelele I'd found in a box at the library, and which Mrs. Vax told me I could have for myself, as nobody else would ever want it.

And so it was that I knew nothing of the women's plans. I pieced the story together later. I record it now so that you may know something of what your mothers did, and why.

The kernel of the idea originated with Mrs. Vax, who offered the library as a meeting place to the mothers before they gave birth. Other women, ones who escaped pregnancy, joined the group as well. Mrs. Vax provided them with materials concerning their situation, and inevitably their interests roamed a bit wider to the circumstances that might provoke such a man as the stranger to be who he was, to do what he did.

Whatever questions the women raised, before and after the children were born, Mrs. Vax found answers for. Over the period of three — almost four — years, various plans were proposed and evaluated. Contact was established with other towns. Quiet routes of communication and barter were established. Maps were made.

The ultimate plan emerged not only from careful deliberation, but also from a bit of luck: a neighboring town had a few weapons that still worked, and somebody found three sticks of dynamite in the bottom drawer of a desk at the gravel pit office.

And so a posse set out in search of the stranger, the procreator, the father. They rode horses gathered from the plains beside one of the towns that was part of their network, a town where women had spent many months capturing and training the horses, then teaching each other to ride. The posse was made up of the best riders and the strongest, fiercest women from all the towns, the women who would have no fear of a fight, yet who were also disciplined enough to stick to the plan no matter what happened and no matter their anger.

It took them five months, but they found him.

They watched him in a town near the coast. They descended at night. They pulled him from a woman he had bound to a bed. He fought them, bruised them, cut them. He escaped to his car and his dogs, but spies from the posse were ready, and the dynamite destroyed the road just in front of him. The dogs died, but the stranger was merely battered and unconscious.

The women broke his arms and legs, then dragged him back to town. They announced their plan and invited anyone to follow them back. A few joined them, but most did not. He had only arrived the day before. The town had suffered many tragedies for many years. The stranger was just one more.

The posse brought him back over many miles through all the towns he had visited. They attended to his wounds, keeping infection away, but keeping the bones broken, the body in pain. He screamed through many nights, they said, and they savored his screams.

In each town, people joined them, walked with them, fed them, bathed them, clothed them.

Finally, after nearly a year away, they returned to our town. Word had circulated through the network that the stranger had been found and his punishment had begun. The excitement spread beyond the women; it was then that even a hermit such as myself could not escape the news. People talked of little else, and in my occasional trips to the store for grains and oils, I heard the tales, which every time got more ornate: the stranger would be brought to us without limbs or tongue, they said; and then they said he would arrive flayed and yet alive; and then they said he had been chopped into pieces and yet his mouth still issued ugly words.

Of course, that was not how he arrived.

The posse rode into town on horses festooned with garlands and ribbons, surrounded by women, men, and children from places far and wide. The stranger lay in an enclosed wagon pulled by eight ponies, a black wagon built like a coffin with windows on its sides and top. He had long ago stopped screaming, his vocal chords shredded, his mouth full of dust. Nurses attended him, healing only what was necessary to keep him alive.

The women removed the stranger from the coffin wagon and brought him to the town common, where other women had set up a table and chair. They lay the stranger across the table.

One of the women from the posse called out to the crowd: "We have asked Mrs. Vax to speak for us."

Mrs. Vax stepped forward. "We have sought something more than justice," she said, "because what would justice be for us? What would justice be for the mothers or their children? There is no justice. There is existence: our common fate, our burden, our curse."

Behind her, women strapped the man to the table with long leather belts.

"We have come to know it is monstrous to bring children into this world. It happens, yes, here and there, now and then. Sometimes accidentally, sometimes not. We all had parents, and though we resented them their weakness and their self-indulgence, we also understood. Some of us have felt the same desires. Most of us. We never hated the children who were born, and even now, after all we have experienced, we cast no blame. We, the born, must care for each other."

The stranger's clothes had rotted during his journey. They were foul and soiled, and only bits remained, bits which were now removed. The nurses cleaned him with soft cloths and soap and water.

"But this man is a monster, a creature undeserving of our care — and worse, a force of evil, of destruction, a creature that spreads and magnifies suffering. We have never seen his like. We hope never to see it again. We must remember."

The mothers all had knives. They moved closer to the stranger on the table, surrounding him. Their movements were obscure to us, but once they pulled away, the effect was clear. They had severed the stranger's genitals and stuffed them in his mouth.

They lifted the stranger up and set him on the chair. The nurses massaged his jaw and throat until, after many minutes, he had chewed and swallowed himself.

They left him in the town common for many weeks. Nurses

attended him around the clock, making sure to feed him just enough, to give him just enough water, to staunch his bleeding, to keep his bones broken and also to keep him alive.

And then one day he was not alive.

The nurses went away, but the corpse remained. No-one dared go near it. Animals chewed at the flesh and bones. The stench hung in the air through days and weeks of putrefaction. Finally, some animal or perhaps some disgusted person hauled the remains off to the woods.

3.

The facts of your existence were never hidden from you. The fate of your father was only spoken of with vague words. "One day you'll be told," they promised you. Mrs. Vax was the one who asked me to chronicle it, shortly before she died. For many years, I could not bring myself to tell the tale. I did not want to think of it. We were all ashamed, even though I have yet to hear from anyone who wishes it to have been done differently.

The women's network dissolved within days of the stranger's death. The mothers attended to their mothering, they took care of each other and you, but the towns had no desire for any but the most necessary contact. You stayed together, always, even though you did not know exactly why. Rivalries erupted, and love stories, too, though none lasted, until one did.

I decided to finish this chronicle on the day of the little one's birth. I began putting my notes into order, the order you see here. It was clear that you needed to understand more than you understood, that you were of the age to know what could be known.

Perhaps, though, you knew more than I guessed — more than any of us guessed.

Three days ago, I had written most of this story for you.

Two hours ago I watched you — all of you, mother and father, uncles and aunts — tear the little one to death in the sand of the gravel pit.

I watched you laugh. I watched you.

You heard me behind you. You turned, one by one, to look at me. You stared at me, smiling, your mouths all dripping with blood.

And in that moment I realized one thing: You have your father's eyes.

ON THE GOVERNMENT OF THE LIVING

They had not lived in this place for long, but it felt longer than they had lived there.

They had lived in other places like this place, and they had moved on.

They often moved on, but they never seemed to move.

This place was just like every other place.

They slept in holes and built hovels in ruins; they shivered in shadows; they amassed collections of cardboard and aluminum and shards of concrete; they built fires in barrels and along the shores of oozing rivers and in the husks of traffic jams; they breathed air gritty with the last bits of broken glass and broken bones; they cast off clocks; they seldom spoke; they never dreamed. They were here, they were now, in this place, a place.

They would not give any place a name, or themselves names, because names were gone now, along with everything else.

This place was a place of ash and sand, a place of burned metal, a place of splinters, a place dwindled long by slow decay.

This was not a place, someone said, it was a memory, faltering, fuzzy.

This was not a place, someone said, it was a feeling, muted.

This was not a place, someone said, it was a gash.

At night, chilled and huddled, with eyes squinted against

smoke from burning barrels, they named what they had lived, loved, hoped, dreamed: the words they would preserve.

My mother, someone said. *Her name was Emily.*

(They remembered and imagined their mother, Emily.)

Popcorn, someone said. *The smell more than the taste. The sound.*

(They remembered and imagined popcorn popping.)

Ben, someone said. *I never had, never knew anybody named Ben.*

(They remembered and imagined never having, never knowing Ben.)

Night after night, the ritual continued.

Now and then, someone was missing or someone was new. There were repetitions. Nearly everyone remembered a favorite pet, usually from childhood, sometimes from later, never from the last days before they came to this place or the places like it, because everyone knew that those days past, and the pets (and other words) trapped forever in them, must be forgotten.

One night, before the setting sun stole the red sky, someone said, "We need names."

Murmurs and whispers cut through the ashen air.

"Without names," the person said, "we will not be remembered."

Murmurs. Whispers.

Someone else said: "We will not be remembered."

Someone else said: "We should not be remembered."

"But," the person said, "our children—"

"Will die," someone said.

"Without knowing our names, their names, our places, our stories. Our children—"

"Will die."

Silence.

Someone else said: "I have no children."

Someone else said: "We have no children."

"All of us," someone else said, "will die."

They did not gather together that night. They sat alone, separate, scattered, cold.

In the morning, they did not seek out puddles and streams in which to wash themselves. They walked through the day covered in ash and sand. Their skin was crusty, their eyes stung, their lips stayed dry, caked, salty. The youngest asked for food and water. The oldest sat stoic.

"Is this the end, then?" someone said. "Is this all we are?"

"We are nothing," someone said.

"We will die," someone said.

"Without names."

"Without a place."

"Here."

"Soon."

A child stared into older eyes. "Who are you?" the child asked.

"I don't know," the older one said. "Who are you?"

"I am not you," the child said.

"Yes," the older one said. "And I am not you. We know who we are then, yes?"

"I know who I am because I am not you," the child said.

"Yes," the older one said.

"I would like a name," the child said.

"There are no names."

"I would like to know about this place."

"Forget this place."

"I would like to remember something," the child said.

The older one was silent for a long time. "There are only words," the older one said, "and none of them are worth remembering."

The child walked away. By the next morning, the child knew childhood was no longer viable, that it was, in fact, an artifact of the deep, impossible past, like *bubblegum* and *fortnights* and *milliners*. Childhood was — always was — something else lost.

The adult felt a moment of nostalgia, then moved on (separate still, alone still, but moving).

Others noticed. Others joined in the movement. Eventually, they found themselves swathed in another night, together. The bitterness had somehow drifted off, much of it forgotten. They moved closer, touching elbows, arms, shoulders. After silence, the ritual began again, tentatively, pulsed with pauses.

Blue skies, someone said.

Pause.

Pause.

The smell of haybales on a rainy day, someone said.

Pause.

Toothpaste, someone said.

Night after night, the words (remembered, imagined) accumulated. Then:

Love, someone said.

First love, someone said.

Lost love, someone said.

Pause.

Laughter, someone said.

Pause.

Lollipops.

Lungfish.

Lollygagging.

Laughter, someone said again. The tone was different this time: urgent, imperative.

Laugh, someone said.

Laugh!

And they did — first almost in silence, as if whispering of something forbidden (like sex in a world no-one would willingly birth babies into, like dreams) — and then with more confidence, more pleasure — chuckles, giggles, chortles—

Laughter.

The sound carried across the dunes of sand and ash, over the tortured steel that slashed the land, through the gritty air, toward the remnants of consciousness out there in a landscape of memory—

And if this were a happy story there would be an epiphany, and voices would rise with their own laughter to meet the laughter, and the whole, desolate world would be united for a moment in human joy—

But here, in this place, in this story—

Laughter cannot penetrate the ash, the grit, the night.

Silence.

Silence.

(Someone smiled at someone else, a sheepish smile, a smile for shadows.)

Silence.

"That's enough for now," someone said.

They huddled closer, deeper into the silence, and soon were asleep.

In the morning, they would move again, and in the night they would not talk, for it was too dangerous, too close to dreaming.

They would move again, still seeking they knew not what.

The adult could not sleep.

Tears welled in eyes. Hands quickly wiped the tears away.

Silence.

There was a moon this night. It had been invisible for weeks or longer, blotted out, but now it had returned to the sky.

The moon burned, coldly, orange.

If this were a happy story, someone would rise with the sun and press on toward something more, something greater, something...

The moon burned.

Tears dried.

No-one slept.

Words crumbled in their minds, each an emblem of the utmost they could know, each now dust.

They were left only with themselves and the universe of night, all unmoving, eyes fixed on sightless eyes, gazing at each other as if admonished from another world.

A LIBERATION

After his mother died, Arthur sold off most of his possessions in a yard sale, then made his way across the world to the city of N—, where his mother had been born, and where he decided he would live out the rest of his life, though he knew nothing of the language or the culture and nobody recognized his mother's maiden name when he spoke it. Within a few months, he changed his name to Akaky, since that is what *Arthur* sounded like when he imagined it in the local dialect, and the kind owner of the café where Arthur spent much of his time said, in the few words of Arthur's language that he knew, "Ah, yes, Akaky, name good, yes, Akaky." The café owner clutched a coffee-stained scrap of paper in arthritic hands, set it on the table where Arthur sat, and, with a plastic ball-point pen that perhaps had traveled as far from its home as Arthur had, wrote the name in the alphabet of the language Arthur did not speak. After finishing his seventh cup of gritty coffee that morning, Arthur thanked the old man and left a few coins from back home on the table. The old man treasured these coins, and Arthur was glad he had gained many at the yard sale and had had the foresight, or blind luck, to be too lazy to turn them into paper money at the bank before he left. Arthur wandered out of the café and to the park of dead trees, where he sat on an iron bench and showed the piece of paper to an old woman who shambled by. "Akaky?" she said, looking up at him. He nodded. She also nodded, then smiled and walked on. And so he became Akaky.

He lived in a one-room apartment in an abandoned building a few streets down from the café. When he first arrived in the city, he found it difficult to tell where one building ended and its neighbor began, because in the center of N— each building was as close to the others as possible, with the few alleys barely large enough for a scrawny person to squeeze through. This design, he learned later, conserved heat and prevented strong winds from blasting all sides of the buildings. In a city as north and as cold as N—, such a design was a matter of survival. Outside the center of the city, most buildings were empty warehouses and massive, abandoned tower blocks, the relics of an old regime that had hoped to relocate citizens to the north to work in the mines. Older residents occasionally told stories of the Winter Massacre, when temperatures plummeted so far that heating systems sputtered and failed, and by the end of a week so many people had frozen to death that the tower blocks became ghostly morgues. For months that spring, the howls of wolves echoed through the concrete halls of massive buildings on the outskirts of the city. Sometime in the summer, the army brought truckloads of prisoners to help clean out the towers. The prisoners hauled, scraped, scoured. Plumbers, carpenters, electricians, and mechanics guided the prisoners. Sawing and hammering echoed for many miles. Soon enough, the apartments were habitable again and the army took the prisoners away, but the buildings remained empty. Winters now were cold, but never quite so cold as they had once been, and there weren't enough people that they would die en masse. Nonetheless, each spring the daylight revealed what winter's darkness hid and ice preserved: lonely tableaux of last days.

Akaky's apartment was small, dim, and shabby, cluttered with furniture left behind by whoever lived there before. He welcomed the dimness during the endless sunlight of summer, and in the winter's darkness he found it comforting to live in a space of shadows. The previous residents must have had a cat or some other animal as a pet, because the upholstered corners of the chairs and the sofa were clawed and torn, and for months Akaky found clumps of hair in corners and under rugs. An iron pot-belly stove stood in the middle of the room, and he fed it bits of wood and garbage whenever he was home, but if he went out for more than an hour, the stove cooled and the apartment cooled. (He worried about the pipes, as he did not know what to do if the pipes froze and burst.) He thought perhaps he should move to an apartment in one of the empty buildings on the outskirts of the city, and so one day when there wasn't too much wind and the temperature was almost pleasant, he walked out to the nearest tower block, a twenty-storey cube of concrete, but he discovered that he could not safely go inside because the building's foundation had shifted, sinking more than a foot into the ground, shattering much of the first floor. Through broken windows, Akaky peered in at a rubble of tiles, sheetrock, wood, metal, and cement. A skeletal staircase dangled in the air.

A few days later at the café, the owner introduced Akaky to a woman who spoke his language. Akaky thought she looked to be a few years older than himself, but he had never been a good judge of age, and in any case the conditions up here skewed people old. Her name, she said, was Zora, or rather it was now Zora, though it had been something different long ago, but so long ago she hardly remembered what it was. Despite speaking the same language, Akaky did not understand some of the words she used, and her accent was one he had not heard before. He wanted to ask her where she was from, but the question seemed impolite. Lacking another subject, Akaky talked about the weather, and then Zora asked him if he had noticed that the buildings in the city were all sinking into the earth.

"Yes," Akaky said. "I saw this on the outskirts. I went looking for another place to live. My apartment is not ideal. I thought perhaps one of the abandoned buildings would allow me a bit more space, though of course there would be no electricity, no running water, I expected that, and I have certainly lived with greater deprivations, and in any case I thought it couldn't hurt to have a look, and so a few days ago I walked out to one of the towers, and I couldn't even go inside because the whole ground floor was destroyed and the building was, as you said, sinking into the earth." Speaking his own language made him loquacious, he realized. He stared at the table and said quietly, "It is all very strange."

Zora sipped a large, steaming cup of tea. She said, "It's sinking. All of it. The towers are simply heavier than anything else, so they're going faster."

"All?" Akaky said. "All sinking?"

"Yes," she said, as if stating an obvious fact, something even small children knew.

"Here, you mean? In the center of the city?"

"This is not the center of the city. We are on the edges here. But yes, the center, too, is sinking."

"No, I don't believe that is true. I wander the city every day, and I have not noticed any sinking."

"Nonetheless," Zora said, "it is sinking. The city is getting warmer, and the frozen ground is not staying frozen any longer. The sea, too, it is coming closer every summer, and though it remains many kilometers away, soon enough it will come closer and closer, and one day it will reach the center of the city. One day, a few years from now, a few decades — one day where we are right now, where we sit, here, this will be underneath the water."

"Well, no matter," Akaky said. "I am not young. It will be after my time."

"The sinking, that is now. But yes, the worst cataclysms will, indeed, come later. Perhaps, though, you will have a long life. If so, you will suffer."

"Yes, but I will not have a long life. I have started smoking. I never smoked before, not seriously anyway, but after my mother died, I decided I would smoke, and so I do. I'm up to a pack a day! And the cigarettes here, I don't know if you've tried them. They're wretched. I think they make them in the mines." From his coat pocket, he pulled out a crumbled gold and red pack of cigarettes. "I must say, one thing I love about this city is that we can still smoke indoors." He picked up a matchbook from the table, struck a match, and lit the cigarette. "I suppose smoke is not much worse than the air that is already here."

"You smoke," Zora said, "to keep yourself from having a long life?"

"I suppose," Akaky said. "I never thought about it before right now, but yes, that would be one reason."

They sat in silence until Akaky said, "Who did you leave behind? Back home? Was there a husband, or children, or…"

"No-one," Zora said. "Once, there were people, but I was no good at keeping track of them, and soon enough I found myself with no reason to stay in any particular place."

"That's sad." Akaky took a deep drag on his cigarette.

"It never seemed so. Not happy, not sad."

"I suppose it was the same for me. After my mother's death. No reason to stay put. I had a wife once, but it was a mistake, we were not in love. Once we realized that, we separated. I don't know where she is now. You said you are not married?"

"I never married."

"Did you ever want to?"

"Look around this city," she said. "Smell the air, let it burn your nostrils. Listen to the breaking buildings, the cracking roads, the silence. What does it matter what I wanted? Or you? We are here. That is all there is to say."

Akaky lit another cigarette. Zora finished drinking her tea and stood up. "It was nice to meet you," she said. "Perhaps we will meet again."

Akaky sat in the café and smoked his cigarette after Zora left, then returned to his apartment. As he prepared himself for bed, he was interrupted by a bark. Akaky often neglected to close the door of his apartment, which was terribly warped and required him to put his full weight against it if there was any hope of it closing, but no person or animal so far had ever come to visit until now, when a dog (something like a beagle but a little bigger and scruffier) trotted in and made its presence known with a few sharp shouts. It then sat down and stared at Akaky expectantly.

"Who are you?" Akaky said to the dog. The dog did not reply. Akaky walked around it, surveying the animal. "Do you have fleas? No?" He leaned in and picked gently at the dog's fur. The dog stood up. "A male, I see. Or a former male. An *it* now. So someone has attended to you in the past." Akaky gave the dog a few pats. "I have pieces of chicken in the refrigerator," Akaky said. "I will make us both sandwiches."

The dog followed him to the kitchen and watched with great excitement as Akaky put chunks of chicken between thin slices of bread. Akaky opened a jar of mayonnaise and smelled it to make sure it wasn't rancid. It wasn't, so he spread a layer over the chicken in the sandwiches. He handed a sandwich to the dog, who ate it mightily.

"Now that we are friends," Akaky said, "perhaps you should have a name. Do you know your name? My name is Akaky. You should have an exotic name, don't you think? Yes, an exotic name. Therefore, I shall name you Arthur."

Arthur looked up from the scraps of sandwich on the floor.

"Hello, Arthur," Akaky said.

Arthur followed Akaky wherever he went, because whenever Akaky had food, he shared some with Arthur. At the café, the owner could not pronounce *Arthur*, so called the dog Sobaka, which Akaky decided was a word meaning *kind, intelligent friend*. The café owner, too, gave Arthur occasional scraps of food. Akaky worried perhaps Arthur would gain too much weight, but Arthur was so demonically energetic that it was unlikely; he spent his days almost constantly moving, running, bouncing. Even in the café, where Akaky warned him to be on his best behavior, Arthur constantly patrolled the perimeter, dove under tables, dashed between chairs, chased rodents from the kitchen, and raced to greet every occasional customer who came through the front door.

Zora finally returned to the café one afternoon when Akaky and Arthur were there, and Arthur immediately fell in love, trying to jump up into her lap, but she gently coaxed him down. He sulked beside her chair, stealing glances now and then, eyes wide with longing.

"How have you been?" Zora asked Akaky.

"Dying by inches," he said, lighting a cigarette. "You know how it is. But now I have a dog."

Zora twirled a strand of hair around a finger.

Akaky said, "And you? How goes existence?"

"I am considering taking a trip out to the sea. I saw it last some years ago, and I would like to return. I thought I might do some painting. I was a painter once. Not a good one, but I enjoyed the work. I have developed terrible fears, however. I am afraid of travel, because I am afraid that when I return, everything will have sunk farther into the earth. Far enough to be, finally, irretrievable."

Akaky nodded. "Seems reasonable," he said.

"Does it? I can't tell anymore. There's too much light. I don't think well in all this light. It is too easy to see the smog in the air, the wreckage all around."

"If you went on a journey to the sea, you would get away from here, away from the city and the mines. The light might be beautiful up there."

"It might," Zora said. "Or it might be more horrible. Horrible in what its beauty reveals of the rest of the world. I don't know if I could survive that."

They sat without speaking, Akaky finishing one cigarette and starting another, and then Zora stood and walked to the door. Arthur tried to follow her, but she paid no attention to him, and she closed the door before he could get through. He stared at the door, whining quietly, then paced slowly through the café.

That night, as Akaky sat in his apartment smoking cigarettes and trying to remember a long poem he had memorized as a child, Arthur wandered through the building. Akaky heard his footfalls and occasional inquisitive barks. The poem was not coming back to him, so Akaky played a game of solitaire with a pack of cards with scratched and faded pictures of penguins on the reverse. He remembered seeing penguins in a zoo once, with his mother. As a boy, he was delighted by zoo animals, and he had been sure the animals shared his delight. Now, he wondered if those animals had ever had a moment of happiness. He looked at the old picture of the penguin on the back of a card and sighed. The zoo his mother had taken him to must have closed many years ago.

As Akaky was beginning to accept that he was not going to win the game and might as well go to bed, Arthur returned, carrying something in his mouth. Akaky could not tell what it was until Arthur proudly placed it at his feet.

A bone of some sort. Long. Perhaps human. A femur, Akaky expected, not that he knew much about bones. Arthur lay on the floor and gnawed on it.

"Where did you get that from?" Akaky asked, trying not to let any annoyance into his voice, because he didn't want Arthur to feel chastised, for if he did, Akaky knew, Arthur would become cautious and furtive. Arthur ignored him. Akaky approached the dog and slowly leaned down. Arthur growled.

Akaky decided it was not worth antagonizing the dog. He went to bed.

In the morning, Akaky discovered that during the night, Arthur had scattered various bones throughout the apartment. They looked like bones from human feet and arms, though he supposed they might be from any animal — remnants, perhaps, of a prehistoric deposit only now surfacing through unfrozen ground. But what of the ones with specks of flesh and blood on them?

Arthur sat amid a small pile of what looked like finger bones. He seemed proud of his work. Akaky picked up a bone. Arthur did not growl. "Where'd you get this from?" Akaky asked. He gestured toward the door. "Where's the bone yard?"

Arthur stared at Akaky, who pointed once again toward the door. Arthur looked at the door, as if expecting a new arrival. "Where are the bones?" Akaky said. "Show me the bones." He started walking toward the door, holding the finger bone out in front of him. Arthur followed. "*I* can't show *you*," Akaky said. "You're the one who knows. You're going to have to lead." Arthur slowly walked past Akaky, then stopped and looked back. "Yes, good boy. Show me the bones."

Suddenly Arthur bounded through the hallway and down the stairs and it was all Akaky could do just to keep him in sight as they descended into the basement of the apartment building, a place Akaky had only ever glanced in at through the door. He had to be careful, because the bottom stairs were covered with debris and the metal railing had separated from the wall. The stairs seemed solid, though, and Arthur hadn't hesitated at all to run through the open door at the bottom. The closer Akaky got to the door, the more pungent the air seemed: thick, both sweet and rotten. Shadows filled the basement, which stretched far beyond Akaky's building, being a basement, it seemed, for the entire block. The only light came in sharp, thin shafts through cracks at the top of the concrete foundation. Though it was a warm day outside, the basement was cool; wet, dripping ice lingered on the wall. Beneath Akaky's feet, the floor was spongy. His boots sank down, the muddy substance rising above his ankle. Fragments of what might have once been a concrete floor drifted like icebergs. He stepped carefully, his balance uncertain in the half-darkness as he walked across a terrain both solid and liquid. With each step he took farther into the basement, the air grew more fetid and fungal. Akaky began to feel nauseated, light-headed, but there was something about the air that satisfied him, like a meal rich with fat.

Arthur plunged his snout into the mossy stew of the basement's floor, wriggled his head, grunted, and brought up a long bone in his mouth. Akaky stepped closer. The bone Arthur joyfully chomped was a human leg, the foot still attached and intact, with rotted cloth, flesh, and muscle falling away as rags and jelly into the muck.

Akaky bent his knees and touched his hand to the damp ground. As he let his hand sink lower, he felt matter amid the mud, objects suspended in melted layers of old earth, bits of stone and concrete but also Arthur's treasure: the bones of corpses, which Akaky soon saw (a blast of sunlight pouring through the many cracks high up in one of the foundation's walls) filled three quarters of the basement's floor and rose in piles at the far end, where, despite distance and shadows, Akaky could see the bodies had been quite well preserved, though rodents had clearly been recently feasting.

He wanted to vomit, but instead Akaky discovered himself laughing. His laughter unbalanced him, and he wobbled, then fell down onto his knees, and laughed even harder. As Akaky knelt laughing, Arthur ran over to him, dragging the leg he had found, and Akaky's laughter shook his whole body. He was unable to help himself, and he feared the force of his laughter might knock the floor beneath him loose, until he plunged down into whatever darkness lay below, like a miner lost to the pit. Soon enough, though, Arthur dropped the bone he had held in his mouth and barked at Akaky, as if telling him his behavior was inappropriate to this place, and Akaky could only agree.

Eventually, once his laughter subsided, Akaky and Arthur together began pulling bones and bodies out of the ground and up into the dusty, fugitive light.

· · ·

Zora heard that Akaky was up to something down by one of the little lakes, but nobody cared enough to go and see what he was doing. "What do you know about Akaky?" she asked Voshchev, who worked at the mine and lived in the building next to hers and sometimes brought vodka to drink with her. "We see him there every morning when we go, every evening when we come back. He's building something."

Akaky had never seemed to Zora like a builder, more a lazy dreamer of shallow dreams, a man with little experience and less imagination: a body taking up space, which made him a good fit for this city in its sinking. Nonetheless, good fit or no, Akaky bored her, and she hated his dog, so for more than a month she had avoided visiting the café. But the cold, dark season was coming and she worried about him. Nobody else in the city spoke the language of her country, and though she was perfectly comfortable speaking their language, talking with Akaky, dull as he was, had given her the comfort of old memories and barely-remembered dreams. If he were in a bad way, he might not make it through the months to come, and she feared for herself — feared his loss might be her own.

She went to the café one morning. Prushevsky, the owner, said he hardly ever saw Akaky anymore. "Hardly ever?" Zora asked.

"Once a week, twice at most. He drinks coffee, eats some bread or a pastry now or then. I send him home with slices of meat, cheese, whatever I have around, but I do not know that he eats it. He is growing thin."

"And the dog?"

"It seems healthier than he," Prushevsky said.

"How does he spend his day?"

"He says he is working on a project at the eastern lake, the one down the hill from the building he lives in. It took a few tries, a few days for me to understand that was what he said. He talked about it at length in his language, your language, but I could not understand, and he drew some pictures on a napkin, which is how I know it is the eastern lake, but more than that I do not know. He seems both passionate and at the end of a tether."

"I am familiar with the ends of tethers. I shall go see him."

"Here," Prushevsky said, "wait a moment while I make some sandwiches for you both, and a few scraps for the dog."

Prushevsky filled a plastic bag with sandwiches, bits of meat, some extra cheese, and a bottle of white wine. "For a picnic at the lake!" he said. Zora thanked him and tried to hand him some money, but he would not take it. "Be good to him, and bring him back if he needs to come back. That is enough for me."

She might have hailed one of the city's few taxis, but decided to walk the kilometer out to the lake, giving herself time to think about what she could say to Akaky, what she might tell him of her recent weeks, whether to admit to him the dull truth of her conversations and assignations or to lie and tell him tales of traveling to the river or, even better, up north to the sea. As she walked, she smiled to herself at what she might tell him of the rogues and rascals she met at the river docks, the scandalous gossip they imparted, and she sighed at the thought of the sea (which she had, in truth, never seen), and how she might describe its vast reach to the horizon, its shifting shores, its seals and whales and polar bears. (Were she to talk of such creatures, though, he would surely know she was telling a tale.) She soon passed the building he lived in, and then the city's streets crumbled away, the orderly design of the city obscured into rubble and ash. She made her way down a winding path along a hill, the lake soon coming into view. She did not see Akaky until she was almost ready to turn back, sure he wasn't there. He and the dog stood at the far end, the dog digging a hole in the ground, Akaky fiddling with something that she could not quite see at a distance, some form, like a tree in a grove, but without leaves. As she got closer, she saw he was not alone, and that the form he had been touching, moving, shaping was a person.

A light wind off the lake carried a scent not only of the lake's water but of something else; not the familiar sulfurousness of the mines, but something sharper. Though unfamiliar, it smelled old to her, as if its source had been underneath the lake for centuries and only now had found its way to the air. As she got closer to Akaky and the people he was with, the scent became richer, almost overwhelming.

Something was wrong with the people. They sat or lay sprawled on the shore of the lake or stood beside metal poles. Akaky moved from person to person, shifting their arms and legs, adjusting each person's position, but none of them moved on their own. As she realized this, she stepped close enough to see that their faces were wounded — or no, not wounded, but rotted away.

"Zora!" Akaky cried with delight, a cigarette dangling from the side of his mouth. "How nice to see you!"

The dreadful dog ran up to her, barking. It sniffed the plastic bag she carried. She held the bag out to Akaky, who took it from her. Without speaking, without acknowledging him at all, she walked to the people — the bodies — he had set along the shore. One was simply a skeleton, its skull the color of old stone. Others looked almost alive, mottled with desiccated remnants of veins, muscles, flesh. The clothes each wore were in better shape than their bodies. The people she had thought were leaning against metal poles were, instead, strapped to the poles with wire and rope. The stench was awful, but less awful than it ought to have been, she thought. Flies swarmed around and between each body in such numbers as to make the air shimmer.

She swatted, slapping her neck and arms and forehead.

"Smoking helps," Akaky said. "The flies don't like it. And it lessens the smell." He blew a puff of smoke toward her.

Zora tried to ask a question, but her mouth would not form words.

"I found these — these — people — I found them in the basement of my building," Akaky said with the excitement of one who has lived for weeks on little more than coffee. "I tried to bring up the ones in the best shape. There's a remarkable range of — of — of *something* here — some of these people, I'm sure they're as old as the land itself — but others, the ones that reek, the still so wretched ones, the rankest, might as well have died only a few weeks ago, a month or two maybe, a year, I don't know, decomposition is not my speciality — some may be miners lost in accidents, or the people from the winters, people the military cleared out of buildings, but that's not the whole story, is it, no, it can't be, there's all the others coming up now, the ancesters, the predecessors — coming up from underneath, as if this is where they have always gone, always ended up, as if this is the place where everyone for all the eons…" His breath failed him.

The dog whined and scratched his snout against Akaky's leg. Akaky said, "Arthur likes the bones, any bones, and he keeps trying to bring them here, but I tell him this is not an ossuary. And we certainly don't mix and match. That would be ghastly."

"What … is it, this place? What are you doing?" Zora said, her voice barely a whisper.

"Doing?" He watched the dog run off, chasing some animal, or perhaps a shadow, in the tall grass beyond the lake. Akaky smoked his cigarette. Finally, he said, "I think of this as a liberation. I bring out the ones I can. I scrounge new clothes for them in my building and a few other buildings that seem safe to enter. I am getting good at eyeing what fits." He dropped the stub of his cigarette to the ground and lit another. "Eventually, perhaps, I will save them all, but there are limits to my energy, to my strength. There are limits. I found a big old wheelbarrow, and I use that to transport them here. I bring out whomever I can, and I try to position them so that they have a good view of the lake. I know it sounds absurd. And smells terrible. And these flies. But don't you think…" He stared out at the lake.

"What?" Zora asked. "Don't I think…?"

"I was going to say, don't you think there's something right about it? I mean, it feels right to *me*, it feels entirely right, but I realize it may seem like I am disturbing them, that I have brought them here against what might have been their will, their wishes. I don't know how they got there. I don't know what they wanted, or even who they are. They could be murderers. They could have been born in caves or in mansions. I do not know anything about them. But still. I would not have done this if I wasn't absolutely convinced. In my heart. No matter who they are, or why they were down there. I am sure this is right. I would not do it otherwise." He breathed deeply.

Zora looked out across the lake at the city silhouetted against the horizon. Smog from the mines tinted the scene yellow. She remembered when Voshchev took her out to see the giant pit of the largest mine, an abyss she could never have dreamed, a perfectly round crater wider than the eastern lake, a structure she knew had been built by people but which her imagination insisted must be something else, something older and stranger than human action, the result of an extra-terrestrial force that pierced a hole in the world. She had turned away from the pit, buried her face against Voshchev's chest, and wept. All the bodies that had ever lived and died in this city would not fill that hole.

"What time is it?" Akaky asked.

"Late," Zora said.

"We should not eat the food if we're here," Akaky said. "The flies. Who knows what germs. We could eat in my apartment, if you want."

"Yes," Zora said, "that would be fine."

They walked slowly back to Akaky's building, the dog following, all silent. She washed in the bathroom while he washed in the kitchen. She was impressed with the water pressure in his building. Perhaps she would look for an empty apartment here herself. Maybe Voshchev would join them, too. Could Akaky and Voshchev get along? It would not matter. The building was large enough that they could all keep to themselves when they wanted. Though clearly the building was sinking — it was already listing enough to the west to be noticeable from outside. Still, good water pressure was rare.

Akaky placed their sandwiches on plates. He poured wine into glasses and set the glasses on the formica table in his kitchen. The apartment, Zora thought, was cozy, though its furniture was all the wrong size for such small rooms. There must be larger apartments in this building, ones with better light. Certainly, there was other furniture around, and this furniture could be moved or tossed in a pile and burned. He did not need to live like this.

They ate in silence. Akaky lit a cigarette. Eventually, Zora said, "Will you take more people to the lake?"

"A few more," Akaky said. "I would like to take them all, but I feel myself fading, and there are so many. I have little energy anymore. I think my heart is slowing down."

"It's strange that the wolves have not found them. There used to be wolves that would wander through the streets of the city. I suppose they've all been killed, though."

"So few animals left," Akaky said. "Just us and the flies."

"And your dog."

"A survivor. Like us."

They finished their sandwiches in silence and sipped their wine.

"The bodies are from this building?" Zora said.

"The basement," Akaky said.

"Perhaps… Yes, I think I would like to see them."

"Oh?" The tone of his voice suggested skepticism to her.

"I was a nurse in a war once, long ago," she said, untruthfully. "Far from here. I have seen bodies in every type of mutilation, every type of rot. Nor does the stench bother me. I have a weak sense of smell. Weak sense of smell, strong stomach."

"Perhaps," Akaky said, "after we eat. Give it a little time."

"Yes, of course. Even with my strong stomach…"

"There are limits."

She nodded and finished drinking her wine. She heard the dog snoring in the other room. In only a few days, she thought, the sun would finally sink away and then begin to rise and set again. She hoped the people at the lake would last long enough to see that. It would rise at their backs and set in front of them. She could help Akaky bring some more people out. Yes, she would do that. Unpleasant work, but though she had not been a nurse in a war, she had done unpleasant work often enough, and dead bodies were familiar to her. She might even recognize some of them from seasons past. "Hello, Yuri," she imagined herself saying to one of the many who had gone away without a goodbye. "So this is where you ended up. Let's get you out of here, shall we? Oh, and Olga Safrova, too. How good to see you again. Is your daughter Masha here? I have so missed seeing Masha." She let the scene carry on in her imagination as Akaky washed their dishes in the sink. It would not be entirely unpleasant work. And, in any case, seldom had she done unpleasant work for much purpose. Here there would certainly be purpose, strange though it might be. Bones and bodies to bring up from the depths. A kind of mining of their own. Mining for what? Some moments of freedom. For the people, for Akaky, for herself, maybe even for the dog. If their luck held out, they could all sit out there one night, perhaps, and watch the shadows lengthen, the light slip away, the bright stars shine through the shrouded sky over the sinking city; and they would know that the sun would rise again, at least once more, before the winter brought its conquering night.

—in memory of Katherine Min

THE BOX

Everything I kept in the box was dead. My fingers trolled the dust and mucas, seeking life, seeking what I had left there in the simple little box, a box far too ordinary to justify its ruby lock.

All dead: the mouse, the butterfly, the toad, the sparrow.

My husband said I should not have expected anything else. Put living things in a wooden box and of course they'll die.

Of course.

They'll die.

He doesn't understand the power of prayer and desire. I tried to fit him in the box — I hacked off his limbs with the saw from the garage, I sliced his stomach open with a kitchen knife (a wedding gift, now that I think of it), I peeled off his face and ground his bones into dust and emptied his veins. I snipped off his penis and testicles with scissors from his desk, then trimmed his fingernails and toenails and hair. Only little bits of him would fit in the box.

I closed the lid and locked it.

I threw the rest of him into the yard for the crows and coyotes to take away.

A week later, he was sitting in the yard, naked, sucking on his thumb, a sparrow resting on his shoulder, a butterfly perched on his elbow and flicking its wings, a toad hiding between his legs, a mouse nibbling his toes.

"You should come inside," I said.

"No," he said. "There's better air out here."

Because he was saying I love you,
something he had never said to them before,
they thought he was saying good-bye.

—Carole Maso

ACKNOWLEDGEMENTS

The sources of epigraphs are: I. Hervé Guibert, *The Mausoleum of Lovers: Journals 1976-1991*, trans. Nathanaël, Nightboat Books, 2014; II. Audre Lorde, "Age, Race, Class, and Sex" in *Sister Outsider: Essays and Speeches*, Crossing Press, 1984; III. Matsuo Bashō, *Narrow Road to the Interior*, trans. Sam Hamill, Shambhala, 2000. IV. Sarah Kane, stage directions from *Cleansed*, Methuen, 1998; end: Carole Maso, *The Art Lover*, Ecco Press, 1990/1995.

The editors who first published these stories took a chance on strange and sometimes difficult material, and I am grateful to them: Andrew Mitchell, Jeremy John Parker, Bradford Morrow, Colin Meldrum, Sean Wallace, Andy Sawyer, and Christopher Barzak. Thank you, too, to Steve Berman for reprinting "Killing Fairies" in *Best Gay Stories 2016*.

Thank you to Chet Weise and everyone at Third Man Books for extraordinary attention, creativity, care, and inspiration. Thank you to Julie Hamel for trusting us with her extraordinary photograph for the cover and to Amy Wilson for creating a beautiful author photograph for an author who hates to be photographed.

"Killing Fairies" owes a lot to conversations over the years with Richard Bowes, and it was written in homage to the style of nonfictional speculative fiction he will forever be the true master of. "Mass" owes much to "The Mappist" by Barry Lopez, *The Mad Man* by Samuel R. Delany, and *Warrior Dreams: Paramilitary Culture in Post-Vietnam America* by James William Gibson. "The Ballad of Jimmy and Myra" owes moments to the movies *Out of the Past*, *Gun Crazy*, and *Pickup on South Street*. "On the Government of the Living" owes it's title to Michel Foucault and his translator Graham Burchell.

Most of these stories were first read by Richard Scott Larson, who offered insightful critique and bolstering enthusiasm. Some of the stories were also read in draft by Rick Elkin and Patricia Sublette, both of whom provided important information about their worlds and experience. All three of these readers' faith in my writing was often stronger than my own, and that faith kept a small candle of ambition burning in me, which led to this book.

I am able to continue to write short stories that make barely any money because I have an academic job that pays a living wage. I am grateful to my coworkers Martha Burtis, Robin DeRosa, and Hannah Hounsell Mallon for making that job not just bearable but exciting and fulfilling. I am grateful to the faculty unions and the whole community of Plymouth State University for support.

I would not have kept at the lonely work of writing strange stories without the support, critique, and camraderie through the years of Katherine Min. That she is not alive to see this book breaks my heart, but I am grateful to her family and friends for doing wondrous work to keep her memory vivid and her legacy strong.

Family and friends make everything possible, and I am lucky in the people who are willing to put up with me. Particular thanks to Jason Burbank & Nilupa Gunaratna, Nora Cascadden, Morganne & Steve Freeborn, Seth Willey, and Ann Thurston, without whose love I would not be.

My mother did not live to read many of these stories, but the title story of this collection exists because she offered me a challenge one day: "Maybe you could try writing a *nice* story." I did my best, kept the murders to a minimum, and gave it the happiest ending I could conjure. I don't think it was exactly what she had in mind, but she said she enjoyed it nonetheless. Her spirit pops up in the story's corners, and probably in all the corners of this book, for she was the audience that mattered most to me from the time when I first learned to shape words into sentences.

This book is dedicated to Eric Schaller & Paulette Werger and Ann & Jeff VanderMeer, whose arts and crafts over the last twenty years have entwined their stories with my own.

PUBLICATION HISTORY

"After the End of the End of the World," *Outlook Springs* no. 6, 2019

"The Last Vanishing Man," *Web Conjunctions,* August 2015

"Killing Fairies," *A Capella Zoo,* no. 15, Fall 2015

"Hunger," *The Dark,* December 2021

"Mass," *Conjunctions,* no. 66, Spring 2016

"Patrimony," *Black Static,* no. 42, October 2014

"On the Government of the Living," *Interfictions Online,* November 2014

"A Liberation," *Conjunctions,* no. 73, Fall 2019

"The Box," *Outlook Springs,* no. 1, Winter 2016

"A Suicide Gun" and "At the Edge of the Forest" were released on matthewcheney.net in 2021 and 2022 respectively. Both were published with a Creative Commons Attribution-Non-commercial-ShareAlike 4.0 license.

All other stories are original to this collection.

BIOGRAPHY

Matthew Cheney's debut collection of fiction, *Blood: Stories*, won the Hudson Prize and was published by Black Lawrence Press. He is also the author of the books *Modernist Crisis and the Pedagogy of Form: Woolf, Delany, and Coetzee at the Limits of Fiction* (Bloomsbury) and *About That Life: Barry Lopez and the Art of Community* (Punctum Books). His work has been published by *Conjunctions, Nightmare, One Story, Weird Tales, Strange Horizons, Best Gay Stories, Literary Hub, The Los Angeles Review of Books*, and elsewhere. He is the former series editor for the *Best American Fantasy* anthologies, and the co-editor, with Eric Schaller, of the occasional online magazine *The Revelator*. He lives in New Hampshire, where he teaches at Plymouth State University.